The Life and Art of Gary Geckleman

Carole Malkin

1. The Fight

While I slept my cot in their bedroom, my parents argued loudly in the living room. Their screams woke me from a deep sleep. Frightened, bawling, I sat up in my cot. Apparently, my mother wanted to run to comfort me.

Dad told her, "He's a six-year-old who acts like a baby because you treat him like he's still in diapers."

"Don't tell me he's a baby," Mom hurled back. "Who are you? Mister Maturity? I love the way you solve your problems."

"I don't want to hear this, Lily. I'm sick of it."

"Go, stay with your girlfriend. You won't have to hear anything there."

"You want me to leave."

"Yes, go!"

"All right."

Hurried footsteps came down the hall. The light flickered on overhead. I saw my father. Usually, when he wanted something, he tiptoed about in the dark and tried to be quiet.

"Daddy," I whimpered, but he paid no attention. My mother stood in the doorway with her hands on her hips while he banged open the closet door. Tugging at the yellow suitcase, he pulled it down from its shelf, threw it on the mattress, unsnapped the latches, lifted the lid.

He rummaged in his drawers. Underwear, socks and shirts flew through the air, landing in the open suitcase. Hangers scratched along the rod as he pulled off slacks and jackets. A badly aimed shoe almost hit me where I sat up in my cot.

My mother tapped her shoe and said, "Don't think I'm going to clean up this mess...I swear, I'm not going to lift a finger...You'll have to hang it all up yourself."

Ignoring her, my father took a carton of cigarettes from a night table drawer, pitched it into the suitcase, then rushed off to the bathroom to get more things to heap inside.

"What are you doing, Dave? Stop this craziness..." Mom said. She was half laughing now like it was all a joke, but she became pale when he swooped back into the bedroom with his toothbrush, hairbrush, and shaving cream.

My mother snatched the toothbrush. Before she could take anything else, my father had flipped the suitcase lid shut and pressed it down. The latches made two sharp clicks as he locked them.

"Dave...stop it...I don't want you to go. I never thought..."

"Don't go, Daddy," I snuffled. "I'm sorry I cried."

My father glanced at me, then jerked hard on the suitcase handle. Thwack! The suitcase landed on the floor. He hurried down the hall with it, Mom and I following.

The toothbrush was still in my mother's hand. She waved it as she talked. "Please, Dave...We can work things out...Don't make me humble myself...Don't do this...Don't...don't go...I'll try..."

Dad stopped at the front door and said in an icy voice, "You made your bed, Lily. Now, lie in it!" He undid the lock.

"Don't let Daddy go!"

My mother put her arms about me. I dove my face into a spot between her waist and chest. She sobbed, "I'm here with you. I'll never leave you...Dave, wait until the morning. Sleep on it first."

My father jerked the door open.

Mom threw the toothbrush at his back. "Walk out, and we're finished."

"Fine," my father said. He walked out the door.

## 2. My Grandmother

No sooner had my father left, than Grandma Etta charged into my life. She moved up from Baltimore and took over our Lower East Side apartment. My mother had to go to work, sewing children's clothing at a factory on Thirty-fourth Street and was exhausted. In the mornings, Grandma Etta dropped me off at my first grade class at John Burroughs. When school ended, there she was towering over the mothers waiting at the gate. Everything about her was large—her height and broad shoulders, her eyes, nose, mouth, bosom, and even the loud voice with which she greeted me with a rush of Yiddish and English words, all tumbling over each other, as I ran to her out-stretched arms.

My mother was too overwhelmed to think about my Jewish education. Grandma insisted I start Hebrew School. So Tuesdays and Thursdays, she delivered me from school to a little classroom above our synagogue where Rabbi Schneider taught a class of a dozen boys. Slender, middle-aged, with a skullcap and a *tzizis*, a ritual undershirt that hung down over his pants, the rabbi peered at us through the thick lenses of his wire-rimmed glasses. Chalk dust covered his thin hands and drifted over his black suit as he wrote Hebrew letters on the blackboard. While his back was turned, we whispered, passed notes and blew spitballs. He didn't seem to notice. In his soft voice, he kept right on talking towards the blackboard.

His goal was to enlighten, transform us from boys to men. Our thirteenth birthday, each of us would be required to stand up on the *bimah*, the platform in front of the synagogue, read from the Torah in Hebrew and give a speech, demonstrating that we'd achieved the desired transition.

With each passing year, Grandma Etta grew more eager about my *bar mitzvah* ceremony. After I turned twelve in May 1961, she and my mother began planning for the event. Then, one evening, while they were drinking tea, and once again, endlessly discussing where to have my party, I told them, "I don't want to be *bar mitzvah*." They went silent, but I didn't care.

I couldn't bear the thought of standing on the *bimah* and everyone staring at me. My feet were large, a preparation for a growth spurt the rest of my body didn't know about yet. Perhaps people wouldn't notice my boat-like shoes. But they would see the angry red pimples on my face; the nervous twitch that my nose and mouth had developed; and, as I read from the Torah, they'd hear my voice crack. Ashamed as I was about how I looked, what troubled me the most was that my father wouldn't be there. He hadn't visited or even called since he'd left six years ago.

Insanely jealous of the other kids with fathers, I'd told them mine was a Secret Service agent who'd been parachuted behind the Iron Curtain into communist Russia. My excuse for his absence sufficed on the playground but a *bar mitzvah* was different. Even a secret agent showed up for his son's *bar mitzvah*.

Grandmother finally mustered herself to utter a weak, "Voss?" Once she spoke, she grew stronger, and cried, "You don't want a *bar mitzvah*?...Hitler would have liked it that a Jewish boy doesn't want to be Jewish...I'm glad my Gur Aryeh isn't alive to hear such things!"

She was always going about my Grandpa Gur Aryeh. He'd escaped to Argentina with his family just one step ahead of Hitler's invasion of Poland, only to have a fatal accident when he got there. While working at a Buenos Aires suitcase factory, he was struck on the head by a falling trunk. I'd been named after him, Mom squeezing Gur and Aryeh together to make 'Gary.' Grandma evoked Grandpa, whenever she thought I wasn't living up to his memory.

Wanting to spare Grandma, my mother hustled me into the bedroom to tell me off in private. A double bed filled the room. She stood on one side, and I on the other, practically backed into the open closet that was filled with her size eight clothes, and three or four of the black sack-like garments my grandmother wore.

"What's this, some kind of joke? No *bar mitzvah*? Stop this nonsense."

I started to reply. "Don't I get to choose?"

"Not another word," she said, letting me know it was useless to protest. "Your grandma is counting on it. She's had enough pain in her life. You're not going to disappoint her."

Although I wouldn't have admitted my reasons for not wanting a *bar mitzvah*, I was hurt that she didn't ask. All that was important to her was that Grandma had decreed that I'd go to

Hebrew School, and that I'd be *bar mitzvah*. That was that! The whole weight of World War II rested on my shoulders. My *bar mitzvah* was supposed to foil Hitler's intentions of annihilating Judaism.

I was furious, but not with my mother. It was much easier to be angry with my fat, clumsy grandmother who barely spoke English.

To spite Grandma, I began sneaking money from the cupboard change jar. Instead of attending Hebrew School after my regular school let out, I went to the movies. I didn't miss every Hebrew School class. But since Rabbi Schneider seemed indifferent to the chaos in his classroom, I assumed he wouldn't notice an occasional absence.

The dark movie theater welcomed me with a stale popcorn and damp wool smell that made me feel at home. A rear projection room shot out beams of silvery dust. Occasionally, at the beginning, I could hear the low, soothing murmur of rotating reels, but once the story started I forgot everything except the beautiful people up on the screen. They never disappointed me. I longed to be like Gary Cooper and John Wayne. The Jewish stuff Rabbi Schneider taught came from Europe where Hitler had killed my Polish aunts and uncles, relatives I would never know, but for whom my grandmother and mother had never stopped grieving. I never knew when one or the other would start crying. Anything could set off a crying jab, an orange, a pair of scissors. Judaism was sad, sad, sad. I didn't want anything to have anything to do with it. The world I sought was up on the screen, glamorous and exciting.

I watched one film after another, believing I was learning about life, particularly about what went on between men and women. When an actress cried, "I hate you" to the leading man, I discovered she meant she loved him. I fell in love with all the blonde actresses: Doris Day, Kim Novak, June Allyson, but my favorite was Marilyn Monroe. I adored her platinum hair, flickering eyelids, and cute, rabbit-twitch nose. Best of all was her breathy voice. I laughed hard when she got caught in a ship's porthole, or when she wiggled her way into a diamond tiara-- "Why shouldn't I have it, Piggy? After all, your wife has *you*!" I completely agreed when she cooed, "I'm smarter than I look." She outsmarted everyone! A fiancée's father accused her of being a fortune hunter. Marilyn fluttered her eyelids and breathed, "Dad-dy." He melted. So did I.

When I stepped out of the theater, it was dusk. Sometimes, there were puddles on the pavement, evidence that while I was inside, a rainstorm had come and gone without my knowing. The stationery man rolled up his awning with a rod; the jeweler took in his rings and watches from the black velvet in his window display. Walter Fisher, the jewelers' son, had died in the Korean War. For the remainder of the war, the family had tried to protect Walter's grandfather from the shock of hearing about his death. They'd even written him letters and signed them 'Walter.'

After sitting so long at the movies, it was hard to walk at first. I didn't always watch where I was going, still bewitched as I was by images from films, like the one of Marilyn Monroe standing on an air vent, her white, pleated skirt billowing up around her legs. I passed the butcher shop with its sawdust-covered floor; the greengrocer's banked wooden boxes of fruits and vegetables. To Enrico's consternation, Grandma always squeezed his produce and tossed back anything over-ripe or bruised. Around the corner was the fish store where, to my humiliation, she bought only fish heads and tails, and then bargained for 'a few cents off.'

Neighbors waved at me--Mrs. Nussbaum, who had a beautiful smile despite her buckteeth; Mrs. Linder who wore her short red hair in a 'pixie' hair-do; Mrs. Kessler who 'frosted' hers, so that it had tiger stripes of blonde mixed into the brown; Mrs. Rosenberg, whom as a small boy, I'd thought had been electrocuted for spying until, to my amazement, I saw her on the street with her husband, another casualty to my imagination.

Still hypnotized by the film I'd seen I climbed three flights to our flat. Children raced past me in chase games Smells of frying onions and simmering stews filled the air. I fumbled with my key, stumbled into my apartment. Grandma Etta's booming woke me from my dreams. "Gar-ye-lah," her garbled name for me, fell somewhere between Gur Aryeh and Gary.

Either she was cooking, cleaning, or collapsed on the living room couch, talking to our little blue parakeet whose cage sat on the coffee table. Grandma Etta doted on the bird; even claimed Tiny had a Jewish soul and understood Yiddish. Carefully, taking the parakeet out of its cage, she stood still as a statue while Tiny flew up and perched on her head.

Grandma's figure was enormous in her rumpled black dress; her skin wrinkled; fingernails cracked and yellow; gray hair tangled in every direction; one earpiece was missing from her glasses. When I was small, she hadn't minded if I watched her change into her housedress. So I knew exactly how she looked underneath her dress. Imagining, her gigantic underpants, pink undershirt over her long, hanging breasts, and corset with laces, straps and metal buckles, I started to giggle. Oblivious to the fact that I thought she looked ridiculous, Grandma Etta responded with a smile.

She was not simply different from, but the opposite of a goddess of beauty like Marilyn Monroe.


The more I adored Marilyn, the more I looked down on Grandma Etta. But I didn't begin to despise her until she— unwittingly, I admit--displayed to the entire United States how un-Marilyn she was. One evening I saw her on "Candid Camera" on our second-hand television set with the 'bunny ears' aerial. I could scarcely believe my eyes. She was afraid of the TV. So how could she be on the screen? Whenever I watched programs like "Father Knows Best"—on every Wednesday at eight-thirty--she hurried outside for a walk or visited the Kesslers who lived next-door. She thought the TV caught people's spirits.

"Candid Camera's" crew had set up a 'talking box' on De Lancey Street, only a few blocks away from where we lived. The tape recorder in the box called out, "Hey, you," just as my grandmother happened to pass by. As usual, she was carrying her big black umbrella. She'd once used it to pommel strikebreakers during a Ladies' Garment Workers Union strike. On another occasion, she'd beaten an exhibitionist who'd displayed himself to her and me on a train. This time, she struck her new antagonist, the talking box, until it fell silent. Then she strode off. She'd appeared on TV for only a minute or two, but that was enough to set our whole neighborhood laughing. Grandma hadn't the faintest notion of the derision inspired by her battle with the 'spirits' in the box, but I could barely hold my head up when other kids teased me.

After this, nothing my grandmother did pleased me. She was a Nobody. Hearing I was going to study a foreign language at school, she begged me to take Hebrew, one of the options available. Instead, I chose French. I wasn't even grateful for the gifts Grandma showered on me, her adored grandson--chocolates, puzzles, and drawing pads and pencils because I loved to draw. How she figured out I would appreciate film magazines, I don't know, but she bought me a few. In one, I read that Marilyn Monroe had been an orphan and felt even more connected to her.

I clipped the Marilyn Monroe article from the movie magazine and put it in a shoebox I kept in the hall closet. The box already contained a collection of my private treasures: matchbooks; cigar bands; a pearl button that flashed and caught the light; a small wooden donkey that moved around and bowed when a button underneath was pressed; a color wheel that gave off sparks as it whirled around; a pair of magnetized tiny Scottie dogs, one white, the other black, that zipped about in every direction when brought near to each other.

After my grandmother's appearance on "Candid Camera," I felt that I couldn't step out of my house without some boy or girl ridiculing me. They'd say things like, "Where are you going? To help your Grandma beat up a garbage pail?" I wanted to run away. I wanted to breathe the same air that Marilyn Monroe breathed. One June afternoon, I cut Hebrew School, and instead of going to the movies, I hopped on an IND train and went uptown. In one of my film magazines I'd read that Marilyn Monroe lived on 57th Street near Sutton Place. Fortunately, like most New York City kids, I was a whiz at navigating my way on buses and trains.

I got off at 57th Street, walked down a busy, wide street with tall buildings. Every passer-by fascinated me: the nanny walking a baby in a high pram; a woman dressed in a light, silvery cape; a man with an alligator briefcase. A chauffeured black limousine rolled by. The man in the back must be important, either the mayor, or head of the stock exchange or even the United Nations. It even occurred to me that it might be my father who, for all I knew, could have become fabulously wealthy in the years since I'd last seen him.

I had to decide which of the buildings was Marilyn Monroe's. Most of them had awnings that extended from the street--over the sidewalk--to the glass doors where doormen stood, sweating in their heavy maroon or green uniforms. I walked down one side of the street and up the other, stopping under awnings to get out of the sun.

One of the doormen was a fat, green-eyed man with thinning hair and a red face. He snapped at me, "You can't hang around here and bother the tenants." This doorman was the only one who begrudged me a few moments in the shade.

It was possible he was just mean, but I decided he was Marilyn's doorman. Her fans must come around all the time, and he was in charge of getting rid of them. I walked a few feet away and even though he glared at me, I wouldn't budge. It was a free country, and I could stand wherever I wanted. The sun beat down. My mouth was dry. My shirt stuck to me.

A cab pulled up. Maybe it was Marilyn. I had to smile at my mistake when an old woman stepped out of the taxi. Marilyn could never be wrinkled, stooped, and walk with a cane. A little white dog with a flat face, pug nose, and long hair, waddled at the woman's heels. A jeweled collar gleamed about the dog's neck. The creature stopped and stared at me with narrow, rat eyes. I wasn't used to dogs. Nobody I knew had one. There wasn't room for more than a gold fish, canary, or parakeet in a small apartment.

My heart pounded, and I shriveled up inside, as the dog began a frenzied, yapping. I felt like needles were piercing my ears.

"Stacey!" the old woman cried. "Stacey, stop it! Stacey, bad girl!"

The dog must have sensed my fear. She darted towards me and leapt. Sharp teeth tore into my pants, piercing the skin on my shins. Over and over, the little dog leapt at me with an insane determination. I tried to get away but couldn't escape Stacey's scratching and biting, any more than I could shut out its hysterical bark.

Grabbing the dog, the doorman locked its squirming body under his arm, and slapped her flat, black nose. Stacey wailed. The old woman hurried over. "Bad doggy," she said, but patted Stacey's head.

Turning to me, she said in a quavering, old lady voice, "Are you all right?"

"I'm okay," I mumbled.

"Take this boy to the lobby, Norm."

The doorman became white-faced, as if he'd been asked to commit a crime, one that might cost him his job. "He's a...a fan, Mrs. Shaw," he stuttered.

"Never mind. Let the boy sit down and catch his breath...And get him a glass of water."

The doorman nodded, opened the door.

I followed Mrs. Shaw into a lobby with mirrored walls, large plants, and leather couches. After the heat, the air-conditioning felt like cool kisses on my neck and face. I sank into an armchair, pulled up my ripped pants to my knees and examined my shins. I was bleeding, but only slightly.

Mrs. Shaw, accompanied by the doorman went to the elevator. After pressing the button, she glanced worriedly at me. I heard her mumble something to the doorman about 'cab fare for the boy to go home.' She snapped open her purse, and handed the doorman some bills, while he handed over the dog. The elevator arrived. The old lady and the vicious animal ascended.

Norm pocketed the money that was meant for me. I didn't protest. Whistling, he came towards me. It was as if I'd tipped him. To my astonishment, Norm was on my side now. We had a common bond: hatred for Stacey. He showed me a scar on his finger. "That little beast bit me here, and another time, on my ankle. What gets me is the little rat probably eats better than I do. Are you alright?"

"Yeah, I'm alright."

"What's your name?"

"Barton," I said. It sounded more glamorous than Gary.

"I'll get you some water, Bart. Wait a minute."

He disappeared through a door, coming back with a large glass of water.

"Another thing about that mutt, it's always shitting on the rugs. Guess who gets to clean up? Yours truly. That's my life. I do all the dirty work...You should go home now."

"Please, I want to see Marilyn Monroe. I want to get her autograph."

"Look, I'm not going to lie to you and say Marilyn Monroe doesn't live here. That's what I usually say to the groupies. But I'm not going to say that after what you've been through." Norm laughed and asked, "Will my autograph do?"

"Yours?"

"I was an actor. I used to do summer stock in the Catskills. I thought it would start me off, and that I'd end up on Broadway. But it didn't turn out that way. In the end, you gotta live. You gotta have a paycheck. So, I clean up Stacey's shit…you know what? Just because you had to put up with that little Stacey bitch, I'll see what I can do for you. I'll talk to Miss Monroe when she comes back. Just don't try and go up and talk with her or anything. Understand?"

"Yeah," I said, barely able to believe my luck. It was worth getting mauled by Stacy to have the chance to see Marilyn. I regretted I'd said I was 'Barton.' Marilyn might write 'To Barton' with the autograph. But I couldn't bring myself to admit to Norm I'd lied. He might get disgusted and chase me away. I'd lose my chance of meeting Marilyn.

"You stay right here, and don't move. You promise?"

"I promise."

Norm winked. He went off to resume his post in front of the building. I was left in the lobby's cool luxury. People passed in and out of the building, a woman with dark green shopping bags marked "Lord and Taylor," a man in a wheel chair and his nurse, a teenage girl. I peered out at the street. A cab pulled up. Norm opened the door, and a blonde woman in black slacks and a long, white shirt stepped out. She wore no make-up, was a ghost compared to what I'd seen on the screen, but still, I recognized Marilyn!

My brains dropped out of my head. Like the little dog, I had to fling myself at her. I rushed out the glass door and when she saw me charging up, she flinched and drew back. Keeping her face turned away from me, she began to sweep past. I wanted to catch her sleeve, but had to be satisfied with a whiff of her perfume.

She was passing through the glass doors, when I pleaded, "Please...please..."

She paused and looked over her shoulder.

My voice came out squeaky and strange. "Can I have your autograph?"

Without a word, she walked into the building, my pal, Norm, following. As she waited for the elevator, he kept talking. His feet shuffled side to side, and he stared at the floor. I wondered whether he was telling her that I deserved an autograph because Stacey attacked me. The moment the elevator arrived Marilyn stepped inside, and disappeared. It looked like she'd walked away while he was mid-sentence.

Norm came barreling back to me, his face beet-red. Spit sprayed from his mouth as he cried, "Why didn't you let me handle it? I told you I'd help you. Now, I'm in trouble. You said you'd stay in your seat. You're a real asshole, kid."

I ran across the street to escape. But once I was planted opposite Marilyn's house, I wouldn't leave no matter how much Norm shook his fist. I craned my head, gazed upwards at the apartment house windows. If only I could catch another glimpse. After a while, a drape parted in a room near the top floor. I saw her silhouette. Then, she disappeared. I hung around, not able to leave because I might see her in the window again, or she might come down to go out.

A few moments later, she stood at the lobby door. Norm's mouth fell open when she beckoned to me. I flew to her side. "Here," she said. "I'll give you my autograph so you can go home." Her voice was flat, with no hint of the baby trill I'd heard in the films. She scribbled her name in a small notebook she'd brought with her, ripped out the sheet of paper and handed it to me. Then she disappeared inside. I studied the autograph. Each 'M' was big, but she'd drawn the rest of the letters with a skipping, nervous line.

I was thrilled. She'd made a special trip down for my sake. It meant so much to me to take home a tiny bit of Marilyn, an autograph that I could touch and kiss—as I wished I could do to the hand that wrote it. I floated back to the IND train station, the autograph in my hand. For a moment, I considered folding the paper and tucking it into my shirt pocket, but I couldn't bear making a crease through Marilyn's name. I descended the subway stairs, not dingy-seeming any more, but mysterious like a path to a temple in India or China. After my meeting with Marilyn, anything seemed possible. Maybe I'd see her again. We'd become friends. I'd move into her apartment, live with her.

On the train, I gazed at the other passengers, wondering what they'd say if they knew they were so close to a young man who'd just met Marilyn. If I spoke to the woman in the pink dress and showed her the autograph, would she think I'd signed it myself? I was bursting to tell someone, but not my mother or grandmother who'd be shocked that I hadn't gone to my Hebrew School Class. Besides, the autograph was a part of my life that I wished to keep separate from them, particularly Grandma.

My grandmother was so ignorant that she didn't even know who Marilyn Monroe was. That was how low and unworthy she was. I came to my stop, left the train station. I hated going back to Grandma Etta after seeing Marilyn. At home, I went right to the hall closet, took out my shoebox and hid Marilyn's autograph among my treasures.

My excursion had taken so long that my mother had already returned from work. "Gary," she called.

I stepped into the living room, saw Mom sitting with my grandmother, and with a visitor. Rabbi Schneider rose and shook my hand.

Grandma sighed while my mother said harshly, "I hear you weren't at Hebrew School. So where were you?"

"At the movies," I mumbled, the only excuse I could think up.

"Where did you get money for the movies?" Mom persisted.

"I borrowed it."

After a thorough interrogation by my mother and grandmother, my sins were exposed. I admitted that I was a hooky player and a thief.

My mother yelled at me. My grandmother paced the room, crying "*Oy vey*...woe to me." Rabbi Schneider lectured.

"Everything that happened in the Bible happens today," he said. "That's why the Bible's alive. In biblical times, we were misled. We bowed down and worshipped the Golden Calf. Today, we turn on the television or go into a movie house and bow down again..."

I stopped listening. It would have shocked Rabbi Schneider to know I was thinking about Marilyn Monroe, seeing her face and hearing her sweet, tinkling voice instead of his. She was saying, "Do I look like a calf?"

Grandma was so afflicted to learn that I'd stolen money that she sought comfort with our parakeet. She slipped Tiny out of the cage. The bird flew about the room from the window ledge, to the light fixture, to Rabbi Schneider's skullcap. While my grandmother chased the bird, and my mother continued making sarcastic comments about my behavior, the rabbi managed to extract two promises from me. I was going to start attending Hebrew School regularly again, and I was going to come to his home the following Friday for the *shabbes* meal, along with my family. I didn't want to do either.

After the rabbi left, I remembered that his wife, Miriam, was French. President Jack Kennedy's wife, Jacqueline Bouvier Kennedy, had French blood, and was glamorous like a movie star. After seeing her on TV, I assumed all French people possessed her *savoir-faire*, a word I'd learned in French class. I couldn't bear the thought of Miriam witnessing Grandma Etta's lack of refinement at close hand.

I wasn't the only one who considered Grandma 'unpolished.' She'd lived with Uncle Ben and his wife, Selma, before coming to live with us. Selma hadn't gotten along with her, complained she was 'uncouth.' Grandma called Selma *'forbissiner*, stuck-up.'

In my heart of hearts I knew I was wrong to be ashamed of my grandmother, that I was *forbissiner* too.

Friday night, we got dressed up and left the house, stiff and careful, trying not to wrinkle our clothes or let the breeze muss our hair as we walked to the rabbi's red brick apartment house. Neighbors stared at us because we were barely ourselves, particularly my grandmother wearing powder and lipstick and with tiny pearl earrings winking in her ears. I wore a pink shirt and gray slacks. My mother, proud of her figure, dressed in the Buenos Aires-style of her youth. She wore a tight skirt cinched at the waist by a wide belt, scooped neck white blouse, stiletto heels. One side of her dark hair was pinned back, and the other fell loose over her shoulder. Her face was powdered white. She'd plucked her eyebrows and penciled in thin lines like bird wings. Her lipstick was bright red.

Miriam answered the door, along with Ellen, her ten-year-old daughter. They were dressed in the orthodox style, in plain dark dresses with high necks, long sleeves, and nearly ankle-length hems. A scarf covered Miriam's hair. She wore no makeup. On the walls of the vestibule were oil paintings of rabbis, one with a long white beard beside a menorah, and another in front of a dilapidated synagogue on a narrow street. They looked disapprovingly at my mother's sexy outfit.

We went to the living room where the rabbi greeted us and invited us to sit down. Mom, Grandma and I sat on the couch, myself in the middle. My mother had to do the talking for the three of us. She asked Miriam when she'd come to the United States.

"After the war," Miriam said and launched into a story about how her aunt had brought her over, hoping she be find a way to get a permanent visa. She'd been fortunate enough to meet and fall in love with her husband.

"When did you come over?" she asked my mother.

"After the war too. I spoke English with a Spanish accent. Strangers thought I was Puerto Rican."

While my mother made conversation with the rabbi and his wife, I looked about at the bookcases, spinet piano, Oriental rug. I spied a number of French knick-knacks: a wooden rooster painted the red, white, and blue of the French flag, with *liberte, egalite, fraternite* written on its base; a porcelain plate inscribed with a blue *fleur de lys* and 14 *Juillet*; a small statue of *Arc de Triumphe.*

On the walls, I saw framed photographs that looked like my mother's from Europe, yellowed and old and taken in a studio with a painted backdrop of a river and trees. But the trees in the painted backdrop of these photographs grew straight up like flames, different from the wide shady ones in my mother's Polish pictures.

Ellen sat cuddled on her mother's lap, and like Grandma and myself, didn't utter a word. My grandmother grew restless, began to stir. She turned towards the side-table beside her. On it was a lamp, and a delicate china figurine, a masked clown in a suit of black and white diamonds. I stopped breathing when she picked it up to examine. She was always dropping things. To my relief she put down the harlequin, unharmed.

Soon we proceeded to the kitchen. Miriam and her daughter lit *shabbes* candles. Rabbi Schneider supervised the hand washing, and prayers over the *challah* bread and sweet red wine. Then the meal began. A white cloth covered the kitchen table. Rabbi Schneider sat at its head. Ellen helped her mother serve. Rabbi Schneider looked on anxiously at the hot soup sloshing from side to side as his daughter carried bowls to the table.

Over the last year, along with my tics and pimples, I'd acquired several aversions. My flesh prickled when I heard my mother crunch into an apple, even though I made the same noise when I ate one. But worse was the way my grandmother sopped up soup with chunks of bread, chewed with her mouth open, slurped whatever she drank. She did all these things tonight, a prelude to even worse behavior when Miriam and Ellen served the main course.

Grandma Etta grabbed her chicken leg in her fist, chewed up the meat, and began crunching and sucking the bone. She made so much noise that everyone noticed. Ellen kicked me under the table, trying to get my attention. If I looked at her, I knew she'd burst into giggles. I ignored her. The rabbi kept talking to my mother like nothing was wrong, but his ears turned pink.

A stiff smile pasted to her lips, Miriam put another chicken leg on Grandma's plate, saying, "There's lots more." She must have thought Grandma was eating the bones because she was starving. But my grandmother always gnawed bones.

"Over in the Old Country, all this food would feed us for a week," Grandma said, then resumed eating.

I couldn't bear her crunching away like a cannibal. It was like she was crushing my bones between her teeth. Cruel words flew out of my mouth before I could stop them. "Why don't you just throw the bones down and eat off the floor?" As if she hadn't heard them, my grandmother grunted and started in on the second chicken leg.

Talk about the weather, Jacqueline Kennedy redecorating the White House, and a cousin of Rabbi Schneider's making *aliyah* to Israel, carried us through the rest of the meal. Small prayer pamphlets were distributed that said, 'Compliments of Stephen Garfield's *bar mitzvah*.' The rabbi led the concluding prayers.

Finally, my mother stood and said, "We have to go, Rabbi. Thank you for the *shabbes* meal." Grandma heaved herself up. I got up too.

Outside, the night was clear with a big orange moon hanging in the sky. The whole way home, my mother spoke only to my grandmother. At the flat, she waited until Grandma went into the bathroom, and then tracked me down in the living room. I had quickly changed into my pajamas, jumped into 'bed'—the couch—and was feigning sleep.

Mom strode across the room, bent down, and slapped my face.

Touching my stinging cheek, I gasped. I was astonished. Neither she nor my grandmother had ever struck me before.

"You deserve it. You're not stupid. So why do you act like a boy with no heart? You insulted your grandma. You insulted her in front of the rabbi and his family. I'm disgusted with you," she sputtered, but kept her voice low so Grandma wouldn't hear.

Lying on the couch, not daring to move, I felt stuck like a pinned bug.

"You should kiss your grandmother's feet She saved my life and yours. And now, she's sick…"

This was the first I'd heard that she was sick. "She's not!" I cried. "She's strong as a horse."

My mother slapped me again.

Afraid she'd hit me once more if I didn't, I gave her a wooden, "I'm sorry."

That didn't mean I believed Grandma was ill. She'd always been her own doctor, had known how to cure herself. Whenever I was out walking with her, she diagnosed people on the street too. A man with a jerky walk had something wrong with his *putz*; the lady with thin eyebrows had a weak heart; the one with a dark color around her eyes was pregnant. In Europe Grandma had learned all kinds of treatments. To her it was obvious an infected boil had to be pricked with a needle so the pus drained. She knew to keep a rash dry, to soak a swelling with hot cloths. When I was sick, she put mustard plasters on my congested chest. If that didn't cure me, she went to a *goyish* Polish woman to get a bag of herbs that she hung around my neck.

My mother said, "I hope you are sorry, Gary. Believe me, everything Mama does is for you. I'm counting on you to act more grown-up. Treat her better. The only reason she keeps going is to see you *bar mitzvah*."


That autumn all I could think about was bicycle riding, and all that my mother could think of was planning my *bar mitzvah*. It was nothing like the previous November when she, I-- and the whole neighborhood--had been excited about the presidential election. Jack Kennedy had beaten Hubert Humphrey in the primaries. Just like during the World Series, people had stood around in stores or on the street, discussing who would win. There'd been excited arguments about whether the country would vote for a Catholic. Some had claimed Kennedy could win, and that in the future there'd be a chance for a Jewish president. Others said they were afraid a Catholic in the White House meant the Pope would rule the country. Even so, Kennedy was considered better than Nixon.

Nixon was called, 'Tricky Dick.' The only one who said he'd vote for him was Mister Spitz, a big fan of Joseph McCarthy. Wearing his Nixon button like a sheriff's badge, he'd stood outside his pool hall, and told anyone who'd stop, "Richard Nixon knows what's what. He learned the ropes from Joe McCarthy." When Jack Kennedy won, the pool hall was closed for a week, as if there was a death in the family. Then Mr. Spitz recovered and continued to corner people and bang them over the head with his political opinions. After the sit-ins in the South to integrate lunch counters took place, he said to anyone who'd listen, "Who do you think is down there, and getting the Colored worked up? The Commies."

Last January, I'd watched the inauguration ceremony on television, and was stirred by Kennedy's speech, "Ask not what your country can do for you. Ask what you can do for your country." Wearing a fitted suit and pillbox hat, Jacky had stood by his side, a model of perfect femininity. Now whenever I saw her on TV, her refinement proved to me the injustice of the slaps I'd received from my mother.

Mom, though, had already forgotten the incident at the Rabbi's. She was in an absent-minded mood when it came to anything other than hiring caterers and halls. Her preoccupation continued throughout the summer and a mild, pleasant autumn.

It wasn't until nearly Thanksgiving that winter blew through the streets. We had our first snowstorm. I bumped my bicycle down the stairs to the low ceilinged, dusty, and cobwebbed basement and threw an old shower curtain over it.


At the end of February, three months before my *bar mitzvah*, Rabbi Schneider decided I needed private tutoring. One evening a week, I received private lessons in his small study. There was a bookcase full of mostly prayer books with black covers so old, that the bindings were half off and the spines showed. The rabbi's desk was piled high with books and papers too. There were two chairs that didn't match. I sat at one that faced a window with a view of a brick wall.

I learned the *parsha*, the section from the Torah called Deuteronomy, which I'd have to chant aloud during my *bar mitzvah* ceremony. Sometimes, I was distracted by the telephone ringing, or by Ellen playing *March Slav* or *Country Gardens* on the spinet in the living room. Since Ellen went to an orthodox school where she met only orthodox kids, I considered her immature for her age. I, on the other hand, was a sophisticated guy from a big-city school. Yet whenever the rabbi told me that soon I'd be a man and would be responsible for everything I did, I trembled at the thought of God noting all my sins, including my angry outbursts at my grandmother.

Rabbi Schneider tried hard to get me to reflect on what it meant to be Jewish. He spoke of how the ancient religion had survived bloodlettings like the Crusades, Inquisition, pogroms and Holocaust. "The reason Judaism survived," he said, "is because of the Talmud. Instinctively people know the purpose of life is to do *mitzvah*. The Talmud gives a guide of how to do good deeds."

"Rabbi," I asked, "How can you be sure you're doing a good deed? Last week, two Jehovah's Witnesses knocked on my door. They wanted to save my soul by converting me to Christianity."

"Those people didn't ask, 'is this a Jewish child?' 'Is this what his mother and grandmother believe?' They have one answer, and they apply it to everyone. In our religion we ask questions."

"But how do you get the answers? How do you know whether you're doing a good deed?"

"You don't, Gary. You just think about things and do your best. Sometimes, you make mistakes. There are even circumstances when obeying the Talmud can be wrong. The Talmud teaches you to analyze and reason things out on your own. Also, it's necessary to have a kind heart to be a *menstch*, a good person."

My lessons stopped when there was a knock at the study door. I had to give way to the next soon-to-be *bar mitzvah* boy who came for private lessons. On the way home from the rabbi's house one evening, I passed the pool hall, glanced through the window and noticed Mr. Spitz, putting up a poster of Jack Kennedy. I was so surprised that I stepped inside to ask him why.

He said, "Today's April 17th, the first anniversary of the Bay of Pigs. I'm commemorating the day with the poster. Jack Kennedy deserves credit. He stood up to the 'Reds.' He supported the Cubans who tried to overthrow Castro…"

I walked home thoughtfully, reflecting on how many people thought they knew what was right for the world, like the Jehovah's witnesses, or Mr. Spitz.


My grandmother had slowed down a lot lately. Even a short walk made her breathless. There were whispered secrets between her and my mother, bottles of pills that appeared in the medicine cabinet. She's not sick, I kept telling myself.

As much as I denied what I saw, I had to wonder whether she'd have the strength to do the big pre-Passover cleaning. Previous years, she'd dusted the moldings, crawled under the bed, cleaned every cabinet and closet, scrubbed the windows, and, before the first *Seder*, changed our ordinary dishes and pots for those we used for the holiday.

Then, one afternoon, I came home from school and smelled *Pine-sol* in the air, saw newspapers protecting the washed floors, and realized the Passover cleaning had been accomplished two days in advance. I went to hang up my windbreaker in the hall closet. Usually this closet was a tangle of shoes, clothes, extra toilet paper rolls, a mop and broom. Not today. Everything was neatly stacked or hung.

I looked it all over appreciatively until I realized that I didn't see my shoebox where I kept my Marilyn Monroe autograph. The autograph was more important than ever. Lately, I'd begun thinking about girls non-stop. I wasn't bold enough to sneak a copy of *Playboy* into the house. Sometimes, when I was alone in the apartment, I drew naked women, but fearful my pictures would be discovered, I threw them away. The one thing I could count on to make me feel great was Marilyn's autograph. A glimpse at it brought her to life. I fantasized that I was her lover. Now, the autograph was gone.

My mother was still at work, and Grandma was taking a break, drinking tea in the kitchen. She drank it morning and night.

"Where's the shoe box with my stuff?" I demanded, standing in the doorway.

It took her a while to realize what I was talking about. "Why are you getting excited about that box of junk?"

"Give it to me. Those are my private things."

"I threw the box away. This is the time to get rid of junk like that. It makes more room."

I rushed to the garbage bin under the sink.

She watched, shaking her head. "Don't bother. I took the garbage downstairs, and the garbage men have already emptied the cans. What are you worried about? I looked in the box. There was no money."

Hating her with all my heart, I blurted, "If you're so sick, why don't you hurry up and die!"

I anticipated a slap like the one I'd received from my mother the last time I insulted Grandma. My grandmother only stood there helplessly wringing her hands while tears slid down her wrinkled cheeks. I ran out of the house. When I finally came back, my mother was home. She spoke cheerfully, said she'd picked up the *bar mitzvah* invitations from the printers.

After supper, she washed off the kitchen table before setting the invitations down. There was a lot of consulting between her and Grandma about who should get one. I wondered whether my father would be invited, but wasn't able to bring myself to ask. I knew my parents were divorced, but didn't know whether my mother had his address, received alimony, had any contact at all with him.

From time to time, I sensed Grandma looking at me as I helped address envelopes, but wouldn't give her the satisfaction of returning her glance. I couldn't forgive her for throwing out Marilyn's autograph. Tossing on my couch-bed later that night, I wished she'd never come to live with us. We wouldn't be fighting. I wouldn't hate myself for telling her, "Drop dead."

Then, a memory pierced me. When she first moved in, I used to ask her, "Grandma, do you miss Baltimore?" I'd been frightened she'd say 'yes,' that she missed Uncle Ben, the way I missed my father, and would go back.

But she'd always answered, "*Oy*, am I glad to get away from that *meshuga*, crazy, Selma." Then, she'd hug me and take me up on a lap that had felt like a big house with a thousand rooms, a place I'd felt I never wanted to leave.

Spring marched into our neighborhood. Leaves and buds sprouted on trees. Doves lined up on telephone wires. The weather turned warm. Laundry dried on clotheslines on the roof. A few boys sneaked up there and set off firecrackers. Kids started roller-skating and biking. My *bar mitzvah* day approached. I dreaded the ceremony at the synagogue, but looked forward to the party afterwards that was going to be held in a nightclub. The word nightclub gave me goose bumps.

Every evening, the phone rang, our guests calling to say whether they were coming. The few times Uncle Ben had visited us from Baltimore, his wife had stayed behind. True to form, Selma wasn't going to attend my *bar mitzvah*. I liked to imagine that roaring blizzards and shifting glaciers had her trapped in the Arctic Circle, while Uncle Ben whom I loved was taking the train up.

When Ben had lived in New York, he'd worked as a welder at a sheet metal factory. Then he'd taken a job as a sign painter in Baltimore where Selma's relatives resided. What my uncle really wanted to be was an artist who drew newspaper ads. When I was small he'd sketched any animal I asked for-- kangaroos, elephants, ostriches, bears, bats. I used to watch how he held the pencil between his thick fingers, how he made the first line, what he did next. I wanted to see how it was done, so I could do it too.

We didn't have anywhere for Uncle Ben to sleep, so Mrs. Kessler, our next-door neighbor, loaned us a fold-a-way cot. When Mom and I went to get it, Mrs. Kessler complained that her daughter, two years older than me, had bullied her into letting her go shopping on her own for a dress for my *bar mitzvah* party. Mrs. Kessler vowed, "Over my dead body, will my Celia show up dressed like a street walker in that tight red dress."

My mother and grandmother bought new dresses too, and went to the beauty parlor for haircuts. Usually, my grandmother cut my hair. But for my *bar mitzvah*, my mother insisted I go to a regular barber. I sat frozen in the barbershop chair as if I were Samson losing my strength. The floor was covered with bits of my brown hair. Grandma believed that anyone who wished to put an evil curse on you could do so if they got hold of your hair or nail clippings. Whenever she cut my hair or I cut my nails, she burnt the clippings in an iron bucket on the fire escape grate. Uneasily, I watched the barber sweep my hair clippings into a pile. I wanted to take them home to my grandmother to burn. Too embarrassed to ask the barber to give the clippings to me, I paid and left the shop.

The morning of my *bar mitzvah*, I woke up and saw my new suit and white shirt hanging on the living room door, a reminder I scarcely needed that today was the day. Uncle Ben lay on the cot next to my couch where he'd gone to sleep soon after his arrival the night before. He was big like my grandmother, had a fighter's flat nose, snored loudly. Since his last visit two years ago, his hair had thinned. He'd gained weight. His heavy cheeks made him look like a bulldog. Later, when we started to the synagogue, he fussed over Grandma as if it were her special day instead of mine. She walked with irritating slowness. I thought we'd never get there.

The little *shul* vestibule was crowded with people who tapped me on the shoulder and said, "*Mazel tov*, good luck." I saw the four Kesslers, my Hebrew School pals, and all the regulars who attended services. Some of the people my mother had invited were only going to come to the nightclub party. Unless you lived in the neighborhood, it was hard to come to two events with no place to stay in between.

A smile fixed to my lips, I said, "Thanks," when people congratulated me. Glancing through the crowd from one corner to another, I kept looking for my father, a futile search. My mother helped my grandmother climb to the balcony where the women sat. At least I had Uncle Ben to sit beside me in the men's section. He held a prayer book. His arm was draped around my shoulder. From time to time, he looked up from the prayer books, turned, and gazed at me. The look in his kind, brown eyes said, 'You'll do fine.'

Light streamed in the windows, brightening the synagogue's high ceiling. Rabbi Schneider stood on the *bimah* in front. Behind him was a purple velvet curtain embroidered with lions and ten-commandment tablets. The curtain covered the ark with the Torah scrolls. Every time I heard the door in the back squeak open, I wanted to turn around to see who was coming inside, but I controlled myself.

The torah scrolls, dressed in velvet cases were taken out of the ark and paraded around. Men, who had aisle seats, kissed the fringes on their prayer shawls, then touched the fringes to the velvet coverings on the Torahs, a way to bring good luck. Uncle Ben's Hebrew name, *Benyimin Yehudah*, was called. He went up

on the platform and read from the Torah. The scroll was too holy
to touch with his finger, so he kept his place with a little silver
and ivory pointer. Rabbi Schneider called me up to chant my
*parsha* from Deuteronomy, the section that begins, "Thou shalt be
whole-hearted with the Lord thy God." The Hebrew letter *tav* was
written larger than the others. The *tav* began the word *tamim*,
whole-hearted. I used the pointer too, placed it on the tav and
began.

With both Uncle Ben and the rabbi beaming at me, the
*parsha* rolled off my tongue easily. I felt inspired, uplifted.
Glancing up at the balcony, I saw my mother and grandmother
with tears streaming down their cheeks. They loved me so much,
had scrimped and scraped to make my *bar mitzvah* possible. I
regretted how cruel I'd been, particularly to Grandma. When I
gave my speech and thanked my mother and grandmother for
their support, I did so wholeheartedly. Uncle Ben presented me
with a prayer shawl. I threw it over my shoulders, and felt like I
was another person, no longer the resentful, ungrateful brat I'd
been up until now.

That evening, I went to the nightclub for my party.
Grandma and I had on the same clothes we'd worn to the service,
but my mother had changed into a turquoise blue taffeta cocktail
dress. She looked gorgeous. My grandmother, in her black dress,
looked pale and drained. Uncle Ben had tried to persuade her to
stay home, but she wouldn't hear of it.

At the nightclub, five other *bar mitzvahs* were being
celebrated simultaneously. Our party made a little island in a sea
of dressed-up strangers, all of us sharing the same gigantic hall.
My mother had reserved tables. She, Uncle Ben and my
grandmother sat at one, along with some distant relatives. These

people were related to my mother's grandfather's brother, Max. I don't think they were blood relatives to us, but I called the women 'Aunt,' the men 'Uncle' and considered the kids my cousins. That's how it was with families that had lost their relatives in the camps. They adopted new relations and included them in their special events.

I sat at a table with my Hebrew School buddies, and a few kids from my regular school. There were more 'relations' at another table, including an elderly couple, the Myers, who'd recently arrived from Buenos Aires. Two women my mother knew from work were seated with neighbors, including the four Kesslers. Mrs. Kessler, who'd threatened 'Over my dead body,' was still alive, even though Celia wore her tight, low-cut, red satin dress. Celia's figure was small and thin, her face, pinched-looking. As a little kid, she'd worn a Davey Crockett hat perched above two ponytails that jutted out on either side of her head. The hat was long gone, and she'd graduated to a single ponytail, lipstick and mascara.

Waiters brought us plates with roast beef, salad and French fries. While we were eating, the lights dimmed and the show began. Schekey Greene, a big burly man with greased-back black hair, came out on the stage and let loose. When he told dirty jokes, some people laughed, and the rest were shocked and silent. Robby, a kid from Hebrew School, was hanging around the bar and handing out drinks to the adults. The bartender turned his back, and Robby brought two bottles over for us boys. In the dim room, no one noticed we'd advanced from ginger ale to champagne. Sweet and cold, its bubbles tickled my nose. Actually, it didn't taste that different from the ginger ale we'd been drinking before. I guzzled it down like it was soda pop.

After Schekey Greene, the two Barry sisters sang in Yiddish, "*Bei Mir Bist Du Shein*." Celia came over and asked me to dance. When we were little kids we used to play that I was her little dog as she led me around with a string around my neck. I'd hated her bossiness, her getting me in trouble.

When she was eight or nine, she used to come over to our apartment to see Grandma's parakeet. "Hel-lo. Hel-lo. My name is Tiny," she'd screech, tapping the cage with her nails. No matter how she begged, my grandmother wouldn't let her take the bird out of the cage.

One evening, my mother took my grandmother shopping. Celia was ecstatic. Throwing open the bird cage, she cried to Tiny, "Come to Mommy." Tiny huddled in the far corner. When Celia thrust her hand in his cage, he darted out and flew up to the ceiling light fixture. The same way she'd seen my grandmother do, Celia held up a finger to lure him down. He wouldn't come. In order to get the parakeet moving, Celia started running around the living room.

Tiny went wild. He swooped to the window and back and forth from wall to wall. I wanted to get Tiny back in the cage before my grandmother returned. I chased and leapt about the living room, but I couldn't catch him.

So, I tried to catch crazy Celia. She was whirling around. I pulled her shirt. She tripped and shrieked so loudly that Mrs. Kessler heard her through the wall, rushed over and pounded on the door. I let her inside.

"What's going on?" she demanded.

Without waiting for an answer, she pushed past me to the living room. The moment she stepped inside, Tiny dove down and pecked her on the nose.

Celia screamed, "Gary pushed me. Look," she held out her glasses. They'd broken when she fell.

My mother and grandmother came home. Mrs. Kessler showed my mother the scratch on her nose, the cracked glasses' lens, and repeated Celia's version of things.

"It wasn't my fault!" I cried.

"I'll pay for new glasses," my mother said quietly.

After Mrs. Kessler and Celia left, I got a talking to from my mother about how 'money doesn't 'grow on trees' and how glasses cost 'a pretty penny.' She knew, having just bought a pair for herself for reading.

The frozen look on my grandmother's face had upset me more than my mother's lecture.

"Grandma, I'm sorry," I'd said.

She didn't notice me, as she whispered to the ruffled blue feathers she held in her hands.

Fortunately, Tiny survived.

By now, I scarcely talked to Celia. Tonight, though, my head was spinning. I agreed to be her partner. We squeezed onto the dance floor. A D.J. played an Elvis song. People danced the Twist. I didn't know how to do it, but it didn't matter. Celia and I flung our arms and legs out, swung our heads, and wiggled our hips. Mrs. Kessler advanced on us, and through clenched teeth, told us, "Don't act so wild." She pulled Celia away.

Back at my table with my friends, I thought it was hilarious when one kid began gargling with champagne, or another put his head on the table, and said, "Wake me up for the naked girls." I glanced at Grandma and remembered a Marilyn Monroe movie where a man puts on a black dress and make-up, and pretends he's a female bass player. Imagining Grandma going up on the stage and twanging a bass, I laughed and laughed.

The next morning, I woke with a headache. There was a vomit taste in my mouth. The toilet flushing, the shower, the kettle whistling, voices talking, made me wince. Even my mother's whisper to my grandmother seemed loud.

"I want you to take your pills."

"It's hard for me to swallow."

I pulled the sheet over my head, kept my hands over my ears. Someone came into the living room. I felt the warm pressure of a hand on my shoulder and swiped it away. My sheet was pulled down. I opened my eyes to a burst of stars. It took a few seconds before I could focus my eyes on a green checked shirt over a bulging belly, chubby cheeks that were red from a razor's scraping, brown eyes beneath bushy brows. Uncle Ben.

"I'm going now, Gary."

"Go-ing? Where?" I managed to mumble, despite my fat tongue.

Uncle Ben laughed. "Where do you think? Home. Baltimore. You've got a hang-over, kid."

"Thanks for coming."

"I want you to have this. Don't get up. Don't move." Ben took two bills out of his wallet and slipped them under my pillow.

"Thanks." I slipped my hand beneath the pillow to touch them. The bills were crisp. Ben must have gone to the bank to get them.

"Are you still drawing, Gary?" His voice was husky. He cared about whether I did.

"Yeah," I said. My face felt warm as if I was blushing.

"Use the money I gave you for paints, pencils, that kind of thing...Don't let anyone stop you...It's a beautiful thing to be an artist."

I heard my mother hurrying down the hall. She stepped into the room, wearing a black and white polka dot dress and white pumps. "You're up. If you hurry and get dressed, you can come with us to the train station and see Ben off."

I couldn't hurry. I couldn't even move. My uncle winked at me and said, "It's too late. We can't wait for him. We better leave."

Voices. Footsteps. I heard my uncle comment on the snacks my grandmother had packed for him. "Mama, this bag is heavy. It's not like I'm going half-way around the world." Grandma had traveled from Poland to Argentina to New York. She knew the number one rule: 'never buy food when you travel. Take your own.'

The door slammed. I took out the newly minted bills Uncle Ben had given me. They weren't two five's or two ten's. They were two twenties. The gifts I'd received as *bar mitzvah* gifts were mostly Israel bonds or checks that Mom made me put in the bank, no ready cash like this. I decided I'd use some of it to buy either chocolates or a pair of nylons for my grandmother. I wanted to show her that I regretted the terrible thing I'd said to her.

I kept denying it to myself, but I knew Grandma was sick....


By July, my grandmother was staying in bed most of the day. My mother began sleeping on the Kessler's roll-a-way, pushed next to Grandma. It was like she wasn't living in the apartment any more, only in the bed. Mom didn't like to go off to work and leave her alone. Since I was on summer vacation, she made me stay.

I felt trapped and unhappy. Every day was boring. With the curtains closed, the room was dim as if daytime had disappeared. Even Tiny, whose cage stood on the bed table now, drooped and didn't have the energy to chirp.

I tried to entertain my grandmother with stories the way she'd once entertained me. When I ran out of my own, I repeated ones she'd told me.

"Remember about your parrot, Grandma?"

She shook her head.

"You were leaving Argentina for New York. Your ship stopped in Cuba, in a harbor. You saw a market on the beach."

"A long time ago, *mein kind*." She closed her eyes.

"Don't go to sleep…don't," I begged, fearing she'd wake up weaker, more confused, perhaps unable to recognize me. "You wanted to go to the market. So you did something *meshuga*, crazy. You jumped off the side of the boat and swam ashore. You were soaking wet,"

She smiled and nodded. "Yes, I remember now. A market with so much junk…tablecloths, straw hats, pots and pans, old glasses…a whole table of used false teeth."

Oh, she did remember. She was herself again. I was thrilled. "And the parrots, Grandma…" I said eagerly.

"The parrots? Ach, there were a lot the man was selling. But only one looked at me like it was begging to be redeemed…what could I do? I didn't have much, but I bought it. I had to float back to the boat on my back. I held the parrot on top of my chest …the bird was a lot nicer than many people."

I laughed, and so did Grandma. Then, sleep overtook her. Her mouth was open, her white hair spread on the pillowslip. She seemed lost in a faraway world. I left the room, came back at intervals to check how she was. After two hours, I resumed my seat in the chair next to the bed.

My mother had Dr. Greenbaum come to check on my grandmother. He was the doctor everyone in the neighborhood used. Normally, Grandma would have objected to being examined. The fact that she didn't showed how weak she was. The doctor wanted to come by every other day. He was a big, bustling man who told corny jokes, and hummed show tunes.

My mother told him, "I want Mama to have the best care. But I'll need time to pay off what I'll owe you..."

"Don't worry. I'm not going to send you any bills. I have patients I come to see around here and can just drop by when I'm in the neighborhood."

"I don't know how to thank you," Mom said, tears in her eyes.

"All I'm asking is that you don't mention I'm not charging you to anyone. Or all my patients will expect the same."

"The man's a saint," my mother declared after he left.

Daily, I sat by my grandmother's side while a second-hand fan that Mr. Kessler had hauled up the steps and installed in the window, rotated with a monotonous sound. Mom tried to pay him a few dollars, but he refused, claiming a business contact had given him the fan for free.

Lethargy filled the bedroom. With every passing moment I was more tired of the waiting, waiting for something to happen.

My eyes closed. I dreamt I was a small boy, sitting on Grandma's lap like I once did. Her housedress felt stiff, pressed and smelled of laundry starch. Her neck was like warm milk; one of her hands smelled of cinnamon, the other vanilla. After a minute or two, I woke with tears in my eyes, sorrowful because I knew I'd never find safe harbor in her arms again.

In the evenings, neighbors dropped by for brief visits with my mother, and to deliver jars of chicken soup, a welcome gift as the refrigerator was nearly empty. My mother didn't cook any more, never even seemed to eat, as that meant deserting the post she took up beside Grandma as soon as she came home from work. I heated up the soup for myself, and made peanut butter sandwiches during the day.

The now lifeless kitchen was so different from the war zone it had been when Grandma was cooking. Like a great warrior, she'd stood cleaver in hand, hacking up chickens and meat. With her big hands, she'd shaped matzo balls or salmon patties, or rolled out paper-thin dough, using only the side of a glass. Every burner had been lit; every pot, out; the pressure cooker, hissing; the air filled with smoke, flour dust, the fumes of cut-up onions, sizzling chicken fat, the stink of simmering gefilte fish. Pots slipped and clanked to the floor. Potatoes rolled across it. Silverware clattered. A fallen spoon meant a child was coming to visit; a knife meant a man; a fork, a woman. "It's a crime to waste food," Grandma would say, picking up a bit of dropped dough, popping it into her mouth, tough, not caring about germs like my mother and I did.

Sipping the soups of others' charity, I thought wistfully of Grandma's wonderful feasts: soups with dumplings; chopped liver; brisket; roasted chicken; stuffed cabbage; *knishes*; *kugel*;

*kasha*; glistening noodles; honey cake; apple strudel. After the first delicious bite of Grandma's food, nothing else had existed, only the happiness of my mouth and belly. I'd taken those perfect meals for granted. I'd taken my grandmother for granted.

While I ate, my mother made lists of things she needed, then sent me to the grocery and the drugstore. I was eager to escape the hot apartment.

Outside, neighbors sat on folding chairs, fanned themselves and gossiped. "How's your grandmother?" they called as I passed.

"She's fine." I hurried away from their probing questions.

I couldn't walk on the Avenue without remembering the walks Grandma used to take me on when I was small. I'd had to hurry along to keep up with her as she'd wandered all over the Lower East Side, including the Ukrainian and Puerto Rican sections. These were neighborhoods my mother considered 'bad' with their uneven pavements, loud music and beer-drinking men hanging around. My grandmother hadn't been scared of anyone or anything except bad spirits' and 'spells'. She'd taught me to not step on cracks or walk under ladders, to say, "*kine horra*, no evil eye."

Even now I saw people as she'd taught me to see them. There, hurrying past on the Avenue, was a *miskeit*, an ugly person; a *minival,* a man who looked like an ape; a *minerval,* a female *minival*; a *schmegeggy,* a not bright person; a *shlameil*, a clumsy loser; a *nudnik*, a pest; a *tukhis lecker*, a phony; a *Galizianer*, a phony but also a charmer, so that it was hard to see the *tukhis lecker* behind the smiling face.

On the way to Temple's drug store, I walked along a path Grandma and I used to take that ran beside the wide, brown East

River. Once, we'd seen fish heads lined up on the sides of steps that led to the street, and on the top stair, a cow's head with coins stuck all over it. After spitting three times, Grandma had whisked me away. She said someone had told her that some Haitians had had a voodoo ceremony, and now she saw what they'd done. For weeks, she wouldn't go near the river again.

But in the end, we went back because the river reminded her of the Vistula where she'd played when she was a little girl. Watching the tugboats chug along, she'd talked about the *shtetl*, the Jewish village in Poland where she'd lived as a child. She'd told me how she had to go to a Catholic School—there was no other--and she was made to bow before the cross. Gangs of Catholic thugs beat up her father and other Jews in the village. When she came to Argentina, she saw the same thing happen there too. Uncle Ben was beaten by boys shouting, "*Yid.*" Whenever my grandmother saw a nun or priest, she waited until they passed, and then spat on the pavement. I became afraid of "Catholic spells," and when I saw a man or woman all in black, I edged closer to Grandma and clutched her hand.

Returning from my errands, I encountered my pale, sad mother. The next morning, she went to work, and I resumed my place by my grandmother's bed. Each passing day, I fell ever more deeply into a well of dreams and recollections about Grandma that were both sweet and painful because I was losing her.

Moments I had hardly ever reflected upon, returned, like the wedding I'd attended when I was eight or nine. My mother and grandmother had plunged into the crowd, leaving me to find someone my age for company. I'd felt so deserted that I'd gone to the lobby and sat by myself. There I was kicking my feet, mad at the world. Then, the doors to the hall swung open with a blast of talking, laughing and music. Out came my grandmother.

"I have to use the toilet," she said in Yiddish. She couldn't read English, not even 'Men' or 'Ladies.' "Where should I go?"

Determined to revenge myself on her, I pointed to the door that said, 'Men.' In she marched and, unfortunately, there was a man inside.

When my mother heard what I'd done, she was furious. "Don't you know the difference between the men's and the women's room?"

Only now, as I sat beside Grandma's bed was I repentant. She wanted to sleep. I wanted her to talk, a sign that she'd recover, that I could make up to her all the ways I'd been disrespectful.

"Grandma, do you remember…" I prodded, reminding her of the big church we'd once passed, at a time when I had no idea what a church was. She'd told me people go inside to hear stories about the Virgin Mary. I'd clamored to hear them, so she'd related her versions.

"Remember you said the Virgin Mary lived a long time ago when there weren't stores, or buses—and she suffered because she couldn't buy bananas, or go to the zoo."

Sick as she was Grandma could still make me laugh. She said in a weak, cracked voice, "The Virgin didn't have heat in the winter. *Nebbich*, the poor thing was always shivering."

The doorbell rang, interrupting our talk. I went to answer it. Mrs. Kessler, dressed in pink Capri peddle-pushers and smoking, had come over with a plate of deviled eggs. She walked into the kitchen as if she were in her own home, put the plate in the refrigerator, then turned to me and said blithely, "Did you hear? Marilyn Monroe swallowed a bottle of sleeping pills. She's dead." Having discharged this news, she asked a few questions about my grandmother. I answered automatically. I suppose she attributed my dullness to my grief for Grandma.

Once she'd left, I sank into a chair and glanced at the calendar on the kitchen wall, noting the date, August 5, 1962. I thought of Marilyn dressed in a low-cut, sparkly pink dress, and singing in a breathy voice that diamonds were her best friends. That Marilyn was a movie fantasy who would never die. The other Marilyn, the woman I'd seen in a big shirt, without make-up, with tired eyes, and who'd made a special trip to give me her autograph, had died. I felt sad for that woman, but she was a stranger. I stirred myself to return to Grandma's bedside.

About a week later, Uncle Ben came up for a visit. He'd come twice in July. Each visit he acted cheerful, gave me a hug, observed that I'd grown, praised the bit of fuzz on my upper lip. This visit, he took me out for an ice cream soda and brought home cold cuts for supper from the delicatessen. After we ate, Ben sent me to sit with Grandma while he talked with Mom in the living room.

I left the bedroom door open, was able to hear Uncle Ben tell Mom, "Mama made me promise to look after you, Lily…Later, if you want to come down and live in Baltimore, I'll do anything I can to help…"

"I don't have any intention of moving."

"Is the doctor still thinking about putting Mama in the hospital?"

"She said that she'd never go to a hospital. She wants to be with us."

My mother went off to bed, while my uncle and I played cards at the kitchen table. It was hot. He stripped down to his underwear. Thick, brown hair curled on his chest and back. The burns from when he was a welder still made tiny, wriggling stripes on his arms, but the scars were no longer red but white. With stubby fingers, he dealt out the cards in rows, and taught me *Pisha-Pesha*. After an hour or so, we went to sleep, he on the couch, me with a pillow and blanket on the hard floor.

From the street came the swish of cars. A car circled the block with its radio on full blast, playing Spanish music. I dreamt of a couple gliding along in a tango. The man wore a dark suit, the woman a red, ruffled dress. Back and forth, round and round, they danced on a circle of black glass. I wanted them to stop, wanted to wake up.

In the morning, my pillow was soaked with drool, my eyelids stuck together. I was confused about why I was on the floor, thought I'd fallen off the couch. Across the room I saw my mother, barefoot in her pink housedress. My uncle had his pants on, but was barefoot and wasn't wearing a shirt. They stood clinging to each other like they would never let go. I knew what had happened.

My mother noticed I was awake. She swallowed, straightened her face like she'd straighten the front of one of my shirts, and came to me. Gently, she kissed my cheek and stroked my hair. "Mama died in her sleep. You can go say goodbye."

"He doesn't have to see her," Uncle Ben said.

"I want to."

I went to the bedroom, feeling like I was sinking into mud. Grandma lay with her eyes closed as if she were peacefully sleeping. I touched her arm with the tip of my finger. She didn't feel cold or stiff. Getting up my courage, I took her hand in mine. The knuckles were red and swollen, the palm hard. "Grandma," I whispered. "It's me. It's Gary. I'm sorry about the times I was mean to you." I sat holding her hand for a long time, until Uncle Ben who'd put on a short-sleeved white shirt, came in and put his arm around my shoulder. "An ambulance is coming to take Grandma away. Your mother wants you to stay next door."

I went next door. Mr. Kessler had left for work at his shoe factory. Esther, the elder daughter, was standing at the sink, sipping coffee. Celia sat at the table stuffing her mouth with scrambled eggs and toast. She put her fork down and blinked at me. Her uncombed hair stuck out in every direction. A cigarette dangled from Mrs. Kessler's lip. She was in her bathrobe. She exhaled a stream of smoke and said, "Sit down at the table. I'll make you breakfast. Anything you want. Pancakes. Ice cream. Cake. Anything."

"I don't want to eat. I just want to be by myself."

"Sure."

She took me to her bedroom, a considerably bigger room than the one the two girls shared. A photograph hung over the bed, Mrs. Kessler and her husband, Herb, as bride and groom. In a corner of the room stood an easy chair with a tasseled pillow, and, on top, a folded blue satin bed spread. Mrs. Kessler pulled down the shades, smoothed the rumpled sheets. "Go to bed," she ordered. "The girls and I are going out. You have the place to yourself."

She took some clothes out the closet, and out of a long, low dresser. I was in the bed now, staring at the fancy, glass perfume bottles, compacts and gold tubes of lipstick on top of the dresser. The door clicked. Mrs. Kessler was gone. I sank into a soft mattress that rose up around me.

All this time, I was crying and couldn't stop. People talk about a good laugh or a good cry, and this was a good cry. I cried from one end of the Kesslers' double bed to the other, lying sometimes on my back, or on my side or belly. My eyes blurred. Sobs lifted me up and down. My lips tasted salty. I pounded the pillow and kicked the mattress. My crying was like an ocean that rolled out faraway, and then slowly back, taking its time.

The ambulance men stamped up the stairs so loudly that I could hear. Fifteen minutes later, they tramped down. Grandma was big. How could they lift her? But they hurried away as if she was light. The following silence stretched out. Eventually, my tears stopped, the way blood stops and a scab forms over a cut.

I returned home. My mother and Uncle Ben smiled 'be brave' smiles at me. I gave a 'be brave' smile back. I went to check the bedroom. It looked so empty with the sheets and blankets stripped off the big bed.

3. My Father

Phone calls were made to say Grandma Etta had died. Uncle Ben placed a notice in the newspaper, announcing a funeral the next day, a Thursday. Although it took place on a working day, a sizable crowd showed up. I hadn't realized how popular Grandma was until I saw all the people, filling the pews at the funeral home.

After the service, most of them rushed off to work, or went home because they couldn't face the long, hot drive to Long Island's Montefiore cemetery. Not many people owned cars. Those who did chauffeured anyone who wanted a lift to the cemetery. Mom, Ben, Rabbi Schneider, and I rode in a black limousine provided by the funeral home.

We parked on the road, entered the cemetery, walked down a dusty path past endless rows of gravestones. The August sun beat down as we stood at Grandma's gravesite. My mother was dressed in a black dress, black stockings and heels. Uncle Ben looked drained. Rabbi Schneider mopped his forehead with a white handkerchief as he recited prayers. I recognized several of our adopted relatives among the twenty or so people gathered, 'Aunt' Rose, 'Uncle' Moe, the Myers, the old couple from Argentina. The Myers held black umbrellas over their heads.

Hearing the crunch of gravel, I turned and saw a couple of latecomers. They stood beneath a tree, and a little to the side of our group of mourners. It wasn't clear whether the couple were with us, or visiting another grave. The woman was slender and had platinum hair like Marilyn Monroe's. The tall thin blond, blue-eyed man resembled my father! He was the last person I expected to pay respects to my grandmother. I remembered how he used to rage at Mom, "I don't want that ignorant woman filling Gary's head with nonsense!"

As I turned my attention back to Rabbi Schneider, I told myself to stop having foolish thoughts, that the man standing beneath the tree was no more my father than his companion was Marilyn Monroe. The rabbi gave black ribbons to my mother, uncle and me to pin on our clothes. Then he slashed the ribbons with a razor to symbolize that we'd 'rent' our clothes. Uncle Ben and my mother said the mourner's prayer, "*Yisgadal, v' yisgadal...*"

I muttered the *Yisgadal* too, but all I could think of was the couple behind us. I turned again to make sure they hadn't gone. The woman was dressed in a black and white print sundress, wide brimmed black straw hat. She took off her sunglasses and smiled at me as if she knew whom I was. I began to tremble. Maybe the man was my father. He looked exactly as I remembered him. Dad had been born in Finland. His father, a Russian Jew, went there on business and became involved with a peasant woman. She bore him a son whom he took to America and raised as a Jew. That person was my handsome father.

My mother put her arm about my shoulder, whispered, "Stop wriggling around."

Two gravediggers lowered my grandmother's coffin into the grave. The taller one scattered the first spade-full of earth on the coffin lid. Then my mother, Ben, and I, and a few of the other mourners took turns with the spades too. Sobs shook my mother. She looked small to me, like she was a child. Uncle Ben took her arm, a signal to everyone to walk away and leave the gravediggers to finish burying Grandma.

We washed our hands at a sink beside the cemetery gate. Rabbi Schneider said we did this to cleanse away the impurities of the cemetery. The hush of the funeral and burial were over. My mother, Ben and I received condolences. People told us, "Too bad we have to meet under such sad circumstances," and, "Etta was a wonderful woman."

The man whom I'd become certain was my father lingered at a distance. His companion approached me, and introduced herself in a voice that wasn't breathy like Marilyn Monroe's had been in the movies.

"I'm Francine, your stepmother."

Her words shocked me. I glanced at my mother, wondered whether she'd registered that my father was here, or that he was here with a second wife. Absorbed in saying goodbyes, she seemed no more aware of Dad and Francine than of the bees buzzing among the blue-flowered bushes by the cemetery gate.

"Your father and I are moving to Florida next week. We wanted to see you before we left. Here's our new address," Francine said, pressing a piece of paper into my hand. I slipped it into my suit jacket pocket. The suit was the same one I'd worn to my *bar mitzvah* three months ago. I'd grown since then, but I'd had nothing else I could wear to a funeral.

People began packing into cars for the return trip. Uncle Ben accompanied the Myers in order to help them into Mr. Kessler's Ford.

Once my mother was alone, my father came up to her.

A puzzled look came over Mom's face. "Dave?" she cried.

"Yes Lily, it's me."

My parents stood frozen, staring at one another.

After Francine went over and introduced herself to Mom, I approached my father. "Dad..." I stammered.

I don't know what I expected. He couldn't say much to me with his new wife and my mother there. It was hard enough to talk, after not having spoken in years. The trouble was, we were strangers. But he was my father, and I expected something.

"So Gary. How are you?" he said.

"Okay."

"How's school?"

"I'm not in school. It's summer vacation. Where in Florida are you going?"

"West Palm Beach."

Francine joined in, and said, "After our decorators are done, I want you to come visit us, Gary."

I nodded.

"Promise?"

"Sure."

My father took out a cigarette and put it in a tortoise shell cigarette holder. I remembered he liked to smoke, but didn't recall him using a holder.

Uncle Ben returned, put his arm around my mother and said, "The limo's waiting." His face was red and perspiring. He shaded his eyes from the sun and nodded to my father. I wasn't sure whether he recognized him.

"Here's Dave and his wife," my mother said, curtly. I could tell she was fuming.

"How are you, Dave? It's been a long time," my uncle said in a friendly way. He put out his hand, first to Francine, then to my father. His calm spread over me like a blanket. Grandma used to say, "After living with that *meshuganah* Selma, Ben can handle anything."

The limousine driver honked the horn, and my father looked towards the road. "Your driver's waiting."

Ben asked, "Do you need a lift? There's room in the limo. Rabbi Schneider went back with Mr. Kessler."

"No thanks, we have our car," my father answered. "Goodbye Lily...Ben...Gary." Dad nodded to each of us in turn. "Let's go, Francine." Francine winked at me.

A big black Lincoln was parked on the road outside the cemetery, its outside as shiny as a mirror. My father opened the passenger door, handed Francine in, then circled around to climb in the driver's seat. The car speed off

"He learned to drive after he left me," Mom spat out, disgustedly.

My uncle helped her into the limousine, and kept his arm around her shoulder as the driver headed towards the expressway. I'd taken the seat beside the driver where Rabbi Schneider had sat before

Behind me, Mom said angrily, "So? What did he want?"

"Nothing, Lily," my uncle replied. "People show up at funerals. He read the notice, or someone told him, and he felt obligated."

"Him obligated? He must have wanted something." In the rear view mirror, I saw her purse her lips and glare as she said, "So Gary, you're ready to run off to Florida?"

"What was I supposed to say?"

"You could have said you were busy. All these years, he was too busy for you. Now he comes! He never liked Mama. Couldn't he let me bury her in peace? It wasn't enough that he showed up. Why did he have to bring along his lady friend?"

The words 'lady friend' brought back memories, her lamenting to my grandmother right after my father left, "Dave found a lady friend." I didn't know whether Francine was the same woman from that time, but my mother thought so.

The rest of the ride, we were silent. For a while, I looked at my reflection in the rear view mirror, trying to ascertain whether there was the faintest resemblance between my father and me. My grandmother, I recalled, used to lift me onto her lap when I was small, and say, "Acck, who is this? He's dark. Not *goyish* hair. Not a little *goyish* nose. Thank God, a *yiddishe punim*, a Jewish face. A Jewish soul…" What she'd meant was that she was glad that I didn't look like my father. Strictly speaking, he was not Jewish because Judaism is passed on through the mother. Everyone, except Grandma, had overlooked this technicality.

The rest of the day, I was in a trance. My meeting with my father had stirred a multitude of memories of the time before he left when he'd taken me to a parade, a 3-D movie, or Steeplechase. I recalled a game we used to play, our hiding behind his armchair, and making believe we were in Finland. Sometimes, he'd thrown a white sheet over our heads and said, "It's snowing." He'd told me about fir forests; hot, steamy saunas; diving into icy water; Lapps who wore thick boots, blue jackets, red, blue and gold hats, and possessed herds of reindeer.

I remembered my mother waking one morning with a fever and sore throat. My grandmother was still living in Baltimore, so she couldn't baby-sit. My father had to fill in.

He took me by bus to a brown building. We rode a creaky little elevator, went to his small office, a room with a light bulb hanging over a desk. My father sat writing numbers in a big book, and punching an adding machine. I sat on a high stool and kicked my feet back and forth. The chair went round and round.

When Dad was done, he rubbed his eyes. "God, I'm beat. I need a cup of coffee." He took me to a large, bright restaurant, crowded with people. An elderly waiter with a white dishcloth tucked in the side of his belt, brought two glasses of water with ice cubes to our table. Then he came back with a plate of green, wrinkly pickles. I bit one. It was so sour that my mouth puckered. The waiter wrote down our order on his pad.

The front of the restaurant was glass with a glass door that opened and let in the cold wind. A big man came in, smoking a cigar. Seeing my father, he cried, "Dave," and headed for us. They started talking. The man leaned forward, one arm on the table. I could see the gold teeth at the back of his mouth.

The waiter banged down plates on the table. Mine had a pink, fat hot dog, lying on top of stringy sour kraut. My father would have to cut up the hot dog for me. I was waiting for him to stop talking and help. The man pulled out a chair and sat with us.

"Sorry Jack, I'm here with my boy," my father said.

"But Dave."

"Another time," Dad said abruptly.

After the man went away, Dad sipped his coffee and smoked. We didn't talk, but what he'd said had thrilled me.

The night after the funeral, my mother and Uncle Ben were talking in the kitchen when I stretched out on the couch to sleep. Mom was still outraged that my father and Francine had showed up at the cemetery.

As I drifted off, 'I'm here with my boy' kept sounding in my ears. Had my father said it because he didn't like the man who'd showed up? Or had he truly desired to be with me? I wanted to believe that he'd once loved me, and despite his neglect, still did. If he and Francine invited me to Florida, I'd be apprehensive, but I'd still need to go and find out.

Two days after Grandma was buried, Uncle Ben returned to Baltimore. He phoned long-distance every other day for a week or two. Then he called once a week. Then Baltimore swallowed him up. We didn't hear much from him or anybody else who'd come to my grandmother's funeral. They had to catch-up with their own lives. While they forgot about my grandmother, my mother mourned her with all her heart.

Wishing to cheer up my mother, I began drinking tea with her in the evenings, the way Grandma had once done. We looked at the pictures from my *bar mitzvah*. Mom loved those photos and even had one of Grandma enlarged and framed. The picture sat on a table in the living room near the couch where I slept. It was the first thing I saw when I woke up.

One evening, a man phoned and asked to speak to her. Mom took the telephone into the bathroom, and closed the door as well as she could with the phone cord in the way. I heard only a few snatches of what she said. "I can't… You have a wife…It's not right for you to say such things to me…" She hung up, came in the living room where I was, and started pacing round in the small space.

"What's wrong, Mom?" I asked.

Mom stopped short. She said, "It's always sad, Gary, when you think the world of someone, and they turn out to be less than you thought."

"Who do you mean?"

She shook her head, refusing to enlighten me.

I wondered who the man had been who'd upset her: her factory foreman; one of the neighbors; someone she'd known in

Argentina; an old boyfriend from before she'd married my father. The voice had sounded a little like Dr. Greenbaum's, but he was 'a saint.' It wasn't likely, it was he who'd phoned.


Towards the end of September, there was a scorching week. September was supposed to be cool, but these were 'dog days,' when everyone went around panting like a dog, and barking at each other. At night, my mother had to leave the windows open to catch the breeze. The neighbors' arguments circled up airshafts, through thin walls and open windows. Mom had trouble sleeping. She'd toss, turn, grind her teeth. After she cracked a tooth, she landed up going to a dentist who discovered she had numerous dental problems. She hadn't had a checkup in years.

To make matters worse, a Hassidic family with eight screeching kids moved in across from us. Mrs. Cooperman, the mother, yelled at the kids to pipe down, but they never did. Worse, the first thing that Mr. Cooperman, the diamond cutter father, did when he woke at five each morning was to put on a cantorial record at full volume, his speakers blasting, "*Yigdal elohim hai...*"

My mother took me along when she went to talk to him. His two huge speakers came up to his waist and took up most of his small living room.

Mom asked him not to play the music so loud in the morning.

He said, "When *HaShem*, the Lord, blesses you with eight children you'll understand."

"What do you mean?"

"I mean, with the music on, I can't hear anything else. I have peace."

My mom was so exhausted that she began forgetting things like paying the electric bill, or turning off the oven. One Sunday, she opened the parakeet's cage to put in fresh water, and forgot the kitchen window was open. Tiny hopped out onto the sill, and flew into the clouds. My mother and I raced downstairs, calling, "Tiny...Tiny." We asked all the neighbors to look for our parakeet. No one could find Tiny, so we went back up. Mom left the windows open on the chance Grandma's beloved pet would fly back inside.

'Look after your mother,' Grandma exhorted me everyday from the photograph on the living room table. I tried. But with her gone, there was no peace-making intermediary between Mom and me, and we fought. Everything at home reminded me of my grandmother's absence and Mom's grief. It was a relief to get out of the house even when my mother wasn't there.

Three or four times a week, I joined my pals after school for rides along the East River. When I went bike riding, I forgot everything. I'd grown so much over the summer that when I rode my old bicycle my knees hung low. If I grew any more they'd graze the pavement. But I made do as best I could.

I rode with the twins Howie and Harvey, and Ben, Robby and Jeff, other guys I knew from last year's Hebrew school class. When my grandmother had seen these boys in their stretched out t-shirts and dirty pants, she'd called them '*die grubbe yinglach*, grubby kids.' I'd been immaculate beside them dressed in the slacks and shirts she'd pressed, and the oxfords she'd polished. Nowadays, I looked as wrinkled and scuffed as everyone else.

We thirteen-year-olds weren't fully men and weren't kids. Balanced in-between, our sleek bodies were perfect for biking. Our group—even I perched on my too-small bike--whizzed by everybody. Grown-up bike riders were slow and clumsy compared to us. The little kids wobbled back and forth, weren't strong. Some even had training wheels.

Walkers jumped out of the way when my friends and I zipped by. We didn't want to knock anyone down, only tried to see who could get closest. Our victims thought they were safe after one of us passed, and then another of us whipped by, and then another. It was fun to scare some guy and then ride away laughing because he couldn't catch us. We made faces, rolled our eyes and pedaled fast. Once we were at a distance, we started showing off and wheeled our bikes in circles, and made the bikes jump. Sometimes we sang Beatles' songs like "Lucy in the Sky with Diamonds," or "Eleanor Rigby." The melodies were strange, different from other pop music.

These autumn afternoons never lasted long enough, particularly as winter neared and night came on earlier. I loved the blue-gray twilight with its blurred shapes and long shadows. We held onto every precious second, continued biking even when a few stars and a sliver of moon showed in the sky. Usually it was Howie who rounded up his twin brother and cried to the rest of us, "Gotta go. Our father's gonna kill us." That was our signal. In cracking voices, we called 'goodbye.' As if Howie had shot off a start-gun, the gang raced off in different directions.

His 'our father's gonna kill us' shot me in the heart. I was jealous the twins had a father who was pacing and glancing out the window, so worried he was ready to 'kill' them.

My mother dragged around, barely heard me the times I told her I needed a new bike. Either, she waved me away with "I can't talk about it now," or told me, "Stop nagging." I was persistent. She walked in from work one evening, and I started talking to her about the bike again.

Her face got red. She screamed, "Why don't you get it into your head? We're barely scraping by!"

I screamed back, "Stop saying we're poor. When Grandma was alive, there was money for stuff. She would have bought me a new bike!"

In a softened voice, Mom admitted, "Yes, she would have. She couldn't stand for you to be deprived of anything you set your heart on. But things are different now, Gary."

"Mom," I asked, "if we're so poor, why isn't Uncle Ben helping out?"

"He would if he could. But he's squeezed on every side. Both Selma's parents are sick. He's paying their medical bills. I don't want to hear you asked him for money for a bike. You understand?

"Yes."

"Don't ask him for a cent. Promise."

I nodded. I'd do what she said. That didn't mean I didn't hate her for telling me that we were poor.

I gave up on the bike, but I thought at least she'd buy me a pair of peg-leg pants. All the cool guys at school were wearing them. I desperately wanted a pair.

My mother's automatic response was, "I can't waste money." We'd been eating supper. She stood up, put her dish in the sink.

"Please, Mom. I really want them. They won't cost that much," I wheedled to her back.

She wheeled around. "Look Gary, you need those pants like you need la hole in the head."

"All you ever say is 'no.'"

"That's because it's hard to make ends meet. You're starting high school next year. I have to start saving to pay for your college. I used up my savings for your *bar mitzvah*. I have dental bills. I'm also paying off what I spent for your grandmother's funeral and her medical bills."

"Medical bills? Dr. Greenbaum didn't send you any bills!" I seized on what seemed a false claim, as if it could invalidate the others.

"No, he didn't send me any bills. But that doesn't mean I won't pay for his visits." Mom's face was flushed.

"But why? You didn't feel you had to before." I couldn't begin to understand why she'd be so stupid as to pay bills she'd never been sent.

Mom said, fiercely, "I don't want to be obligated to anybody. Just remember, Gary, nothing's free in this world!"

"Sure," I said, although I didn't have the faintest idea what she was talking about, only that she wasn't going to give me anything I wanted, not a bike, not peg-leg pants.

I pushed my plate away, walked off, thinking of ways to get away from her--hitchhiking to San Francisco, where I'd wear a feathered hippie headband, and take L.S.D.; becoming a Hollywood stunt man, jumping from moving cars and out of burning buildings, and making friends with the movie stars I adored; running away to Florida and cruising around in my father's big Lincoln. He didn't seem to have any money problems.

I went to the closet to look for the suit I'd worn to Grandma's funeral. If she'd been alive and well she would have taken it along with everything else I'd outgrown over to a family she knew with three boys younger than me. But the suit was still there, and so too the slip of paper in the pocket with my father's Florida address

Later, while I was watching television, my mother came in, turned off the sound and told me, "I want you to understand why I can't buy you the pants."

I stiffened.

"My boss laid off a couple of operators at work today. What if I lose my job? I'm worried." Tears stood in her eyes. She wiped them away with the back of her hand.

"I'm sorry," I mumbled. Her news terrified me. Since Grandma died, my mother wasn't her old self. If they were looking for someone to fire next, it was bound to be her.


When Eleanor Roosevelt died, I circled the date on the calendar, November 7, 1962, just the way I'd noted the date Marilyn Monroe had died. Everyone in our neighborhood was fiercely devoted to Mrs. Roosevelt. My mother had bought the *New York Post* in order to read her column. Hearing about her death on the news, Mom burst into tears. "She helped the little people," she sobbed. She was upset the rest of the evening.

The next day, when Mom came home from work, her eyes were red as if she'd never stopped crying from the night before. I assumed she was still sad about Mrs. Roosevelt. We ate supper without a word. The only sounds were the clink of our forks against the plates and the click-click of the wall-clock's minute hand, going round.

My mother cleared the table. I got up to leave the room, but she said, "Stay a minute, Gary. I have something to tell you."

"What is it?"

"I lost my job."

I gulped.

"You're not to worry. It will be all right. I'll get work. I was tired of that shop anyway." She began washing up.

"Maybe Uncle Ben will help us."

"We'll manage," she said, turning towards me. A glass slipped from her hands and shattered on the floor. I tried to help clean up the glass. "Leave it," she cried sharply. "I'll do it myself."

In the living room, I tried doing homework, and watching television, but couldn't concentrate. As far as I could tell, everything was going to fall apart. Soon, my mother and I were going to be truly poor. Soon, we might not have a place to live, or even enough to eat. Drawing was the only thing that relaxed me.

Mom finished cleaning up in the kitchen, came in, and sat down nearby while I sketched. I thought she was admiring my skill. She surprised me by saying, "I wish Ben hadn't put all those ideas about being an artist in your head. You should train for a profession that brings in a good salary."

"Like what?"

"I don't know…be a dentist. You should look at the bills that guy sends me."

"I don't want to be a dentist! I like to draw."

"Okay. Be a draftsman and draw blueprints. You can take a drafting course when you start high school next year."

"That's not the kind of drawing I like to do."

"Grow up, Gary," she said with exasperation. "Artists don't make any money. Do you want to be poor your entire life?"

Later, I heard her pacing in her bedroom. In the morning, the cantorial music blasted from the big speakers at the Cooperman's place. Mom left the house to look for work while I dragged myself to school. After school, I came home to our empty apartment. Taking my sketchbook, I sat in a chair near the living room window to have good light. I didn't know what I wanted to draw. My pencil made light passes over the paper while I searched for an image. I ripped up a lot of the stuff I drew. One sketch pleased me, a small bird, his head cocked over his shoulder. It was a picture of Tiny, my grandmother's parakeet. He'd escaped these sad rooms as I dreamed of doing.

A fantasy popped into my head, that I sent my parakeet drawing to my father After his friends--people with big cars like his--saw my framed picture on the wall of Dad's Florida apartment, they clamored to buy my artwork. The checks started pouring in. I became the breadwinner for Mom. I put aside my sketchbook, didn't want my mother to catch me drawing.

After two and a half weeks, I was more panicked than ever because my mother still didn't have a job. I had to do something. Having been forbidden to appeal to my uncle, and not knowing what else to do, I finally wrote to my father. I begged him to let me come visit as soon as possible. Until I saw him face-to-face, I didn't want him to know my purpose. People ignored charities that wrote asking for money. A second wife might toss out a written appeal to her husband on behalf of his first wife. I had to tell Dad in person that Mom had lost her job and needed his help.

I had only to mail my letter for my mother walk in a few hours later, wearing a new white angora beret, her cheeks rosy from the cold. "Guess what, Kidd-o? I have a new job."

I stared at her.

She smiled. "I told you I'd get one."

"Where?"

"You're looking at a Klein's saleslady. It's exactly the right place for me. Thank goodness, I won't have that factory foreman breathing down my back."

I ran and threw my arms around her. "That's great, Mom." It was such a relief that she was working again.

On the weekend, I didn't have school, so I dropped by Klein's to see how Mom was doing. The moment I stepped inside the big department store on 14th Street, I was swept up by a pushing-shoving mob. I could barely breathe. Customers stampeded from one table to another and pawed over big jumbled piles of marked-down handbags, nylon stockings, sweaters, and other bargains. I pushed through to the escalator but not before a cosmetics saleslady accidentally stung my eye with a spray of perfume.

My mother worked on the second floor in the ladies' department. It was almost as crowded as the main floor. Here women raked through racks of dresses while a little bell rang ding-ding-ding. One woman charged out of the dressing room and screamed, "Joel, where are you?" A small boy ran up to her, grabbing her around the knees. It took me a while to spot my mother. She drifted absent-mindedly among the racks and didn't look as if she was going to sell anything to anyone. I slipped away before she saw me. I was upset, feeling sure she was going to be fired again.

I kept checking the mailbox to see whether my father had answered my letter. To my relief, the week after Thanksgiving I found an envelope addressed to me. Francine and Dad had written inviting me for the Christmas vacation and included a check for bus-fare.

I showed my mother the letter when she came home from work. She said, "What do you want to get involved with them for?" We argued about the trip to Florida trip for days. Finally, Mom told me, "I can't fight with you any more. You want to spend time with your father. Go! Get it out of your system!"

Five minutes later, I was at the kitchen table, writing Dad and Francine to tell them I was coming.

Mom poked her head in the door. "You're writing to them?"

"Yes."

"It's a long ways to Miami. Ask them if you can stay three weeks."

"But school's only out two weeks."

"You can take an extra week off if you promise to make up the work."

"Thanks, Mom." I jumped up and hugged her. I knew she didn't want me to go. But now that she'd given permission, she was generous. I could spend a long stretch with my father.

The pre-Christmas rush had begun at Klein's. Mom was working long hours. Three evenings later, she came in bearing two big bags. "I don't want you showing up there with raggedy underwear," she said as she unpacked bags with underwear, socks, pajamas, pants and shirts that she'd bought with her ten per cent employee discount. She borrowed a brown suitcase from Mrs. Kessler that wasn't worn out like our yellow one.

My father wrote back saying that a three-week stay would be fine and included his phone number. I let him know when my bus would arrive.

I'd never been on a vacation, out of the state of New York, or separated from my mother. In the John Burroughs school library, I found a book about Florida, read it, and wrote down the things I wanted to do: see the Everglades, alligators, swamps; ride in a glass bottomed boat; visit Miami and the Keys; go to the beach. When I was little, my mother used to take me to Brighton. We'd go with Mrs. Kessler and her girls, ride on the rattling, hot, crowded train, our swimsuits beneath our clothes, our arms loaded with bags filled with sandwiches, thermoses, towels, blankets, extra clothes, pails and shovels.

Dad's letter had said, "the ocean's in our backyard." All I'd have to do in Florida was step outside in a bathing suit, a towel draped about my neck. I hoped to learn to swim. Neither my mother nor I knew how. The most either of could do was wade out a little and jump the green waves. My father though, was an excellent swimmer. I recalled him plunging in the ocean, and swimming far out beyond the rocks, the only swimmer visible on the horizon.

The day before I was to leave, my mother said, "I boasted to my friends at work that I have a thirteen-year-old son who is traveling all the way down to Florida on his own."

I was pleased to hear her say 'my friends at work.' She spoke affectionately about her supervisor, called her 'Shirley.' I figured that if Shirley didn't like Mom, she'd have fired her by now. Mom was going to keep her job.

I relaxed, lost myself to a whirlwind of thoughts about my trip as I packed my clothes, sketchbook, pencils and toiletries. That night, I went to bed, thinking of palm trees, sandy beaches and sea gulls--and of my father. I wanted to see him, but was nervous about how that would be. At least, I wouldn't have to ask him for money.

At three o'clock the next day, my mother and I took a bus that let us off a block from the Port Authority. Fierce winds pulled and pushed us along as we walked towards the terminal. Entering a side entrance, I had to walk around two bums, dozing on the floor. I held my breath so I wouldn't smell the urine stink their trousers exuded. My mother and I became part of the crowd hurrying through the terminal's underground hallways. Puerto Ricans, Haitians, Chinese, Hasidic Jews thrust past us, loaded down with luggage and packages. Here and there, I saw joyful reunions, tearful separations. A crew-cut soldier and his girlfriend kissed passionately. A woman said loudly to an old man, "Dad, hold on until I come back next month."

Mom and I came up to a doorway marked "49," the number of my Florida-bound bus. It was also the year of my birth, and that seemed lucky. Outside, we found the red and white bus, it's trunk open, and motor thrumming. My mother pressed an envelope into my hand with my tickets and some spending money. The driver threw luggage in the side-compartments of the bus and started collecting tickets by the door.

"Have a good time," my mother whispered, coming along with me on the line like she was a passenger. Her coat fell open. Somewhere in the terminal, her button had dropped off. She noticed the loss, lamenting, "I'll never find a match." When it was nearly my turn to board, Mom ordered, "Call me the moment you get to your father's."

"I promise."

"Call me every day!"

I nodded, climbed up the bus steps, and went down the aisle to the rear of the bus where I took a seat on the backbench over the motor, higher than the other seats. That seemed a cool place to sit. I watched the remaining passengers get settled. The driver loosened his tie, adjusted his rear view mirror and shifted into gear. I looked out the window to wave to my mother. Her hand rose but only got as high as her mouth. Tears filled her eyes. She mouthed, "I love you." The bus pulled out of the terminal. If we'd stayed a moment longer, I might have rushed back to her.

We left the city's dark, old buildings behind for orchards with bare-branched trees, snow-covered fields, an occasional cow, horse, and barn. My backbench took the shocks, bounced me up and down. After a while, I changed seats. Just the way my grandmother would have, Mom had packed me a big bag of food with cheese sandwiches, hardboiled eggs and fruit. I was too excited to eat.

My seatmate was a middle-aged salesman. "Where are you going?" he asked. I loved saying, "I'm going to visit my Dad," words I'd not been able to utter before.

I slept cramped up, off and on. My neck was stiff. In the morning, the bus stopped at a diner. I threw my bag of food in the garbage and bought a hamburger and French fries, the greasy food Mom had warned against. She'd have been horrified to know I was eating it for breakfast, washing everything down with coca cola. It tasted delicious, particularly because I had skipped supper the night before.

As we sped on, the weather became warm and sticky, so different from the winter cold in New York. I saw cotton fields covered with spidery threads, trees by spooky-looking Spanish moss. When the first palm trees appeared, I gasped. They were much taller than I'd imagined, looked like fantastic, huge flowers from the dinosaur age. We didn't pull into the West Palm Beach terminal until the late afternoon.

A bum was stretched out on a bench. At a distance from him, a woman sat with two small children. I didn't see my father. Not knowing what to do, I just stayed where I was. A tap on my shoulder made me jump. I whirled around. It was Dad. Tan, his blond hair lighter than ever, he was dressed in pale green silk shirt, brown pants, and matching shoes with a perforated design. There was a mother of pearl "D" on his belt buckle. He looked like a movie star to me.

I didn't know whether to hug him or shake his hand. He didn't give me a hint. The moment passed, and I did neither. I felt let down.

"Thank you for bringing me, Dad," I said.

He gave a little laugh, picked up the brown suitcase, and said, "Thank Francine...Let's go."

I had to hurry to keep up with his long-legged stride. Outside the terminal, I saw the Lincoln. Dad unlocked the passenger door. I climbed in and sank into the plush seat. He turned on the engine. Frosty air-conditioning replaced the Florida mugginess. I put my hands over the dashboard vent to feel the stream of cold air. After a few blocks, we left behind the littered streets and the dusty, little stores around the terminal, and turned onto a highway. On one side of the road were new apartment buildings, some still under construction, with cranes towering over the sites. On the other side was the ocean. Foamy waves hit against the shore. Seagulls screeched. I spotted a white boat on the horizon.

I asked my father, "Are you still a bookkeeper?"

"I'm retired," my father replied.

That surprised me. He wasn't old, only in his forties.

Dad turned off the highway, driving us up to one of the new buildings and into a parking garage in its basement. "Well, this is it," he said, turning the motor off, taking my suitcase out of the trunk. I followed him up to the lobby. He stopped to check his mail. Only a few names marked the shiny, brass letterboxes. My dad and Francine were among the first tenants. I breathed in the sharp smell of new paint, plaster and carpet, so different from my building's stale air, the decades of long accumulated odors of cooking and rot.

At home, I used stairs. Here, there was a mirror-lined elevator that whizzed us up to the top floor. My father led me down the hall to his door. "We picked an end apartment," he said, "to have ocean views from two sides." Slipping his key in the door, he warned me to be quiet. "Francine's napping." When I'd met her, she'd looked younger than my mother. I wondered why she needed to nap. But of course, unlike Mom, she had the leisure to do so.

I entered an apartment with chrome and white leather furniture, glass topped tables, white carpeting, bright paintings. Nothing was mismatched, frayed, cracked, or cluttered like at Mom's apartment. My mother squeezed what we needed into too small a space. Here nothing accumulated in piles, was thrown across chairs, or hung on doorknobs. The glass walls made it seem as if we were floating in the sky. I saw a lot of mirrors: gold framed; circular; rectangular. If a strand of my hair happened to fall out of place, I'd know it at once.

I was overwhelmed by the view of the Atlantic Ocean, by how different it looked when seen from high up, by the restless rolling beneath the green, glassy surface. "Wow, look at the ocean. You live right near the beach, don't you, Dad?"

My father smiled, and said, "Not bad, is it? Let me show you your room."

I'd expected to sleep on the living room couch, the way I always did. But I was going to have a room to myself. The den, the room given to me, had a television, dresser, easy chair, built-in bookcases, and paintings of a hunter, fisherman, and golfer. There was the kind of couch that opened up to a real bed. The bed was made up with soft blue sheets, pillows and a velvety blanket.

Off the den was my very own bathroom. It had a shower but no bath, the same as at home. I wondered whether Dad remembered the years we'd lived in a flat that had had neither bath nor shower. When we'd wanted to bathe we'd used the kitchen laundry tub, located next to the stove. My mother still laughed about how she used to soak herself and stir a pot of soup at the same time.

"Unpack while I check on Francine," my father said.

There was more space than I needed in the dresser drawers and closet. I sank down into the easy chair and looked at the view from my window. The sky was changing from pink to deep red, looked lit up. From another part of the apartment came murmured voices. Some time went by. I felt timid about leaving my room, but was about to so when Francine showed up with her cloud of platinum hair, little turned-up nose and pouting red lips. Her green silk bathrobe shimmered like water. I wished I could touch it.

"Hey, you," she said. She smiled, dimples showing in her cheeks.

How should I greet her? Should I call her, Mrs. Geckleman? Francine? Mom? It seemed safest not to call her anything. "Hi," I said.

"How about some supper? I'll go whip up something."

At home, we ate in the kitchen. Here, there was a separate dining room, but Francine called it 'the sunroom.' The three glass walls, the pots of leafy, green plants made it look like a hot house at the Botanical Gardens. Seated at the wrought iron table, we ate grilled salmon, a salad, and rice. I couldn't take my eyes off Francine. She didn't look as much like Marilyn Monroe as I'd thought. Her eyes were brown, not blue. She had a narrower face. Her figure was skinnier, except for a little potbelly. Although not Marilyn Monroe's identical twin, she was, nonetheless, beautiful.

Exhausted from the trip, I kept yawning. My father told me to go to bed. In the den, I stripped to my underwear, but was too tired to put on my new pajamas. 'Shhh, shhh,' the ocean whispered. Quiet wrapped around me like cotton, so different than the noise at home, the roar of traffic, the Cooperman kids screaming, televisions blaring through thin walls.

I dozed until a light in the hall flashed on, shining through the crack where my door met the floor. Soft voices sounded as Dad and Francine neared and went past. A toilet flushed, and flushed a second time. The light went off. The apartment settled into darkness.

Then the noise of creaking bedsprings.

"Ohhhh," he moaned.

"Ahhhh," she cried.

My body went rigid. I put my pillow over my head to shut it out. At last, it was over. Or rather it was over for them. It took a while for me to relax. I finally fell asleep, slept on and on, so comfortable, lying in my own bed, wrapped in blue sheets light as a silk cocoon.

In the morning, there was a tap on the door. I opened my eyes. Where was I? Oh yes, I was at my father's. This was the den. There was someone standing in the open door, dressed in a pink shirtwaist dress, and with a blue terrycloth robe draped over her arm. "Time to get up, Gary."

Francine crossed the room to open the blinds. I shut my eyes and rolled over. "Hey sleepy-head, don't go back to sleep on me." My mattress dipped and rose as Francine sat down beside me. Her hand shook my shoulder. As I woke more fully, I realized that I'd forgotten to call my mother the night before. She'd have been up, waiting to hear I'd arrived safely. By now, she must think I was kidnapped or dead.

"I was supposed to phone my mom last night. She'll be…"

"Whoa...slow down," Francine told me. "I can't make out what you're saying."

I explained again.

"You're all excited about nothing," Francine interrupted. "Your mother phoned while you were asleep. She knows you got here."

"Can I call now?"

"Now? Doesn't she work?" Francine glanced at her tiny, gold wristwatch as if to check how many hours I must wait. "You'll phone tonight."

"Where's my dad?"

"Dave ate breakfast and went out, but he'll be back to take you to the beach." She handed me his bathrobe and went off to prepare my breakfast.

It was thrilling to wear something that belonged to my father. The robe's hem fell to my ankles. A year ago, it would have dragged along the floor. I hoped, one day, I'd be as tall as him.

In my bathroom—jubilant that I had one all my own--I used the toilet, brushed my teeth. At home, the toilet needed to be flushed twice to get everything down. The pipes rumbled. Rusty water came from the tap when it was first turned on. Here, everything worked the way it was meant to.

On the way to the kitchen, I peeked into the master bedroom. As in the living room, everything was white: walls, furniture, rug, and the satin spread covering an enormous bed. Light streamed through the windows, striking mirrors on the wall-to-wall closet, over the dresser, on the door to the bathroom. I proceeded to the kitchen, a room with white walls, counters, cupboards and pantry. In a special niche was a washing machine and dryer. Francine didn't have to carry the laundry out like my mother. Mom considered white an impractical color. It showed the dirt. But what did that matter when you had a washing machine right in your apartment?

Francine stood at a counter across the room. Her pale, pink lipstick matched the color of her dress. She had on a delicate gold necklace and tiny post earrings. "I bet you never had fresh-squeezed orange juice," she said.

Fresh-squeezed was the only kind I'd ever had. My grandmother or mother would never have bothered with diluting or measuring concentrate. But since Francine seemed excited about giving me 'a first,' I lied and said, "No." It turns out she used an electric machine to squeeze the oranges. To make me an omelet, she got out a battery powered electric needle to prick the eggshells. *Zzzzz*, it vibrated and mixed the egg and white inside each egg. All Francine had to do was crack the shells and empty them directly into a hot skillet.

At home, breakfast was something to finish fast so I could rush to school. Usually, I had cold cereal in a chipped bowl. This morning's breakfast seemed grand to me as I sat down to it in the sunroom. There were eggs, warm toast, orange juice, coffee. Everything tasted delicious. Francine had her meal with Dad, but she stayed to keep me company. Mom never felt obliged to sit with me. Francine, though, treated me as an honored guest.

To entertain me, she opened a breakfront cabinet in the corner of the sunroom, showed me souvenirs from an around-the-world trip she'd taken with her first husband, Joe, a department store owner who'd died of a heart attack. Each treasure brought back memories for her, the cruise down the Danube, 'the Palace on Wheels' train ride in India, the African safari. There were carved ivory, miniature animals and dolls, cups and saucers. My life was full of people who'd fled to the United States from Poland or Argentina.

Francine was the first person I'd met who traveled abroad for pleasure. Perhaps one day, I too would travel fearlessly. Doors were opening, my world expanding.

Why I could even talk about my father. My mom preferred me never to mention him. She'd said not to discuss him outside of the family and 'let people know our business.' With Francine, the most natural thing in the world was chatting about Dad. I dared to pose questions, asked, "How did you meet my father?"

"I met him through my cousin. Your Dad was his bookkeeper. I happened to be at the shop one day, and there he was. The moment I set eyes on Dave, I knew he was the one."

"When was that? How long ago?" I wanted to know if my Dad had known her before, or after he walked out on Mom.

Francine wagged a finger at me playfully. "What's this? The third-degree? Ask your father." She glanced at her wristwatch. "Oh gosh, I better hurry. I have a hairdresser appointment."

It wasn't mere flattery when I exclaimed, "You look good already." I meant it with all my heart.

"Thanks. But I need my tune-up. Men never understand. Women have all kinds of tricks to be beautiful. We have to work at it...Not men. They're either good looking or not...Your father's always the most handsome man in a room. He doesn't have to do a thing." She wrinkled her little nose. "Is that fair?"

We both laughed.

"Speaking of your father. Where is he? He promised to take you to the beach. Can you keep busy until he shows up? Say, you must feel filthy after that long bus trip. You haven't bathed yet, have you? Why don't you take a nice leisurely bath?"

"My bathroom doesn't have a tub."

She smiled, kindly. "Mine does. Use it whenever you like. By the time you're dressed, your father should be home."

"Thanks," I said. I'd never had a soak in a real tub, only had used the laundry tub when I was little.

Francine and Dad's bathroom had flickering gold streaked pink wallpaper, a cart piled high with thick towels, a pink marble counter. Best of all was the tub with its shiny brass swan faucets. I turned them on. Water streamed from the beaks. There was a shelf full of glass bottles with oils, crystals, and bubble bath. I held each to the light, studied the colors and took sniffs. Finally I emptied purple liquid into the tub. Frothy bubbles floated on the bath water. A sweet, fruity scent filled the steamy air. I stripped, stepped in the bath and soaked a long, long time.

Finally, I climbed out and threw a velvety towel around me. It was so much softer than the worn, scratchy ones at home. The soles of my feet sank into the thick bath mat. Blazing lights lit the over-the-sink mirror. I wiped away the mist with a washcloth. Using Dad's razor, I shaved off the peach-fuzz on my upper lip. Then, I splashed my neck and cheeks with his tangy Old Spice cologne. I went back to my room to put on a fresh outfit. Everything I'd brought was new, but I wished Francine, not Mom, had picked out my clothes. I wanted to look debonair like my father.

My father returned and took me to the beach, a short walk away. Dad was fair, afraid of getting burned. He wore a wide-brimmed hat and long-sleeved shirt. I was in a bathing suit, working on my suntan. I wanted to look good when I returned to New York.

Before coming to Florida, I'd imagined meeting beautiful young girls in bikinis, but as we strolled along, I didn't see many people my age. My father said the tourists were in Miami. Here, there were older people, many retired. Even so, I enjoyed looking at the women's bodies. I saw a fat, gray haired woman dipping a foot in the waves and pulling back. She scooped some water up and splashed her thighs, then got more to splash on her neck and enormous, hanging-down bosom. The old lady looked like Grandma Etta.

After about twenty minutes, my father asked, "Do you know how to get back to the apartment on your own?"

"Yeah, sure."

"Good. I have to go."

"But why?"

He explained that Joe had left Francine property and investments. Dad managed the books, kept an eye on the properties, talked to her broker. After jabbering on about all he had to do, he pressed an extra key into my hand, and took off.

I was crushed. He'd told me he was retired. I'd assumed he'd spend every single day with me! I spread out a towel I'd brought onto the sand and lay down. My face grew warm. Little black spots floated before my eyes. Tomorrow, I told myself, would be different. Dad would give me swimming lessons. If a master-swimmer like my father taught me, I was confident I'd soon learn. Or maybe, he'd take me to the Everglades. Francine would come along. The thought of our little family together cheered me.

I shook sand out my towel, threw it around my neck, and began to hike along the shoreline. The water was calm, flat, and shining. A large boat in the distance made me think of Grandma's story about swimming with a parrot back to her ship. Probably, she'd made the story up. But I wanted it to be true. Then there'd be two great swimmers in my family, even more reason for me to become one too.

An old man had set up a folding easel by the ocean. I watched him brush paper with water, then drip down spatters of color that spread into beautiful shapes. He asked me whether I liked to draw. I said yes.

"Get your sketchbook and come draw next to me."

"Not today. I have to go home now," I said, moving on. I didn't think I'd be able to draw beside someone. For me, drawing was private.

I strolled back up the beach, thinking of '*die grubbe yinglach.*' Wouldn't those boys be amazed to see me living in a fancy place right near the ocean? There wasn't a soul in sight when I entered the apartment house. Riding up in the silent elevator, I had a pang for the Lower East Side where it was hard to step out your door without someone saying hello. I hoped to see Dad or Francine at the apartment. No one was there.

My skin was sandy. I bathed in the swan bathtub a second time! Luxuriating in the large tub, I fantasized about a large-breasted girl in my school to whom, I'd never spoken. I'd heard she dated high school boys. That seemed unfair to the boys her age, like me.

After dressing, I took out my sketchbook and ended up sketching my father and Francine's bed. When I was done, I went to the kitchen for a snack, made myself a bowl of cold cereal.

As I was eating, I heard a noise, looked up, and saw a heavy woman in her fifties in the kitchen doorway. She wore a flowered smock and slippers, and was staring at me.

"Who are you?" she asked with a clipped Jamaican accent.

"I'm Gary…Mr. Geckleman's son. Who are you?"

"I'm Alicia. I clean."

"How did you get in?"

"The Mrs. gave me a key…Why I didn't see you before?"

"I'm visiting from New York."

"You come all that way…a long trip…why you sitting by yourself?"

She talked and laughed, and feeling lonely, I tagged after her as she lugged the vacuum cleaner and cleaning rags from room to room. Alicia moved slowly and with a calm, rocking motion. I enjoyed watching her. Her frizzy, graying hair was braided and pinned to the top of her head in a crown. It was the same style hair-do I'd seen on my grandmother in photos taken in Buenos Aires. When she was done cleaning, she changed from slippers to shoes, put on a scarf, and got a large purse from the hall closet. "Goodbye, Mr. Geckleman's son," she said, then slipped out the door.

I went to the den, turned on the television, and sprawled on my just-made bed. I was crazy about Annette Funicello on the Mickey Mouse Club. In the last year, her figure had filled out. Even with mouse ears, Annette looked sexy. I didn't care that the show was for young kids. Another of my favorite shows was American Bandstand. Watching it, I was inspired to draw some of the dancing couples. In one sketch, I made the boy's pants black, matching the girl's dark top. Her skirt was white, the same as his shirt. The checkerboard made them fit together like a puzzle.

Francine returned and called, "Hello, I'm home."

I barely heard her over the noise of the TV. Throwing down my sketchbook, I snapped off the television and raced off though rooms Alicia had made immaculate. Francine was in the kitchen, making a pitcher of iced tea. The sun streamed in the window, lighting her beauty-parlor-perfect platinum hair.

"Where's your father?" she asked.

"He had business to look after."

"I see." For a moment her mouth pursed with dissatisfaction, but soon she was smiling again. She picked up a tray with the pitcher and two glasses, carried it to the living room, and set it on the coffee table. Gracefully, she sat down on the couch. Her hand patted the seat beside her. "Right next to me," she said. I sat down, took my glass.

For my mother and grandmother, tea had had to be steaming hot even on summer days. "A *glassel* of hot tea," my grandmother would sigh happily and place a sugar cube between her teeth for the hot water to dissolve. I was thrilled by tea with ice cubes, so cold that the outside of my glass was damp. Francine took her tea with a sliver of lemon. I had milk. I loved watching the milky white color uncurl and swirl through the dark tea, hoped to try to capture the same effect in a watercolor painting.

"Aren't you going to mix it up?" Francine asked, putting her bare feet up on the glass and chrome coffee table. My mother kept to the European style and didn't shave her pale white legs. Francine's were smooth and tan.

Whenever she left the house for excursions to shop, have lunch with friends, visit her masseuse or manicurist, Francine called out to my father and me, "Well, I'm leaving you two on your on. Now you boys make up for lost time," I would have liked to, but Dad kept slipping away the way sand on the beach slid through my toes. When he came back from his 'business,' he wanted to read his *Miami Herald*, listen to jazz, or read a new library book. There was a big one he'd checked out, a history book written by Ariel and Will Durant. His elusiveness disappointed me, but we had a whole three weeks for him to warm up.

Meanwhile, I was having a good time. I enjoyed walking on the beach. In the bright sunshine, everything became a shimmering blur--a kid's pail and shovel, a bright red Frisbee whirling through the air, the throbbing ocean, the little sea birds rushing over the mud on tiny, thin legs.

After a few days, I began to recognize people on the beach. I used to run into a mother with two young children. One morning, they were standing by the shore. The kids had written messages, put them in glass jam jars, and were trying to get the waves to carry them out to sea. Their jars kept coming back. The mom asked me to watch the kids, while she waded far out to throw the jars. She seemed to have more success. An hour later after she and her kids were gone, I found one of the jam jars back on shore. I took off the lid and read the message.

"My name is Jeremy. I'm seven years old. If you find this, can you please write to me? Here's my address."

I decided I'd write back, but to make it exciting for the kids, I'd say the bottle had rolled up on a desert island on which I lived near Tahiti, and that I'd given my letter to the captain of a passing American ship to mail in the United States. Walking home, I made up more things for my letter, that I had a hump on my back as big as a basketball, that I could do imitations of animals, and that I smelled like cooked fish.

A couple of homosexuals were at the beach every day, gentle souls, so different from the gang of tough Puerto Rican homo kids who used to hang around the local high school in my Lower East Side neighborhood. In the autumn, my pals and I had biked over to the schoolyard and played basketball. But when the homo gang showed up, they chased us away. The boyfriends in the gang dressed like guys. Their 'girls' shaved their eyebrows and drew in dark, thin lines in pencil for brows, and they wore lipstick. My friends were afraid of them. We didn't dare call them fags.

Seeing me stroll along the beach every morning, the homo couple began waving to me, as did several other regulars. I got to know an old guy with a metal detector. I liked to walk along with him. It was amazing the haul he made of money and watches. I also talked to a man named Gus who made sand sculptures. One was of a mermaid lying on her side. She had pointed nipples. Her long hair swirled around over her back. I spent a long time watching Gus spray his creation with glue and water, then brush it with egg white, and sprinkle it with salt.

"Aren't you worried someone will kick it over?"

"I just do this for fun," Gus laughed.

The next day, the mermaid was gone. The waves had washed her away. The hot sand burned my soles as I walked off. I waded into the water to cool them. Waves bubbled up around my ankles.


The only times I seemed to see Dad was when Francine was present like when we went out to meals at restaurants. It wasn't the same as being alone with him, but I can't say I didn't enjoy these occasions. Mom and I never went out to restaurants, and certainly not to ones with wine stewards, and with waiters who pulled out upholstered chairs and unfurled linen napkins. The restaurant visits were as much a novelty to me as my soaks in the big bathtub. I was dazzled by nearly everything, including the mild weather, so different from what I would have had to endure in New York. When I talked to Mom by phone, she told me it was snowing, the streets icy.

My first conversation with her, she'd said, "How is everything? Are you enjoying yourself? Are they treating you okay?"

"It's great! Really great!" I'd described the room I had all to myself, that I could walk to the beach in five minutes—no hour's ride by subway like in New York—and that there was a dishwasher, washing machine, dryer, and a panoply of fascinating small appliances, like the electric needle that mixed eggs in the shell.

Even the way Francine cooked seemed unique to me and worthy of mention. Worried about her weight, she bought the lean, expensive cuts of meat, like sirloin, and trimmed every bit of fat away. I went on and on about how she used spices with names I'd never heard of like tarragon, oregano, saffron; how she served exotic fruits, mangoes and kiwis; how she used a cookbook with French recipes.

When I was done, Mom was silent. Like my grandmother, she used only salt, pepper, chicken fat and ketchup to spice her dishes; considered fat a delicacy; bought whatever was cheapest in the store, things like liver, chicken legs, fish heads.

"Mom, are you there?"

She blurted, "It sounds like if there was a machine to wipe a *tukhis* with toilet paper, they'd have it."

Hurt by her retort, I wanted to get off the phone, and told her, "I'll call you tomorrow."

To my relief no one objected to my daily long-distance conversations to New York, a sign that sufficient money promoted congeniality. A bigger phone bill wasn't going to thrust my father and Francine into ugly scenes where threats were made, ultimatums given. When my father was living with my mother, he used to hate the way she'd call Grandma in Baltimore nearly ever day. Once, he'd rushed into the house, the just arrived phone bill in his fist. The moment my mother saw him, she shrank back, while my father informed her in a cold voice, "I'm going to institute a new system. Every time you make a phone call, you have to write it down and write down how many minutes you talk." My mother started to laugh, he told her, "You don't like that? I could just get rid of the phone."

Every conversation with my mother, she'd say to me, "Tell me how your father's treating you."

The truth was after a week in Florida, I was scarcely closer to achieving the warm, loving bond with him that I wanted. But I always said, "Fine."

To my chagrin, Mom told me, "You can change your bus ticket and come home early. I want you to know that, Gary."

"I just got here!"

"Keep it in mind if you start feeling like you want to come home."

The second week I was in Florida, I noticed my mother sounded cheerier than she had for a long time. I was glad but baffled too. Wasn't she grieving Grandma like before? Didn't she miss me?

I had a fantasy that I didn't dare speak aloud. Of course, I wouldn't, couldn't abandon my mother. But if only a robot Gary could go to look after her in New York, while I remained in West Palm Springs for a few months more. How I admired, adored, savored the material things I was experiencing. My life in New

York was threadbare in comparison. Here, I felt sophisticated, particularly after Francine announced she was going to throw a cocktail party.

A cocktail party! On the Lower East Side, people might have a celebration with *schnapps* for some important family occasion like a circumcision or engagement. But no one there had a party for no special reason. Nor had anyone there ever even pronounced the word 'cocktails.' Until now, I'd thought such things only took place in movies.

Francine spent an afternoon on the telephone calling friends and inviting guests to her gathering.

"Hello Barney..."

"Pearl, this is Francine..."

"Hi Larry..."

"Sylvia, it's me..."

That evening as we ate dinner at a restaurant with red-flocked wallpaper, white tablecloths, and gleaming dishes, Francine informed my father she'd invited a woman she'd met in her Hadassah group.

"Ask anyone you want," my father said, sipping his white wine.

"Many of the women in Hadassah are older than me, but I don't care. The point is Hadassah's an organization that attracts a better class."

"Ah, the better class," Dad muttered.

Francine turned to me. "In Poland, my family had *yikus*. Do you know what that means?"

I shook my head. *Yikus* was a Yiddish word my grandmother had not taught me.

"It means class. We were looked up to as fine people. I'm not ashamed of being Jewish. There's a country club here in West Palm Beach that won't let Jews join. We have our own country club..."

Dad looked bored as if he'd heard this discussion many times before. He lit a cigarette, gripped his holder between his thumb and middle finger. Inhaling deeply, he kept the smoke down a long time before he slowly blew it out towards the ceiling.

The next day while my father was out, Francine and I settled onto the living room couch for iced tea and a talk, an afternoon routine for us now. She brought up the subject of *yikus* again, saying her father had been a respected small businessman and a Talmudic scholar before the Nazis forced him to flee Poland. Francine had been only ten. Her family had gone to London, then made their way to the United States. People acted snooty. To be an American-born Jew was the highest rung. Next was to have immigrated before Hitler came to power. As refugees, her destitute parents were the lowest of the low. When Francine was eighteen she married Joe, a man thirty years her senior.

"Money is important," she said. "In this country, people look at the way you dress, where you live, the kind of car you drive. On that basis, they decide in an instant whether you deserve respect. Joe took care of my parents, gave them a comfortable old age. And, I was a good wife to him. But once he died, I felt I had the right to choose any man I set my heart on. The moment, I saw your father, I knew he was the one."

Francine's voice drifted off as if she were in a dream, scarcely aware of me sitting beside her. I didn't press her again about whether she'd taken up with my father while he was still married to my mother. I didn't want to know any more.


Saturday was the cocktail party. In the morning, Alicia showed up and got the apartment sparkling by dusting, washing floors, and vacuuming. My father was in and out, bringing grocery bags with food and bottles of liquor. He loaded club soda in the refrigerator while Francine, dressed in a loose *muumuu*, stood at the counter, preparing party snacks.

Her *Mix-master* whipped. Her *Moulinex* sliced. Her dishwasher swished. I was put to work peeling and slicing hardboiled eggs for *hors d'oeuvres*. I peeled shrimp too, a forbidden food by Judaic law. I'd never handled shrimp before. A pile of pink shells accumulated at the bottom of the sink. Francine showed me how to push them down the drain and run the buzzing garbage disposal.

My father jumped in the shower, forgetting he was supposed to buy stuffed olives and toothpicks. So I went out to the store, not the big one to which he would have driven the Lincoln, but a little, nearby grocery. A dusty paper donkey piñata hung in its window. The dark haired clerk didn't speak English. When I returned home, I found Alicia gone. Francine was sitting on the couch in a bathrobe. She'd showered, and now, she was painting her toenails with pink polish. Her left foot was lifted onto the coffee table, little cotton balls stuck between each toe. Looking up, she smiled. "Go shower and get dressed for the party." I dressed in black slacks and a plaid sports shirt. Excited, nervous about attending my first cocktail party, I got the shirt buttons wrong and had to do them over.

Francine was dressing while I waited in the living room with my father who wore a pale blue shirt, white slacks and white loafers. Dad leafed through a newspaper but put it down when Francine appeared. She wore a filmy white dress. Her skin looked pale, her hair, teased and puffy. Her skirt swished about her legs. She, Dad, and I were ready. The apartment was immaculate, the refreshments prepared. There was nothing more to do but wait for the guests.

"Oh no," Francine cried and gagged. Unable to make it to the bathroom, she threw up on the white rug. A streak of vomit stained the front of her dress too. Bursting into tears, she cried, "My dress is ruined."

Dad leapt up, rushed to her, put his arm about her shoulder. "I'll take it to the cleaners tomorrow. It's not like you don't have a closet full of dresses."

"They don't fit any more."

"You'll find something. Just get yourself washed up."

"There's no time. It's not just the dress. The rug needs to be cleaned before people come."

"I'll take care of that mess. Don't worry, Fran. People aren't going to show up on time. They'll come fashionably late. You've got a half hour, at least. Take a bath. Relax. And if one or two come while you're dressing, so what? I'll cover for you until you're ready."

There'd been times when Francine hadn't come to breakfast, and my father had carried her ginger ale and dry toast to eat in bed. One morning, I'd watched her writing down a list of questions for a doctor's appointment with a specialist ninety miles away in Miami. When I'd asked what was wrong, she'd told me, "It's routine woman's stuff." Later, she came home, boasting, "I'm fine. Strong as an ox." Her words had reassured me. Now, I felt worried.

From the master bath came the whoosh of bath water, from the kitchen, doors and cabinets opening and shutting as my father gathered what he needed to clean the rug. I wondered what Francine would change into.

I was familiar with all her clothes. One morning when no one was around, I'd gone exploring, hoping to find out more about my father. Entering his and Francine's bedroom, I'd slid open the wall-to-wall closet. Flowery sachet had scented the air. Along the floor were neat lines of my father's oxfords and loafers, and Francine's sandals, and high heels. My dad's shirts, trousers and suits had hung to the left. Opposite were Francine's clothes. They'd glimmered pale lavender, pink and green. I'd run my hands over a silver lame evening gown, a lace over-blouse, and Japanese kimono.

"Is she all right?" I asked my father when he returned to the living room

"Yes, yes. Right as rain," he said, busy emptying a box of baking soda over the vomit, drying it with a hair dryer, and then whooshing up the mess with the vacuum cleaner. A brown stain remained. Dad scrubbed it with a bristle brush and a pail of hot soapy water. It was reassuring that he wasn't rushing Francine to the hospital. The party was still on. She must be fine.

I took a turn with the rug too. Finally, the stain disappeared. Our victory wasn't complete. The room still stank, and my father asked me to go get perfume.

The door to the master bedroom's bathroom was closed. Through it, I could hear the splashing noises Francine made as she climbed out of the tub, and as the water emptied into the drain. I stood over a collection of cut-glass bottles on the dresser. Chanel #5 was a small, square one with a pale, yellow fluid. I took that one to my father.

"Perfect," he said as he held it up to read the label. He began flicking drops here and there. The scent made me sneeze. Dad burst out laughing. I felt closer to him then I had since coming here.

"Well, what do you think of the swans?" he asked.

"Swans?" My face burned. Not wanting to stain the sheets on my bed, I tried to reserve my jerking off for when I was in the tub. Just the sight of the 'swans' gave me an erection. Did my father know what I did in the bath? "What...what swans?" I stammered.

"The swans. The ones in the tub. You must have noticed. Never mind. There's the doorbell. The better class has arrived!" Thrusting the little perfume bottle in his pants pocket, he went off to welcome his first guests just as Francine emerged from their bedroom.

Dressed in a navy skirt and beige blouse, she called to the couple who arrived, "Oh hi." She rushed up to them, put out her cheek to be buzzed.

Dad's greeting to every guest who arrived, was, "What are you drinking?"

Francine introduced me to her dentist, then her accountant. I met her realtor, and a short, fat podiatrist named Doctor Berman, the husband of Francine's Hadassah friend. Everyone asked me a question or two-- "Enjoying your stay?" "How old are you?" "When are you going home?" Soon, I was left on my own as conversations began about people I'd never met, and about investments and travel which I didn't know anything about either. The dentist and accountant discussed how you had to see Portugal before it was ruined. The realtor, his mouth half full of one of Francine's canapés, declared that Turkey and Thailand had already gone downhill.

While making the rounds to freshen drinks, my father observed, "Everywhere is spoiled."

I liked that remark, as if he'd seen and been all over. I was still in his good graces for helping clean up the vomit, so I followed Dad to the kitchen and asked, "Will you make me a drink?"

"Why not?" He filled a glass with ice cubes, poured in tonic and a jigger of gin.

I gulped my drink down. Back in the living room, I felt lost, and wished somebody would talk to me. Luckily Francine gave me something to do. My job was to pass around platters with shrimp and thin cucumber slices on crackers, cubes of cheese, little rounds of toast with smoked salmon. I was the waiter, and Dad the bartender. Every chance he could, he sipped on his own drink.

Francine called, "Dave, come talk to Doctor Berman."

The podiatrist had a loud voice and seemed like a wise guy. My father didn't go over, only muttered, "I need more ice," and disappeared.

I followed him to the kitchen. The counters were littered with open jars, crumpled paper towels, empty cans, plastic wrappings, and dirty plates. Dad grinned, lifted his glass like he was toasting and tinkled the ice cubes, saying, "Made your escape too?"

"You don't like the party?"

"I'm not complaining. There's plenty to drink." He didn't object when I took one of the glasses he filled and began sipping another gin and tonic. I thought that he'd liked me better if I drank, that I'd seem less like a little kid, unworthy of his attention.

Francine came into the kitchen, saying she'd popped the button on her navy skirt. She pulled her blouse out to let it hang loose over the waist.

"My dear wife," my father said. He paused and licked his lips. They looked dry and cracked. "How do you put up with Berman? If I was his patient, the moment he bent down to examine my toes, my reflex would be to kick him in the mouth."

I tittered.

Francine said, "He's a *doctor*."

"So?"

"Did you go to medical school? Where's your M.D.? When you have a M.D. you can criticize him."

My father sighed. "No M.D. No license to practice witticism."

"You mean *criticism*."

He laughed. "There's hope for you, my girl."

I laughed too.

Francine turned on me, hissed, "What are you standing there for?"

Of course, she was tense because of the party, but her impatient tone was a dart in my heart. I liked her a lot, wanted to be in her good graces. "I ran out of stuff," I said, thrusting my platter towards Francine to show it was empty except for a few lettuce leaves.

She dug into the refrigerator for the remains of the smoked salmon, ripped off the wrappings and dumped it on my plate along with some crackers. "Here you are," she said and sent me off. In a little while, I saw Dad back in the living room. He'd switched to drinking orange juice. I wondered whether he'd doused it with vodka, whether he'd allow me to have a third drink.

The arrival of a new guest distracted me from my speculations, a slender, swarthy man with black curly hair and thick eyebrows joined closely over a strong nose. He wore wire-rimmed glasses. The reason I noticed him was because he gave Francine a long hug that looked like it would never end. When I asked my father who it was, he said, "It's her brother, Tony." Brother and sister were so different in appearance, although both were good-looking. I watched Tony make his way around the room, hugging all the women and shaking hands with the men. He seemed to like everyone, including Doctor Berman, whom he called, "Doc."

My turn came. Tony gave my hand a firm squeeze and looked into my eyes. "So we're finally meeting! I've been meaning to get over here to see you. I'm sorry it took so long." To my amazement, he acted like I was important. Thank God, someone was paying attention to me.

"Let's see. If Fran's your stepmother, I guess that makes me your uncle. Well, maybe more like a big brother. Fran's the older one." Ha, ha, ha. He laughed a lot. His laughter was a bubbly waterfall, flowing over me. And when he wasn't laughing, he flattered me with his confiding tone. "My sister has me managing one of her apartment houses, but that's not going to be forever. I have plans. You know how it is...Everything changes. That's what makes life exciting. Don't you think? I hate getting stuck at anything too long...But it's not bad being here with the great weather, the beach, the tennis and dancing. What do you like, little brother? Do you enjoy golf? I could take you over to the country club."

"Gary!" my father called from across the room. I went up to him, and he asked, "What's Tony saying?"

"Nothing special."

The guests began leaving. Francine stood at the door, hugging everyone. Dad and I stood to one side, nearby. My father ignored Tony's wave, and his goodbye. Either he was too high to notice, or he didn't like him, just like he hadn't liked Uncle Ben, his first brother-in-law. Tony winked at me. Half out the door, he called, "Hey Dave, you've got a terrific kid." My father ignored him.

After the last guest left, Francine turned to Dad and said stiffly, "I'm going to lie down."

"Are you nauseous again?" Dad asked with concern. "You rest...Gary and I...we'll...we'll take care of..."

Francine interrupted, "That's the least you two can do." She walked off to her bedroom, shutting the door behind her.

My father lay collapsed on the living room sofa, watching me move chairs back in their places, clear away crumpled napkins and dirty glasses. I was tipsy. A tray of used plates that I carried to the kitchen, slipped from my hands and crashed. There was glass all over the floor. I disposed of the larger pieces, then ran a wet paper towel over the floor, getting up glass that sparkled like dust, too small to pick up by hand. The thought flitted through my mind that I ought to phone my mother. Usually, I phoned her this time of day. Then I forgot. I was distraught that I had broken the dishes, that Francine would be angry.

Later, I was watching television when I heard a knock at my door. "Come in," I said. Francine came in and turned off the television. She'd changed from her blouse and skirt into the green silk bathrobe

"We need to talk," Francine said, sitting down at the foot of my bed.

I dreaded rebukes for my getting drunk, and for my breaking her dishes. But what she said was completely different from what I'd expected.

"I thought you came down here to get to know your dad better. But you're hardly ever with him. I hope your mother didn't prejudice you against him."

I didn't like her mentioning my mom. Besides, what she said was unfair. I'd tried to spend time with Dad. I'd wanted to tour around with him, had hoped he'd teach me to swim. Whenever I'd asked him to do so, he'd been pleasant, but unavailable. I'd given up on expecting anything more than, "Not today...Another time."

"You're not a little kid any more. I think you should know why your father didn't see you all those years. It's because of your mother. Let's set the record straight. Your father tried. He sent you a train set. Did you know that? An expensive Lionel train set."

"I don't remember any train set."

"Of course, you don't. Your mother mailed it right back."

Her words confused me. How could Mom send back a gift meant for me? I didn't understand why my father didn't try again with another present or a phone call. But maybe he had, and I didn't know about it. "I'll try harder to spend time with Dad!" I said, hoping that would satisfy her.

"Well, that's all I wanted you to hear. Do you promise?"

"Yes."

A smile lit Francine's face. She bent and kissed my cheek. I was relieved. We were friends again.

"Dave's a shy man. You have to be the one to reach out to him, Gary," Francine said, cupping my chin in her warm hands, raising my face so I had to look into her brown eyes. "Pressure him. Push. Insist he absolutely must spend a whole day with you. Tell him if he tries to run off, you'll grab him and tie him up with chains." She laughed. The dimples in her cheeks appeared.

Once more, I promised to try to do what she wished. I was so glad she liked me because I adored her. In this moment what had been a fantasy, seemed possible. Why couldn't I live with her and Dad permanently? I'd visit my mother of course, phone every day, the way I did now.

The following morning, I woke up far later than usual, probably affected by the alcohol I'd drunk. My father hadn't been struck down the same way. He'd woken early and had already left. So had Francine. I ate a breakfast of toast and juice, although it might as well have served as my lunch. The phone rang. I hoped it was Dad calling, that I could convince him to spend the day with me. Francine would see that I was making an effort.

I picked up the receiver, and a man's voice said, "Hi, Gary. How are you this morning? Did you sleep well? What are your plans today?"

"Who is this?"

"It's Tony. Don't you recognize my voice?" He sounded hurt that I hadn't.

"Your sister isn't here."

"Francine isn't the reason I called."

"Dad's gone too."

"Wait a minute. Ha, ha. You're the one I want to talk to. I've got some time free. Do you want to go to the country club and play golf?"

" I...I..." I stuttered, surprised and grateful he'd thought of me. But I had to explain that I didn't know the first thing about golf. Otherwise, we'd get out on the course, and he'd be disappointed, or even angry.

"Don't say a word," Tony interrupted. "I'll be over in ten minutes."

Not long after we spoke, I heard him at the door. He had his own key and had let himself in. "I'm here," he called. I went to greet him. His sunglasses were hooked over the neckline of a pale yellow shirt. He wore checked slacks, a blue cap, tan and red golf shoes.

"I don't know how to play golf," I said.

"No problem. It'll come naturally. All you need is for me to give you a few pointers. Come on. Let's get going."

I felt swept up by him and his enthusiasm. It was exciting to go off in his red, two-seater convertible. Tony drove fast. A breeze whipped my hair. I pretended I was with my Dad, the person with whom I'd wanted to spend my day.

"So where has Francine and your father taken you so far. Miami? The Everglades?" Tony asked.

"I've been going to the beach here."

He raised his thick eyebrows and clucked his tongue in a comical way.

"On your own?"

"Kind of."

"They must have shown you Palm Beach."

"Aren't we in Palm Beach?"

"We're in *West* Palm Beach. The town next door is Palm Beach."

"No. Not yet."

The car made a sharp turn. My head nearly hit the windshield.

"Where are we going?"

"I'm going to show you Palm Beach."

I loved the way he'd decided in an instant.

While we toured through a neighborhood of mansions, Tony said, "The owners of these homes come down for a few months in the winter. It just kills me seeing these magnificent places unoccupied the rest of the year. In the spring and summer, I drive around here and feel tempted to move into one of the empty houses." Ha, ha. "If only I could get away with it, I'd do it in a second. The trouble is, there are burglar alarms. Another problem. The gardeners." He gestured towards a man in a gray uniform who stood on a ladder trimming a bush. As we sped by, Tony waved to him. "They're clipping the hedges and mowing the lawns all year round. I should get a job as a gardener, and then, well, maybe I could cut the wires on the alarms, and live the good life. What you say? Do you want to live in one of these mansions too?" Ha, ha.

"Sure, let's figure out how to break in" I said, joining in his laughter, trying to sound cool and daring like him.

On the way to the country club, Tony passed a golf course, and said, "Look. That's where the club is that won't take Jews. Francine was livid when she heard. She wouldn't even drive down this street. Not that she or your father were interested in golf or any of the other stuff. But she went and bought a membership at the Jewish country club 'to spite the anti-Semites.' Fran never used it, so she signed it over to me. With every game of golf I play, I fight anti-Semitism." Ha, ha.

Tony drove up a circular driveway, past a spray of sprinklers that watered *a* lush lawn. After he parked the car, he entered a long, low building, walked over a plush blue carpet. There was a separate entrance directly into the lockers, but he'd wanted to show me around. Tony put his finger over his lips. We had to be quiet. A wedding was in progress in the banquet room. Through a half-open door, I glimpsed a bride in a white gown, and a groom in tuxedo. Once we were in the locker-room Tony tossed his head and sang, "To the alter. Just like sheep to the slaughter. To join the army of married boobs."

He took his clubs from his locker and carried them outside. It was a perfect day to be on the course. The sky was blue, cloudless. Tony waved to people, and whispered in my ear which ones were big shots. Then he got down to work, teaching me about the different golf clubs, the woods, iron and putter. I was to choose one or the other based on how far I wished to hit the ball, or whether it landed near the hole, or on flat grass, a depression, high grasses, bushes, or in water. Demonstrating the proper grip, Tony showed me how to stand with knees loose and bent. Wiggling his hips from side to side, he swung and hit the ball high in the sky and far over the grass. It landed by a clump of trees, not far from the first hole.

I took a golf club, and tried to do everything he'd demonstrated. My club sliced through the air but missed the golf ball. "Let me help you with your swing," Tony said. He came up behind me, put his hands over mine. "Relax," he said. I managed to move my arms and twisted my torso like Tony showed me. My next try, I connected with the ball. It was thrilling.

Tony said, "You're a fast learner."

After we walked the entire course, Tony bought us glasses of coca cola at the snack shop. The little restaurant with small round tables and wire-backed chairs overlooked the greens. Tony sprawled in his chair, his legs stretched out in front of him, crossed at the ankles. His big laugh made us look like we were having more fun than anybody else.

A couple at a nearby table looked over and smiled. I imagined them saying, 'What's going on? We wish we were in on it.' I wondered whether they assumed Tony was my father. He was young looking. They probably didn't think so. I wanted my real father to be here with me. When I'd told Dad that I didn't know how to swim, he'd laughed and said, "I'm amazed that a boy your age doesn't know how." I'd been in Florida two weeks already. If I was 'a fast learner,' how easily he could have taught me by now.

"Tell me about yourself, Gary. What do you want to be? Doctor? Lawyer? Or Indian chief?" Ha, ha.

I poked at the ice in my glass with my straw. "I want to be an artist."

"Artist! Well, that's great. An artist like Michelangelo?"

"Commercial artist." I said commercial artist because it was a way to make money—but all I wanted to do was draw. When I drew, I entered a private world. Everything became alive and revealed secrets to me. Before drawing the palm tree that I passed everyday when I went to the beach, I'd assumed its widest point was at the bottom. But when I sketched the palm tree, I discovered the wide, bulged out middle of the trunk, texture of the bark, fresh leaves on top and scruffy ones below. When I drew, I was like a once blind man, discovering the world.

"How'd you decide to be a commercial artist?"

"My Uncle Ben wanted to be a commercial artist. I take after him."

"That's great. I love art. Not that I can draw." Ha, ha. "But I love paintings. Once, I met Picasso. I was in France, and we were introduced. Do you know who he is?"

"He's a great artist." It seemed like Tony was teasing me, but I said, "What was Picasso like?"

"Delightful. Charming. A wonderful friend..." Ha, ha. "Now, I'm talking to the next Picasso. Right Pablo?" He gave me a playful poke in my arm.

On the drive home, he said, "There are some good art schools in New York, Pablo. There's Cooper Union and the Parson's School of Design. You'll have to decide which one is for you."

I was glad he was taking me seriously, yet sad too. My stay in Florida was nearly over, and my father hadn't once asked what I wanted to be, or discussed how I might prepare for my goals, or how he might help.

Tony parked the convertible, accompanied me upstairs. Francine was home. Tony told her he'd taken me to play golf. "Geckleman, Jr. and I had a great time." Francine told him she had a headache, and he left.

There were no flirty smiles from Francine to me, no light brushes of her fingers to my chin or hair, no light chatter. "I thought you were going to spend the day with your father," she said coolly, walked off to get her purse, and said, "I have to go buy some groceries." I wanted to follow and ask, but didn't have the guts. Why did it mean so much to her that my father hang out with me?

After she was gone, I went to watch television. My room felt stifling. Before I knew it, I was on my way to take a bath. The tub filled. The bathroom steamed up. Slipping into the bubbly, sweet-smelling bath, I reached out to turn off the gushing faucets. One of the swans came off in my hand. Since it was only ornamental, I was able to shut the water. Why didn't the swan break off after I left for New York? I'd only dipped myself in the bath for a second, but I leapt out, streaming water onto the floor. The faster I got away from the scene of my crime, the better. I hurried back to my room and got dressed.

Dad came home before Francine. He had a routine of removing his sunglasses and taking his keys and billfold from his pockets and leaving them on the hall table. A couple of times, I'd seen Francine stopping at the table and slipping bills into his wallet.

I went up to him and said, "Please Dad, let's do something together tomorrow." I wanted to tell Francine that he'd promised when she returned.

"Maybe. We'll talk about it in the morning. I'll figure out then what I'm doing." He went into the kitchen for a glass of water.

I followed. While he was running the tap, I pleaded, "Dad, take me to the beach tomorrow. I want you to teach me to swim. I have to know how. I don't want to drown if I'm in a boat and it turns over…or if a wise guy pushes me in the water."

Dad was supposed to say, 'About time you learned. Lucky you came down to Florida so I can teach you.' But all he said was, "Let's see what the weather is like tomorrow. It might rain. I think the forecast was for rain." He threw back his head and gulped down half a glass of water like he was dying of thirst. More slowly, he drained the rest, and got an aspirin and swallowed it too.

"But if it's nice, can we?"

"Let's talk in the morning. I've got a headache." Wincing, he touched his forehead lightly with his fingertips. He left the kitchen, walked to the living room.

Trailing him, I begged, "Take me with you tomorrow. I want to be with you."

Dad barked, "Don't act clingy!" He reached for the newspaper on the coffee table. I saw a tremor in his hand.

Later, my father, Francine and I ate supper together, looking out at an orange sun dropping into a green ocean. The sky on the horizon turned pink, red, then purple. Forks clinked against plates. I helped myself to mashed potatoes. Francine slid the bowl an inch or two to the side, to exactly where it had been before I'd touched it. I helped myself to lemonade. She did the same with the pitcher. She seemed nervous, twisting and turning her diamond engagement ring. Her first husband had given it to her, not my father. I wondered whether she'd already noticed I'd broken the swan faucet. She didn't mention it, and I didn't have the courage to tell her.

After she cleared the dishes, I found a moment alone with her in the kitchen. I told her what had happened when I'd spoken to my father earlier.

"I'll talk to him," she said in a firm voice.


"You could have mentioned the faucet broke," Francine told me at breakfast. She said the words carelessly, but I could tell she was angry. I assumed Dad was too, but he turned to me and said, "How about going to the beach with me?"

I stared at him, astonished.

"That's what you want, isn't it?"

I nodded, unable to speak, so overjoyed that I was almost in tears. 'I want to be alone with my boy,' rang in my head.

After breakfast, Dad dressed, then got his Panama hat and his sunglasses and called, "Come on." He wore navy pants, a blue and white striped shirt and white loafers. It was clear he wasn't going swimming. I was disappointed, but I didn't dare object. He might change his mind about spending time with me.

As we rode the elevator down to the lobby, he said, "So you broke one of the swans."

"It just came off in my hand. It wasn't on purpose."

"I know. I know." He smiled broadly, almost like he was glad I'd done it.

Outside, Dad lit a cigarette, narrowing his eyes against the bright sunshine, inhaling deeply. His long fingers were yellow from nicotine. "Want one?" he asked and held out the green and white pack.

"Thanks."

"So you're grown up enough to smoke?"

"The other kids at school smoke."

"Don't be in such a hurry. I wished I'd never started smoking...or drinking."

"Okay, Dad. I won't smoke. Just don't ask me if I want a cigarette."

He nodded. "Fair enough."

At the beach a man was throwing a stick into the sea for a cocker spaniel to fetch. The dog's shiny black coat gleamed in the sun. The man whistled. The dog jumped out of the water, scattering drops in every direction. The waves looked gentle. We passed two boys tossing a ball, and my father, stretched out his arm and caught it. He threw it high into the sky. The pink ball went up, up, up towards the sky.

"Great throw, Dad."

My father grinned. He was in a good mood. One of the kids raced to catch the ball. Dad and I walked on.

"You're going back on Saturday, Gary?"

"Yes."

"Less than a week, and then you leave. The time flew by...How is your mother?"

"All right," I answered automatically.

"You look like her, you know. Every time I see you, I see her face."

We walked in silence for a while. I didn't want to pretend or lie to him. I said, "After Grandma died, Mom was crying all the time. She lost her job, and she had to get another. I tried to help her, cheer her up and stuff, but you know..."

"What?"

"We were fighting."

"That's too bad."

"When I call her on the phone from here, she sounds all right. I'll tell her you asked about her."

"Do that."

We walked past a picnicking family, past a boy making a castle, emptying a bucket of sand and patting it all around. Sand was getting into my shoes. I was hot. Sweat dripped down my back. A screeching seagull flew overhead.

My father took out his cigarette pack, shook one out, lit it, and started to smoke. But after a puff or two, he offered the fag to me. I hesitated. It might be a test to see if I was going to obey what he'd said before.

"Take it, take it." Dad thrust his cigarette towards me. I took it and he lit one for himself and took a drag. "Well, I think a drink's in order for me." His voice sounded strained.

I thought he meant we'd get cokes. We left the beach for little side streets with shops that displayed swimming goggles, flotation tubes, flippers, and souvenirs. The cigarette smoke stung my lungs. I coughed and threw my butt in the gutter. I kept looking for a soda shop, but before I found one, my father stopped in front of a bar.

"Sam's" had no windows. The door flew open as a man left, and I saw a dim interior with a long wooden counter and black walls lined with shelves of bottles and glasses. My father held onto the door so it didn't swing shut.

"It's time for you to go home, Gary."

"Buy me a drink."

"You can't go in. You're under age."

"Let's go somewhere else."

"I need something now."

"I'll wait for you. I'll wait right here."

"Suit yourself."

The door closed behind him. Glancing at my watch, I hoped Dad would come out. But five, ten, fifteen minutes, went by. I thought about leaving, but didn't want to go back to Francine. She'd be angry I hadn't stayed with Dad. I might even receive a lecture about the stupid swan faucet. Opening the bar's door a crack, I slipped through into the darkness. Nobody noticed me, not my father, not the bartender, or the customers sitting on their bar stools. By the flashing light of a *Coors* sign, I made out a fat man, an old guy with two hearing aids, a man with a protruding red growth on his forehead. There were other people further back in the shadows. I couldn't see them as clearly. Dad had a tiny shot glass. The fat man beside him sipped a glass of beer.

Everything was in slow motion. When one man made a remark, there was a long pause before someone croaked an answer. The man with the bump growing on his forehead was talking about some land he'd wished he bought.

"Just forty miles from here. And so rich they take in four crops a year."

"Four?" the fat man asked suspiciously.

"I said four crops, Bob. You so fucking tanked you can't hear?"

"I can hear all right."

"You all should catch a ride out there. Get out there just after the sugar cane harvest, when they're burning the stumps. What a beautiful sight. And you know what? That dirt's so shit-rich, it catches fire too. Looks like the goddamned Fourth of July. If I didn't have a cracker of a brother-in-law I'd have me a piece of it."

"Who do the crackers hate worse, the Catholics or the Jews?" the old man with two hearing aids asked, like all he'd caught was the word 'cracker.'

"The Jews," bump-on-the-head answered.

"Nope. Them Jews just come down part of the year. Crackers don't know the Jews good enough to hate them."

To my surprise, my father threw back his head and laughed. Didn't it bother him to hear how these jerks talked about Jews? He made it look like he hated Jews too. Besides, the others were lushes. One had a flushed, dazed face. Another mixed up his words. Grandma had told me about peasants who'd get drunk and then run out and beat-up Jews. To me, the people sitting with my father were frightening. I wanted to get both of us outside and away from them.

"Dad!" I cried,

He turned on his bar stool and glanced at me. "I thought you went home."

The bartender, a short man with a pencil-thin moustache, asked, "You got a son, Dave?"

"Guilty as charged."

"I'll be damned. You sure kept it to yourself."

Everyone perked up. They sat there discussing what 'a sly one' my father was for never mentioning his kid 'all this time.' I'd thought he'd just gone into the first place he could find to get a drink, but he was a regular like the rest of them. He'd spent hours sitting in this dark place, barely moving, listening to stupid talk. That sickened me.

"Please Dad, let's go. What are you doing with these *shickers?*"

I used the Yiddish word for drunkards, figuring only my father would get it. But Bob, the fat man, was insulted. "Who ya calling names in that foreign gibberish?" He slipped off his bar stool, stood there like he couldn't figure out what to do. "I'll teach you." He unbuckled his belt, slid it from the loops on his pants waist, whipped it over his shoulder.

It would have come snapping towards me, but my father grabbed Bob's raised hand from behind, forcing him to let go of the belt. It dropped to the floor. "You're leaving, Bob," Dad said.

Bob was drunk, confused, like he was waking from a dream. "Where's my belt? My pants are falling down."

My father kept pushing him towards the door. "Go home...Sleep it off...Get out of here." With each shove, I thought the fat man was going to topple over. Then he was outside, the door slammed against him. There was a scuffle as he tried to push in again.

"Just give me my belt," he whimpered.

The bartender came out from behind the counter, picked the belt off the floor, and passed it to my father who handed it outside. That was the last I saw of Bob.

"Do you drink Coke?" the bartender asked me. I told him I did, and he got me a coke and an ice filled glass, saying, "You can't drink at the bar. Go in the back."

My father put some money on the counter, took his whiskey, and we went to a booth. I poured the fizzing soda into the glass and took a sip. The ice knocked against my teeth. My finger ran along the tape covering a rip in the vinyl-covered bench on which I sat.

"You're not supposed to be here," my father said. "When you finish your coke, go home."

With one finger I circled the wet ring my glass had left on the table. "Dad?"

"What?"

"Why'd you have me come down here and visit?"

"What are you getting at?"

"You ignored me the whole time."

"It wasn't me who asked you. Francine invited you. She thought it would make me...happier. Now, she sees it's not working, and she's disappointed."

"You're sorry I came, aren't you?"

No answer. Dad leaned back, took another sip of whiskey, kept it in his mouth a couple of seconds, then swallowed. I watched his Adam's apple bob up and down. It was like I was invisible. All he could concentrate on was his whiskey, his glass—the next swallow.

"I...I...I...hate you," I cried.

"You don't understand, Gary. I didn't want you to see me like this...I didn't want..."

I jumped up. His voice followed me, as I ran outside. I passed bathers going to the beach, loaded with piles of blankets, towels, and carrying folding chairs. Racing by, I almost knocked over an old men on crutches. *It wasn't me who asked you. Francine invited you.* I meant nothing to him. 'Sam's' was more important. Francine had thought if I came to Florida, he'd stop drinking. I was supposed to save him.

At the apartment house, a woman was placing new plants in the lobby. White-haired, in a striped shirt and red slacks, she directed while a black man wheeled a large potted palm in on a gurney into a corner. She turned to me, said, "What do you think?"

"Good," I said. The sound of my voice surprised me, It was someone else talking, someone calm.

The apartment was empty. I went to the den and turned on the television. Two people jumped up in down in clown costumes. One had a large nose and turned down mouth. I stretched out on my bed and tried to absorb the fact that my father was a drunk. His nose didn't get red. He didn't stagger around or slur his words. But he still was a drunk. The 'D' buckle on his belt could well be for 'drunk.' At the cocktail party, he'd gotten juiced, so he was friendly to me. When Francine thought I could keep him out of trouble, she was too. I'd never mattered to either of them.

Hearing the door open, I assumed Francine had come home. Someone was standing in the door to my room. I looked up and saw glittering glasses, dark curly hair, a friendly, smiling face. It was Tony. He'd let himself in with his key. At least, he cared about me.

"Are you alone, Pablo?"

"No one's here."

"Still in bed?"

"I've been out," I stammered, then broke into sobs.

Tony snapped off the television. "What's the matter, Gary? What happened?"

"My father...he never wanted me to come here."

"He told you that? Or did Francine?"

"My father..."

Tony came over, put his arms around me, stroked my back. I was grateful for his soothing, "It's all right...cry...get it out...you've had a hard time."

When I resumed my self-control and tried to pull away, Tony wouldn't let go. He told me, "You're a great kid. You need someone to be close to you." But it felt weird. I jerked away with all my strength and freed myself.

"What's wrong?" Ha, ha, ha.

"Nothing."

Tony came towards me again.

"Leave me alone!" I cried.

He froze. "Oh, I see. You're a cold fish…like your father." He stared at me, as if waiting for me to apologize. When I didn't, he left.

I curled up in bed, pulled the covers up high. All I wanted to do was go home where there was no Tony, Dad, and Francine, where there were no swan faucets. My mother didn't need ridiculous swans to bathe. I don't know how I got through the rest of the day. Nearly every moment, I felt overwhelmed by what I knew: my father was a drunk; Francine had been using me; her brother was weird.

The next morning, I looked out the window. Although the sky was gray with large, heavy clouds, Francine and Dad had gone off. I wanted to walk on the beach before the storm came. I was scarcely out the front door when it began to rain. The beach was out so I went back upstairs.

A clap of thunder broke like a drum roll. I glanced outside and saw the rain coming down in sheets. I couldn't wait for my stay in Florida to be over so I could be back with my mother. My in-doors day went by slowly. Every few moments, I glanced at the clock, wanting time to fly by. I looked forward to calling Mom after supper and hearing her voice. If only I could talk to Grandma. I'd thought I'd left my grief for her behind in New York, but it came rushing back this afternoon. I recollected how my father had looked down on her. His contempt for her made me furious.

When I was a small boy, I'd once told Dad, "Grandma said that a lady gave birth to a fish." He'd stormed into the kitchen and raged to my mother, "Did you hear, Lily? Women are giving birth to fish. See the kinds of things that stupid woman

tells our son!" My mother had tried to explain that Grandma
didn't like to use the word 'miscarriage,' but Dad stayed angry,
adding 'the fish story' to his other resentments. He was overjoyed
when Uncle Ben had said he was moving to Baltimore and taking
Grandma with him.

Francine came home. The rain had streaked her makeup.
She gave me a cool 'hello.' I'd disappointed her. She scarcely
said a word until my father appeared, and we ate dinner.

After the meal, I called home, using the telephone in the
den. There was something odd. The phone clicked when I began
talking, like someone was picking up another receiver.

Mom chattered away about how it had warmed up in New York, and
how she'd taken a long walk along the river, and the air had been so fresh. I
thought of kind things she'd done. When our relatives, the old couple from
Argentina, first came to New York, she'd helped them find a place of their
own. On the weekends, she'd taken them places on the bus or subway. They
loved my mother. She went to a lot of trouble for people, including me.

"I have good news," she said. "The Coopermans bought a house in
Monsey. They'll be leaving soon. Let Mr. Cooperman play his loud music in
the woods. He can wake up the birds instead of us."

The cheerfulness she showed in every recent conversation continued
to surprise me. Maybe that was because she knew the time was near to when
I'd be coming back. Or had she become used to my being gone, and was
getting along fine? Maybe she enjoyed not having me around, always
fighting with her.

As I was saying goodbye, I heard another click like
someone was hanging up. I realized Francine must be the
eavesdropper. Dad wouldn't have been interested enough to
listen.

On Saturday afternoon, I had my bag packed and was ready to go. Francine gave me a warm goodbye. I guess it was easy being nice, knowing I was going to disappear. My father drove me to the bus stop in the Lincoln. The sights of West Palm Beach went by in a blur, the new construction, ocean, rows of palm trees. We'd barely exchanged a word since that day in the bar.

He surprised me by saying, "I had two cups of coffee today. Nothing else to drink."

I didn't answer.

"Gary..."

Again, I said nothing, wouldn't make it easy for him.

"Don't tell your mother I drink."

"All right, I won't."

"Thanks," he said, sounding grateful. He told me, "I should have taken you around more, but I was preoccupied. Francine isn't herself. Don't blame her for anything. She tried to have a baby for a long time but wasn't able. That upset her."

"What about you, Dad? Do you want a baby?" I asked. I was sure that he'd ignore another kid, the way he did me.

My father said, "She's pregnant."

I should have figured it out. There'd been Francine's nausea; her visit to a Miami specialist; the little bulge in her belly, although she was so conscious of her figure. A few days ago, she'd come home with new clothes that she called 'tents.'

My father parked the car in front of a pawnshop. Its windows were covered with a metal grating like other stores in the run-down neighborhood near the terminal. He carried my suitcase inside and helped me find my bus.

The engine was on, and the driver was collecting tickets. I got in line behind a pack of boy scouts in khaki uniforms, boys younger than myself.

"Do you want a coke or a 7-up?" My father glanced at his watch. "There's still time."

"No thanks."

He slipped a ten-dollar bill into my hand, the only bill he'd had in his wallet. I realized that Francine must dole out his money little by little so he wouldn't drink too much.

"Good-bye," I said.

"Well, good-bye Gary. I wished you'd had a better time."

I didn't expect him to hug me, and he didn't.

The bus driver called, "All right, you all, it's time now."

I found an empty place on the bus, slumped down and didn't glance out the window until the bus was on its way. The boy scouts jumped from seat to seat like monkeys. After a few shoving matches, sandwiches flipping through the air, a boy sitting on a ripe banana planted on his seat, and the scoutmaster screaming his voice hoarse--the scouts quieted down.

It was the same long, boring trip as before, the bathroom and hamburger stops, change of bus drivers, endless highway. People fell asleep even before it was dark as we passed from state to state. The further I was from Florida, the more I focused on my mother and how much I loved her.

In Philadelphia, the scouts shoved each other to the front, whooping and excited, and got off. I'd overheard one of them say they were going to see the Liberty Bell, and later, the Capital. The bus seemed empty without the boys, even though more passengers had got on. Outside, rain pelted down as we drove up the New Jersey turnpike. The sky turned from black, to gray, to white. It was morning. The rain stopped. The highway pavement smoked with steam. I could barely see a thing.

The news about Francine's pregnancy had kept me worked up the entire trip. In April, I was going to have a brother, or sister.

This child would be brought up like royalty, having every luxury, a separate room, beautiful clothes and toys, a private nurse. Until only four days ago, I'd have been wild with jealousy. But now, there was a pain in my heart...I felt so sorry for that baby.

## 4. My Own Place

As my bus pulled into the Port of Authority, I saw my mother semaphoring a warm greeting with both arms. The three weeks in Florida was the first time we'd been separated. I'd missed her more than I'd realized, knowing now that she was the only one I could count on. I blew my nose, wiped the tears from my eyes, before leaving the bus to fling myself into her arms so hard that she stumbled backwards.

"Hey, what's going on?" she said, laughing.

I said nothing, wouldn't let go of her.

Gently, she pulled away. "Is something wrong?" She studied me intently. "How were things between you and your father?"

I recovered my voice. "Great," I said. Having promised my father I wouldn't reveal he was a drunkard, I felt obliged. Besides, I was ashamed to say that he'd treated me like I was a stranger who meant nothing to him. I didn't want anyone to know about it, particularly not my mother. She'd phone Florida, yell at my father. He'd know I'd betrayed him.

I collected my suitcase. My mother and I left the Port of Authority. Standing at a city bus stop, I delivered a speech I'd prepared during the trip back to New York. "Dad and I went to the beach. He took me to see the swamps and the alligators. We did a lot of cool things. Francine was nice too…" This speech was meant to allay any suspicions Mom might have that I'd been mistreated.

Last year, I'd had a black and blue mark on my arm because a teacher pinched me for dawdling in the hallway. Instead of going to work one morning, my mother marched over to the school and yelled at this teacher who, as usual, was in the midst of supervising the kids as they went to their classrooms. "Don't you dare lay a hand on my child…The next time you pinch Gary, I'll give you two pinches…" The kids broke the queues they were supposed to walk in, gathered in a crowd, and cheered my mother. I'd felt like hiding.

Our bus pulled up. We climbed on, paid, took seats. On the ride home, I stared out the window. In only three weeks I'd forgotten the noise, dust and confusion of New York. Buildings were covered with metal scaffoldings. On the street, people rushed about with briefcases or bags of shopping. Workers wheeled racks of clothing through the thick traffic. A Puerto Rican boy who looked my age bicycled along with a pile of cardboard boxes tied to his fender. A red scarf trailed from one of the boxes and kept catching in the bike's spokes. Yellow taxicabs zigzagged and cut off other cars. Brakes screeched. Horns blasted.

Not once in Florida had I ridden on public transportation, the life-blood of New Yorkers. I was accustomed to smooth-riding privileges in a Lincoln. Like a half-remembered dream, I watched people climb on the bus, observed the driver take off quickly, nearly knocking the standing riders off their feet. I'd become accustomed to privacy while I rode, resented the loud voices, scents, random touches.

A wild-eyed woman started screaming at a bearded old man. "I hate you for what *your* people did to *my* people."

In a heavy Spanish accent, the old man asked, "What did *my* people do?"

"Oh, my mistake. It's not *your* people."

I cringed, but an amused smile flickered across my mother's lips. When I was a little kid, she would take my hand in hers on a bus or train, performing a ritual only she understood. Her thumb tapped my thumb, then each of my fingers in turn. She took my hand and did her ritual now, as if because we'd been separated, she had to speak me in this more primitive language. I wondered whether she believed my gibberish at the bus stop. I couldn't tell. Once again, she struck me as far more cheerful than when I'd left her three weeks ago.

She began to talk about how she came to enjoy living on her own. "I got used to coming, going, and eating meals at odd times. Now that you're back, I'll have to remember things like closing the bathroom door..."

"It sounds like you enjoyed my being away." Tears I'd held back before, swam up into my eyes. I blinked, brushed them away with the side of my hand. The shops and cafes of the Lower East Side came into view.

"In a few years," my mother mused, "you'll have to live your own life...and I'll have to live mine...I have to get used to your not being around...You have to become more independent too. That's life...Children grow up...They go off..."

Her words bewildered me. Before I left for Florida, I was the center of her life. Now, she preached that we have independence from each other.

All I had to do was step into to our flat to realize how much I'd changed. I could dispense with the swan bathtub, white rugs and furniture, and fancy restaurants that I'd experienced in Florida. I knew I didn't want to live with Dad and Francine--an option not open to me anyway. Even so, I found it difficult to come back home after having had my own room. Mom had spoken about us becoming more independent. The reality was, our flat was tiny. We were intertwined like wriggling worms in a fisherman's can.

In Florida, the views of ocean and beach had enhanced my sense of space. Here, most of our windows looked out at airshafts or brick walls. I didn't even have a bed of my own. The couch wasn't mine until my mother finished watching television.

The loud noises coming through the thin walls increased my sense of confinement. The Coopermans, the main noise culprits, weren't going to depart until April. Meanwhile, the kids shrieked all day, and the diamond cutter's huge speakers jolted me awake early every morning. I cursed him, then cursed myself for being so spoiled. No matter how I tried, I couldn't get over yearning to have somewhere where I'd be unobserved, could relax and feel free.


At school I made a few new guy friends. Milt Shorestein, a popular kid, finagled me an invitation to my first party, one where girls would be present. I was thinking of girls all the time, continually undressing them in my thoughts. Sex was driving me crazy. There was a big discrepancy between what I imagined doing to girls, and what I actually got to do. I hoped this party would change that.

It was at the home of a girl named Lonnie—short for Ilana. Lonnie's mother was a brunette, her father a thin man who smoked a pipe and wore a button-down-the-front sweater. When I arrived at their apartment, they were in the little entrance hall, putting on their coats. I received a pinch on the cheek from the mother and a handshake from the father before they left to go to the movies.

Feeling scared, I sauntered into the noisy living room. There was a grand piano in an alcove and some boys, including my friend Milt, were sitting on its bench or standing nearby. Milt wore a bowtie. His father ran a men's haberdashery shop. I had on a t-shirt and slacks. I wished I'd put on a dressier shirt.

Milt and the other boys acted nervous and laughed a lot. Across the room, the girls, dressed in nylons, heels, and make-up, squeezed together on a long brown couch. Everyone snacked on the cokes, pretzels and potato chips on the coffee table.

Someone put on a 'Peter, Paul and Mary' record. Lonnie was thin and dark and had short, curly hair in a 'poodle cut.' She was dressed in a tailored white shirt and short red skirt. She was in my English class. I wanted to dance with her. Not that I knew how. I figured I'd just sway to the music, and press my body against her. But the girls started dancing with each other. The boys hung together and watched.

The close dancing I'd hoped for with Lonnie, never took place. The next day, I phoned her to ask her out on a date. It was the first time I'd phoned a girl, but I was determined. I wanted to have my first boy-girl kiss, and perhaps more. The moment I heard her voice, my heart started to pound. I hung up.


By April, the accumulated dirty winter snow along the sides of the street melted. *The Mirror*, the newspaper my mother had begun reading—until recently she'd been a devotee of *The Post*--advertised Easter hats, and displayed photos of chicks, rabbits and painted eggs. My mother did spring-cleaning, dusted, mopped, picked through our closets and dressers for wool clothing. She gave me an armful of wool slacks and sweaters to haul to the cleaners.

I walked past the little shops on the Avenue. The sun was shining brightly, the sky clear blue with a few wispy clouds. People walked by with a zing I hadn't seen all winter. Kids roller-skated. The lady who owned the dress store had a Puerto Rican guy washing her shop window. His squeegee squeaked on the glass. White curtains flapped like flags in the wide-open windows of the apartments over shops. I noticed a few old people. Mr. Krauss tapped his cane along the pavement. Mrs. Moore used a metal walker. I hadn't seen them for months. They'd stayed inside when it was cold, afraid to 'thin their blood.'

Young mothers wearing mini-skirts and tottering along on high platform shoes, wheeled baby carriages with infants I hadn't seen before. I wondered whether Francine had delivered her baby yet. I hadn't heard a word. But, I wasn't expecting that a Nobody like me would receive a birth announcement. Maybe it was for the best, as I hadn't told Mom about the pregnancy.

Why trouble her? She was so happy. At last the Coopermans had begun to prepare for their move to Monsey, a suburb popular with the Hasidim. Boxes stood in the hall outside our apartment. Pot handles stuck up out of one; another was filled with toys; a third with books, topped by a dish drainer.

On an early Sunday morning, three men wearing skullcaps and *tzizis,* undershirts, showed up with a van that had the word 'dry cleaning' stenciled on its side. Mr. Cooperman's bearded friends spent the day helping him carry down his furniture. Amidst all the commotion, the children ran wild. Their rushing up and down the stairs sounded like a cyclone.

It took my mother a while to realize someone was knocking on our door. She opened it. There was Mrs. Kessler. Unlike Mom, Mrs. Kessler wore slacks instead of dresses, smoked *Winstons*, could even blow smoke rings. Today was one of her 'frosting days,' meaning she was presently undergoing a treatment to put gold stripes in her brown hair. Before dropping by, she'd put on a special shower cap with holes, pulled bunches of her hair through and brushed on a foamy bleach. Then, as she always did, she'd come over so she could chat with Mom until her prescribed time in the shower cap concluded. They settled at the kitchen table for cups of coffee. I joined them.

Mrs. Kessler flicked cigarette ash into her saucer, and said, "In a week or two, Mr. Huber's going to plaster, paint, put in new appliances. He'll rent the place at double what he charged Cooperman."

"You think he'll raise our rents too?" Mom asked. She hated the way Mr. Huber squeezed money from the tenants; how he returned her polite 'good evening' with a gruff, wordless grunt. In the summer, the landlord dressed in only an undershirt, not a shirt. To appear half naked seemed disrespectful to her.

"I wouldn't put it past him. Look how he tacked on an extra fifteen dollars a month when Mrs. Jackobson put a television aerial on the roof. Well, if he raises us, I'm complaining to the Rent Control Board."

"Mrs. Cohen complained. He still talks about it as if she'd stuck an ice pick in his heart."

"Yes, I heard he blames her for his heart attack."

Out in the hall, the move was in full swing. Heavy footsteps sounded, kids cried, a man shouted, "Watch out for the mirror." We heard a tinkling noise that sounded like glass was shattering on the hallway's tile floor.

Mom and Mrs. Kessler ignored the commotion, and ignored me. I didn't mind being invisible. Their gossip, and the relish with which they told stories, fascinated me.

"Lilly, did you hear what happened two blocks over?"

"What happened?"

"Mrs. Rosenthal, the one who shows up at the synagogue on the High Holidays with the big hat. She was in the lobby of her building getting her mail, when this punk kid pulls out a knife and says, 'Stick 'm up.'"

"It's a sad day when it's too dangerous to get your mail."

"The worst part is about the ring, Lilly. It wasn't enough to take her purse. He wanted her ring."

"She couldn't get it off?"

"That's right. He grabbed her finger and twisted. Yesterday, I saw her with her finger in a splint. Actually, she'd lucky. I heard of a case where they cut off a finger to get a ring."

"Animals...Can I offer you another cup of coffee?"

"Thank you, but I have to go Lilly. My hair's done."

Mom accompanied Mrs. Kessler down the hall. At the door, they bid each other goodbye, said how much they'd enjoyed the company and conversation.

"Too bad you have to rush away for your hair," Mom opined

"Whenever we talk, Lilly, I think—who has to read a novel?"

"I feel the same way."

Mrs. Kessler squeezed my mother's hand, then stepped into the hall.

Two Hasidim in rolled up shirtsleeves angled a brown sofa out of the door of the Cooperman apartment. "Out of the way, Lady," one cried.

Mrs. Kessler pressed against the wall, holding her shower cap in place.

At nine that evening, I looked out our front door. The hall was clear; the door to the Cooperman apartment, open a crack. I peeked inside, called, "Hello," to make sure no one was there. My voice echoed back. They'd all gone. I wanted to see how the place looked when it was empty. I switched on a light, and strolled through the rooms. The last hairpin, the last bread crust, the last torn rag had disappeared.

I noticed a key on the kitchen counter that must have been left for the landlord. I tried it on the front door. The key fit. I locked the door, slipped the key in my pocket. Mr. Huber wouldn't notice if one were missing, as he had extra keys for every apartment in the building.

At home, my mother was curled up on the couch, watching the Ed Sullivan show. "Where were you?" she asked.

"I wanted to see whether the Coopermans were gone."

"Are they?"

"Yes." I fingered the key in my pocket, feeling like the proud owner of a home.

"Good. Whatever the new tenants are like, they can't be worse."

On the television screen, Kate Smith, a heavy woman in a long, dark, sequined dress, was singing, "God Bless America."

Her high soprano swept through the living room. Forever grateful to the refuge she'd found in the United States, Mom turned her attention wholly on the performance. Sitting down on the couch beside her, I hummed the words to the song. I was in a good mood.

With Mr. Cooperman's speakers gone, I had an extra hour and a half of sleep the next morning. I felt more alert at school. At lunchtime, I lined up in the basement cafeteria, bought a sandwich and milk. As usual, I headed with my tray for a seat beside Jeffrey Lumpkin who was skinny, had buckteeth, thick glasses and frizzy hair.

We'd met in Gym, and become friends because of our names. In Europe, in places where everyone spoke Yiddish, our names would have had dignity. But in America, transformed by English meanings, they were ridiculous. He was called Lump at school. I was Gecko. We banded together as fellow sufferers.

Jeffrey swore he would never change his inherited name, no matter how much scorn and ridicule was heaped upon him. He despised the high school girls in our neighborhood who'd had plastic surgery to achieve smaller, more American noses. I was too cowardly to tell him, but I didn't share his commitment. After all, most of the movie stars I adored hadn't kept their original names or noses.

After a few bites of my sandwich during lunch, I set it aside so that I could check for the key I'd pocketed the night before. The key was an open sesame to what I needed, a place of my own. There would be risks--Mr. Huber's fury, my mother's fury. I could be arrested for trespassing. I didn't care. Up until the time that the renovations began, the place was mine.

Jeffrey interrupted my reverie. "What's going on Gecko?"

Nothing, Lump," I lied. The empty apartment was my secret!

After school, I went home and looked about to see what was worth taking to the deserted flat. At the top of my mother's closet were an old pillow and a ragged blanket that she didn't use. I took them, as well as a glass, plate, box of crackers, and my sketchbook, colored pencils, and charcoal drawing sticks. If the landlord found my things, he'd assume the Coopermans had left them behind. As long as no one found me occupying the flat, and Mom didn't notice she was missing stuff, I wouldn't get in trouble.

The hall was deserted when I let myself into the next-door flat. I walked through the rooms, put the plate, glass, and crackers in the kitchen. I ate four crackers, washed them down with water, rinsed out my glass. In the living room, I spread the blanket on the floor, plumped up the pillow for a seat, and began to sketch. Without curtains, the light in the flat was bright. I drew the long, curling shapes of the radiator pipes, adding leaves as if the pipes were tree branches. A deep calm filled me.

I didn't want to stop, but I had to get home before my mother returned from work. Otherwise, she'd question me about where I'd been. There were no noises coming from the hall when I put my ear to the door. I slipped out, locked the door, turning the knob to make certain the door was secure. The next day, I went back. This time I brought over a towel, worn bath rug, and a candle and matches, in case the electricity was turned off.

I became more reckless in what I took. My mother didn't seem to notice. It took her three days to catch on that her hassock was missing. "Where did it go?" she asked, squinting at the empty place in front of the easy chair. Then she noticed a couch pillow was gone too. The things I'd taken had no value, so I couldn't claim a thief, other than me, had stolen them. I was compelled to reveal that I was furnishing the other apartment. I couldn't look her in the eyes, waited with bowed head for her anger.

I expected her to call me a thief, to say I'd set her up to be humiliated in front of her enemy, that beast, Mr. Huber.

To my astonishment, my mother laughed. "So you have a club house. What do you do there?"

"I draw. I read...I'll bring everything home that I took."

"I don't need those old things...I suppose it doesn't hurt anyone if you hang out there for a few more days."

"You don't mind?"

"I should, but I have to laugh when I think about putting one over on Mr. Huber. Just don't let anybody see you going in and out, or someone's going to object. And don't bring any of your friends over there. People will hear you talking."

"I'll be careful." I was glad I hadn't told Jeffrey about the place, or he would have been over there with me every day.

I thought my occupancy of 'my club house' would be temporary. But something unexpected happened. One night, Mr. Huber had a second heart attack. He died in his sleep. After the funeral and the week of sitting *shivah*, I expected his widow to expel me from the Cooperman flat. But there was no eviction. As far as I could tell, Mrs. Huber was weighed down by responsibilities. Mr. Huber had left her four properties to manage, our building, two in Brooklyn, and one in the Bronx. It seemed

like she'd forgotten about the Cooperman apartment. I was
thrilled to continue my tenancy.

"You're over there a lot," my mother said.

I tensed, thinking she was going to curtail my hours or end
them.

Mom continued. "As you have some place to go, do you
mind if I go out at night?"

"I don't mind," I blurted, assuming she planned to work
over-time at Klein's.

At first she was away on the occasional weeknight or for a
few hours on the weekend. "You're working hard," I told her,
delighted that she was able to put away extra money. Gradually,
she began going out more frequently.

For the first time, TV dinners made their appearance in
our house. Mom taught me how to cook them. I pulled back the
tin foil slightly to let the steam escape while the dinner cooked in
the oven. Two to three nights a week, I dined alone on dried-out
chicken and rice, and cardboard-tasting carrots, and string beans.
My grandmother would have been horrified to see me eating
meals that didn't use fresh ingredients.

I didn't feel neglected, barely noticed the terrible meals--
or that Mom wasn't around much. I was preoccupied with my
private digs, and the secret drawings I did there. I'd never have
done them at home where there was always the possibility of my
mother showing up. I didn't want her to find me sketching naked
women.

I desperately wanted to know about the bodies of my
teachers at school, girls in my classes, mothers of my friends. I
drew them, attempting to discover the contours and size of their
breasts, color and quantity of their pubic hair, shape of their

nipples. Drawing gave me intimacy, delight, arousal. Like in
Florida, I had a place to indulge my sexual fantasies. There wasn't
a swan bathtub in my flat, but all I required was privacy.

At home, there was no private place to keep my drawings.
No matter where I might put them, inevitably, my mother would
have found them. Unable to bear destroying them, I hid them in a
kitchen cabinet at the Coopermans' flat. But I knew Mrs. Huber
could send in workmen at any moment. In my mind's eye, a
painter or carpenter gave them to her; everyone in the
neighborhood heard about them; my mother had the privilege of
personally examining them. It was too dangerous to keep these
sketches.

I brought over the old metal bucket in which my
grandmother used to burn my hair and nail clippings. It pained me
to do it, but I burned my nude drawings. In the days to come, I
never left a drawing of a naked woman behind. These creations
became ash, infants born and cremated on the same day.
Gradually, I came to see that like hair and nails that grew, there
were always more drawings. My art was inside me, not in a
particular picture.

My infernos liberated me. I became a reckless artist, took
more chances, knowing my mistakes would soon be incinerated.
One afternoon, I came home from school, went over to my
clubhouse, and did something that I'd never dared do before. The
bedroom had a full-length mirror on the closet door. I pulled
down the shades, took off my clothes and began to draw myself
naked. This was the first time I'd drawn a male nude. I felt
detached as I studied my body, saw it not as mine, but as an object
I was drawing. Lightly, quickly, I roughly sketched in my
shoulder bones, spine, hips, legs, and skull, carefully erasing these

lines as I began to flesh out the drawing. The sketch grew more life-like. I shaded in the light fuzz of black hairs running like an arrow from my navel to my crotch, drew my cock and balls.

As soon as I was done, I threw on my clothes. My hands trembled as I buttoned my shirt. I felt triumphant. I'd crossed a border. From now on, I could draw anything I wished.

One time, I slipped out of the Cooperman flat, and locked the door, unaware of anyone else in the hallway. Feeling a tap on my shoulder, I whirled around and saw Celia Kessler. She drew towards me, brown eyes wide behind her glasses. In her excitement, a spittle of spit shot from her mouth, as she demanded, "How'd you get the key to the Cooperman's?"

My belly clenched. Celia was the last person in the world I'd choose to trust with my secret. Now, I was at her mercy. I wondered how she'd blackmail me, possibly confiscate my apartment, or at the very least, insist I share the place with her.

To my relief, a tour around the Cooperman apartment satisfied her. She promised she wouldn't tell anyone about my staying there. I was grateful. Whenever I ran in to her, I took the time to exchange a few words.

In the beginning of June, while I was at the Cooperman's flat I heard a noise behind me. I jumped up, whirled around, thinking I'd see Celia. I saw a pimply-faced man in a t-shirt and stained khaki pants. He stood in the doorway to the living room, sucking a red lollipop. Remembering I'd locked the door after arriving, I realized he had to have let himself in with his own key.

"Who are you?" I asked, filled with dread. I knew who he was. Mrs. Huber had sent him over to begin renovations on the flat.

"Who are you?" he shot back, and set down a metal tool case. His lollipop stick bobbed up and down. "How'd you get in?"

"The door was open. I heard some noise and wanted to check to see everything was all right."

He looked at the hassock, blanket, pillow, and drawing things I'd just been using. "You're a bull-shit artist, aren't you kid?"

"I'm not. I really…"

"If you don't want me to tell Mrs. Huber, take your stuff and get out of here."

I grabbed as many belonging as I could carry, and disappeared.

Over the next four days, I encountered workers who plastered and painted the rooms of my former clubhouse. Three men struggled up the stairs with a new stove. Two others brought a thick roll of brown carpet that filled the air with the sharp smell of new wool. From the outside hall, I watched these men drop the roll on the Cooperman's living room floor with a thump. As far as I could see, every scrap I'd brought over to make the place mine was gone.

"We got work to do. Get lost, Kidd-o" one worker told me. The other shut the door in my face. It was the second time I'd been kicked out of the Coopermans.

At home, I listened to them nail the wall-to-wall carpeting into place. Every bang, reminded me I'd lost my secret refuge. My grandmother, of all people, had once regaled me with stories about Jesus. I thought of the two carpet guys as the Roman soldiers who'd nailed Jesus to the cross.

Seeing my sad face when she came home that evening, my mother, tossed off, "It's amazing that you had your clubhouse for three months." She didn't understand my loss. The other apartment was a place where I felt free, creative, a grown up man.

My finals were in two weeks. I had no private place to study. If I spread my textbooks on the kitchen table, Mom made me relinquish the table so she could serve a meal. Because I was home now, she'd begun staying home more, but she seemed unaware of my needs. If I studied in the living room, she turned on the television for her nightly watching. True, she put the volume on lower than usual, but the noise still disturbed my concentration. I couldn't claim the bedroom either. She would traipse in to hang up a dress she'd ironed, humming to herself, barely aware I was trying to study.

It seemed like she was always ironing dresses lately, or polishing her high heels, or--something completely new--dabbing perfume behind her ears. I should have suspected there was something unusual going on in her life. But I didn't. My mother was like the air I breathed, every breath automatic. I needed air, but didn't take much notice of it.

The phone rang one evening as I was studying for the next day's American History final. I picked up the receiver, said, "Hello." The caller hung up. I didn't give it a second thought. There were a lot of weird people in New York who made crank phone calls. Kids like me did too. I'd telephoned Lonnie a few months ago and hung up.

Five minutes later, the phone rang again. This time, a man said, "Is your mother, there?" When I said "No." he hung up without leaving a message. I assumed he was a salesman. Insurance salesmen, in particular, phoned a lot.

The following day, I took my American History exam. In the evening, there was another phone call. This time Mom was home, but I ran to get it, eager for a break from studying Algebra, the last subject in which I was going to be tested. A man, sounding like the one from the day before, asked for my mother again.

"Who's calling?" I said.

Mom came up, took the receiver from my hand. She retreated into her private phone booth. I could have stood by the closed bathroom door and snooped, but was afraid she'd catch me. I went to the living room and tried to study Algebra again.

After she hung up, I called from the living room, "Who was it?"

"A friend."

I followed her to the kitchen. She filled the kettle, set it on the stove. A blue-yellow flame flared as she lit the burner.

"Someone from work?"

My mother put a teaspoon of loose tea leaves into a teapot. "Are you having tea, Gary?"

I shook my head to let her know I wasn't.

She put away the box of tea leaves, set out a single cup and saucer.

"You didn't answer me, Mom."

She lifted the whistling teapot, poured boiling water into her pot, and sat down at the table.

I took the opposite chair.

"He's not from work."

Mesmerized, I watched her pour tea into her saucer, blow on it, take a sip. "Who is it? Where'd you meet him?" I pressed. A story was unfolding. Was it possible she had a boyfriend? As far as I knew, there'd been nobody since my father left her. And now…

"A friend at work introduced us."

"When?" I asked, recalling her dress pressing, perfume dabbing, rolling her hair with newly purchased curlers.

"Oh, a couple of months ago "

"Why didn't you tell me?"

"Because…because I'm just getting to know Bernie."

"Bernie," I echoed. We didn't need a Bernie. We were all right with just the two of us.

"I'll tell him to come by. You can ask him whatever you want to know?"

"Sure, Mom."

I left her to finish her tea, tried to return to studying Algebra for the next day's test, but the x's and y's swirled like my thoughts. I wished I could go over to the Cooperman flat. A few hours in my own place would have calmed me. Except it was no longer my place. I didn't have the key any more, had thrown it in the garbage.

Sitting down in the classroom where I was to have the Algebra exam, I put two number two pencils on my desk. It was hot. Sweat poured out of me. The classroom filled with kids. My friend Jeffrey sat across from me, Milt, four seats behind

Mrs. Gordon, my Algebra teacher, stood at the front with a black board and an American flag behind her. She warned us, "There will be serious consequences if you cheat. You might not be able to matriculate to high school in September..." All I wanted was for her to shut up, and for the test to start so I could get it over with. She took out a stopwatch, said the reason she used one was to get us ready for the Regent exams we'd take in high school. Staring at it, she clicked the button and finally said, "Begin. Good luck."

Everyone bent over their examination and scribbled away. From outside came the sounds of cars going by, kids' voices, pigeons' cooing. Otherwise, the room was quiet. Mrs. Gordon didn't make a sound as she walked up and down the aisles. I noticed her only when her shadow fell over my desk. That made me shrivel inside as if she was accusing me of cheating. It was a relief when she passed on and stopped by another student. Finally, she was at the front of the class, calling out, "Stop."

I handed in my test. I thought I did well, but you never could tell. What I marked as the right answers could have been wrong. All I wanted to do was race out of the school building and run home.

Mrs. Kessler and Mrs. Cohen were standing outside my building. They were watching movers unload furniture from a big van. Silent, jaw-clenched workers lugged furniture upstairs. Tables, dressers, lamps, twin beds and mattresses disappeared into what had been my place.

Mrs. Kessler popped in that evening to talk to my mother about the twin beds. Orthodox couples slept in separate beds. Mrs. Kessler worried there'd be another Hassidic family with a gang of loud children.

A frail-looking elderly couple moved into the vacant flat two days later. They taped their names on the downstairs mailbox, Adele and Morton Zipperstein.

"We'll have peace and quiet," Mom sighed. "Those two will lay in bed all day, poor things."

They were angels for a couple of days, probably dazed from the effort of the move. Soon however, they recovered and showed their real natures. They were constantly shouting at each other in their cracked voices. With the thin walls, Mom and I heard everything. One of the Zippersteins opened a window; the other slammed it shut. Then it got reopened. If the wife wanted to go to sleep, the husband blasted the television.

He'd lock himself in the bathroom and she'd bang on its door and scream, "I'm bursting."

"So burst," he'd say.

When he went out for a newspaper, she'd yell, "Go out and never come back."

"Have a heart attack while I'm gone," he'd cry and slam the door behind him.

It was worse when their son, Arthur, and his wife, Beverly, came over. Arthur was a professor of Economics at Queens College. He'd show up once or twice a week with his wife. Mr. Zipperstein called her 'the *shicksa.*' The moment Arthur and Beverly left, he started blaming his wife. If she'd raised Arthur right he wouldn't have married a *shicksa.* She screamed back it was his fault. Didn't he know their son did everything to spite him?

Because of the Zippersteins, I began to appreciate the large, noisy Cooperman clan. Not a one of the Coopermans had been mean. I wasn't such a dolt as not to know the flat they'd vacated had never been mine. I would have eventually accepted losing it if more decent people than Adele and Morton had moved in.

My mother went over to talk to them, explained politely that their voices carried. "We hear everything," she said pointedly. Her visit made things worse. As if to spite her, they shouted all the louder, acted more viciously. In frustration, she grabbed a shoe, banged it on the wall. They banged back with their canes, and longer and louder than she had. Mom shuddered at the fracas. "Stop it," she pleaded to no avail.

She was upset about the harpies next door, and I was upset about her having a boyfriend. What did it mean? Was this Bernie going to live with us in our tiny flat? I imagined some fat idiot sprawled on the couch watching wrestling matches, drinking beers, ordering my mother and me around. At night, I'd hear him bonking with my mother, the way I'd heard my father and Francine.

Maybe we'd have to move to his apartment or a new place. My school would change. Everything would change. I'd have to get to know new kids and teachers. Would Bernie hate me? Betsy Stockfed, a girl in the next house, had a stepfather who beat her. Once, she'd shown up at school with a black eye. Everyone whispered about the way she was treated, including the teachers.

What if my mother got knocked up? Probably, the baby would scream all the time like the Cooperman baby. Would Bernie take off? Grandma wasn't around to take care of a baby. Mom and I would be stranded, but she'd never give up a baby. Not my mother. One of us would have to stay home and baby-sit. She needed to work and earn money, unless, I quit school and got a job that paid more than hers. That wasn't likely.

My mother wasn't dumb. I couldn't understand why she didn't figure out all this stuff herself. I imagined her justifying what seemed like a betrayal to me. 'I'm doing this for you, so you'll have a father.' Well, I had a father already. I hadn't heard from him since we said goodbye in Florida. Fathers, as far as I was concerned, weren't necessary. Not for me, at least.

I still hadn't met Bernie, only exchanged a couple of words over the telephone. Our first telephone encounter had taken place the night before the two old bags showed up to take over next door. I was inclined to believe, that one way or another, Bernie was going to be as horrible as them.

5. Bernie

As soon as school let out, I started going from store to store, asking if anyone needed an errand boy for the summer. My hope was to earn enough to help my mother out with expenses. She'd see she could rely on me and didn't need Bernie. Mr. Springer at the hardware store, Mr. Rosenbaum at the stationery store, Mr. Temple who owned the pharmacy, and several others, turned me down. They wanted someone over sixteen who could get working papers. I envied the kids who'd passed their sixteenth birthday. Working papers were a passport that I wouldn't be able to get for two years. With working papers you could find a job and earn money. You could even have a vacation in the Catskills while you worked as a busboy or waiter. Grossinger's, The Concord and Kutcher's were the big, fancy Jewish resort hotels. Guests came from wealthy suburbs like Westchester. I'd heard the teenage daughters of the rich guests hooked up with the working guys, and that there were make-out parties around the pool at night.

But I was stuck in the city. My friend, Jeffrey, went to his uncle's farm in upstate New York. Milt worked at his father's store. Even Celia was gone. The Kesslers had rented a summer bungalow in the Catskills, with Mr. Kessler commuting by bus for the weekends. Mom told me, she'd heard that their place was a one-room cottage without a stove or sink, and the cooking was done in a shared kitchen. Still, she was envious that they "breathed fresh air." If she could have afforded it, we would have gone too.

With no job, no friends around, and nothing to do, I was bored and lonely. My mother was still disappearing several nights a week for dates with Bernie. I dreaded meeting him.

One evening, she came home from work and started cleaning house. "Don't get everything in a mess tomorrow," she said.

"Why?"

Mom paused in her dusting. "Bernie's going to pick me up here tomorrow. It will be the first time he sees the place. I don't want it to look like a pig pen."

"I might not even be home tomorrow," I said petulantly. "So don't worry about me making a mess."

"Be here! I want you to meet him."

I was restless the next morning. Over the last couple of months, my mother had told me alarming things about her boyfriend. He'd married a Jewish woman, divorced her; then married a *shicksa* show girl whom he divorced too; then married another show girl and divorced her. Three times divorced, yet Mom had begged me last night, "Keep an open mind."

Not wanting to hang around the apartment and think about Mr. Three-time-loser, I hopped on an uptown bus. A kid at school had told me how to get free tickets to talk show tapings. I'd already seen interviews with Tony Curtis, Jerry Lewis, Arlene Dahl, and other celebrities on television. But viewing such people on TV wasn't the same as seeing them live. At a 57th Street office, the guy handed me a Johnny Carson Show ticket, saying it was against policy to say in advance which star was going to appear on the show. I looked forward to finding out.

An hour later, I was ushered up a flight of steps to a theater balcony, along with a crowd of shabbily dressed individuals who looked like vagrants. They shuffled along, several unshaven, a few smelling badly, no one talking. Probably, each of them had nothing better to do in their lonely lives but be part of a TV audience. That certainly was true for me. Up in the balcony, I and the other ticket-holders followed our cues to laugh or clap. A guard watched over us, ready to throw out troublemakers. We were invisible to the television cameras, unlike the well-dressed tourists with teased hair and suits who sat below in the mezzanine.

Connie Francis was the mystery guest. Every word out of her mouth was sophisticated and witty. I lost track of everything but her. At the end of the show, I made my way down the stairs in a daze. The blazing June heat outside brought me back to reality, all the more bitter because of the hour of escape in the theater. On the bus ride home, I slumped down in my seat, thought about the stifling summer days ahead with nothing to do. From there, I skidded into thoughts about my father. He hadn't bothered to let me know whether I had a brother or sister. In April, elegant printed birth announcements must have gone out to 'the better class.' Only I, the brother, had been excluded.

That evening, my mother called me into her bedroom. "Can you zip me?" she asked. She had on her black and white polka dot dress. I zipped it. "Keep me company while I finish getting ready." I watched her smooth her nylons, the unshaved hair on her legs flattening beneath the mesh She held onto the dresser, and eased one foot into a white pump, and then the other. Standing before the closet door mirror, she brushed her hair, powdered her face, applied eyeliner, shadow, mascara, red lipstick. Arching her back, she pushed out her bosom. I wondered if she was trying to look like a showgirl since that was the type that had attracted Bernie before.

The doorbell rang. "You get it," she said in a flustered voice.

I opened the door to Bernie Ackerman, a short, muscular guy. His hair--including his Elvis Presley-type sideburns—was all the same black color, and looked dyed. He wore a bright silk shirt with swirls of blue and green; high-heeled boots that made him seem the same height as my mother; a diamond pinkie ring that cut into my palm as he shook hands. He accompanied me down the hall to the living room with a bow-legged walk.

A voice in my head pronounced, 'Not a member of the better class.'

"Hot today, ain't it?" he said, taking a seat on the couch.

"Do you want a glass of water?" I asked, so Mom wouldn't criticize me later for not being polite.

He shook his head. Noticing a copy of the *Mirror* on the coffee table, he said, "That's my paper."

Now, I knew why Mom had changed newspapers. "My mother used to read the *Post*," I said gloomily.

"I'm not a big reader. Usually, all I want to know are the racing results."

"Uh-huh," I grunted. My father sometimes labored through the *New York Times*. Mom was taking a big step down.

"Wonder what's taking your mother so long?...Guess she wants us to get acquainted."

The burden of initiating another subject was on me. I noticed a small, white scar at the side of his mouth, pointed to it, and said, "How'd you get that?"

"A horse at a racetrack kicked me. Lucky it wasn't my eye. I always had good luck. A lot of times I thought I was a goner, but I came through."

I'd hit on a subject he liked. He listed his near-escapes, that he'd been robbed, hit by a car, had a tumor cut out of him. To him, his survival proved he was lucky; to me, he seemed a magnet for trouble. I noted he didn't mention his marital troubles among his disasters.

"Are you a jockey?" I asked.

"I was, but not any more. Jockeys have short careers. Especially if they put on a few pounds." Bernie patted a potbelly. "I have a different job at the race track."

At this point, my mom walked into the living room, and said, "Not just a job. He's the manager." She sat down beside Bernie, crossed and uncrossed her legs. The perfume she was wearing filled the room with its scent. When I had the chance, I was going to throw away the bottle. No, then she'd just buy more. Better to pour half down the drain, then top the bottle with water so it stank less.

"What took you so long, Lil? I thought you got flushed away in the little girls' room," Bernie laughed.

My mother laughed too, something I couldn't bring myself to do. The remark had been idiotic, not witty.

"Well, Lil, ready to go?"

"I just have to get my purse." With a jerk of her head, my mother signaled I was to follow her. In the bedroom, she whispered anxiously, "What do you think of him?"

I shrugged and said, "He's all right."

She squeezed my shoulder in gratitude.

The truth was, I thought he was vulgar. Even if he wasn't, I couldn't put my faith in a guy who'd been divorced three times. Sooner or later, he was going to hurt my mother.

The next morning, my mother hurried off to work, while I lazed in bed. I didn't feel like getting up, but the ringing phone brought me to my feet. I picked up the receiver.

A man's voice said, "Is this Gary Geckleman?"

"Yes."

"This is Mr. Temple from the pharmacy. If you still want a job, come in and we can talk."

"I do! Thank you. When can I come?"

"Right now."

I had no working papers, so I wasn't officially hired. My only earnings were to be my tips. I began delivering prescription drugs. I'd long outgrown my bike, so I went everywhere on foot. The work had me running through streets and up and down stairs. Sometimes a customer would ask me to go over to the newsstand to get them a newspaper or to the grocery to pick up a carton of milk. I earned a little extra by doing these favors. They'd take time, but Mr. Temple never made a fuss if I returned a little late.

Sometimes, he took out a little white bag, filled it with a string of rock candy and gave it to me so I'd have something to suck on as I ran around. Or before I went home, he'd give me a bottle of a brand of hand lotion or a shade of lipstick that wasn't selling well and tell me to bring it home to my mother.

During slow times, he leafed through his stamp collection album. "You can learn a lot from stamps. They teach you about history, geography, art," he told me. "Look at this one of the Palomar telescope." He launched into a talk about the development of the telescope; how the street outside the observatory was called *The Avenue of the Stars*; how this commemorative stamp was the first of its kind. Before that stamps had been mainly of presidents.

When a customer came into the store. Mr. Temple snapped to attention. The white tunic he wore looked crisp and immaculate, like him. He believed that one could be 'a professional' in any job, even if you were only a delivery boy.

He liked to talk to me about 'the finer points' of my job, and advised me once, "Don't ever look at the amount someone tips you. Just slip the coins in your pocket."

"Why's that?" I asked.

"It's more classy to not look. Besides, you'll never resent someone for being a cheapskate."

I took Mr. Temple's advice, didn't know how much I'd earned until the end of the day when I counted my tips. At home, I stacked them on the kitchen table, making piles of dimes, nickels, and quarters. Mr. Temple was right. It all averaged out. If one person gave too little, then someone else made up for it.

Mom sat across from me, watching. My working impressed her. "A man earns money. Now, you're a man," she said. She brought home a new shirt and pair of pants for me from Klein's--"You're going in front of people. You have to look nice" She'd even urged me to eat more--"You need your strength."

I loved any extra attention she could spare. Most nights, she was flying off with Bernie, giving me a breathless, 'goodbye' as she left. They ate out, went dancing, took in shows on Broadway or at Radio City Music Hall. Mom bought a slinky black dress, sling back heels, and a little rhinestone clip for her hair. She was having the time of her life. One weekend, Bernie drove her out to the country, and they stayed overnight. That infuriated me. Afterwards, I could barely bring myself to say 'hello' to him.

With every passing week, he was around more than ever. Sometimes, he came by to fix stuff in the apartment. He brought a new washer for the kitchen sink, a replacement 'ball' for inside the toilet tank, oiled hinges, cleaned out a clogged drain, leveled a table leg. Mom was thrilled.

When she complained that the Zippersteins' screaming was driving her crazy, he volunteered to fix that too. I don't know how he did it—was too proud to ask—but Adele and Morton reverted to the quiet, angelic souls they'd been when they'd first moved into the Cooperman flat.

I hated Bernie for being a know-it-all. He fixed what was broken, managed to get the best deals. One night, he took both my mother and I out to an Italian restaurant in Greenwich Village. Of course, he knew everyone. The waiter gave him a big 'hello,' then led us past a bar to a semi-circular booth with a high-backed green leather bench. The manager came over to greet Bernie. My mother and I were introduced.

Everything in this restaurant was large, from the big menus covering the table, to the huge hamburgers, the platters of French fries, and the bowls of tomato sauce with ladles. Bernie made sure Mom and I noticed. He also pointed out the black sample cases on the floor under the seats of other customers, and said, "Out-of-town salesmen know where to get the best food at the lowest prices."

Of course, he was only boasting about himself. I didn't know how Mom could stand him.

The anniversary of my grandmother's death was coming up, the time when a headstone would be placed on her grave. There was to be an 'unveiling ceremony.' Uncle Ben was coming up from Baltimore. My mother was overjoyed about seeing him. She said he'd surely stay over two or three days. We hadn't seen him since the funeral.

Bernie was going to attend too. To me, he was a stranger who didn't belong at our ceremony. He'd never even met Grandma. But Bernie had a big, shiny, aqua colored Buick with a silver grille. We needed him to chauffeur us to the cemetery.

The night before the unveiling, Uncle Ben arrived at our flat with a little sports bag and a gift of pears from the tree in his garden. His face was puffier, his belly more bloated. "I got fat, didn't I?" he said. He gave a little snort of embarrassed laughter as my mother assured him that he hadn't. We went to the living room.

Mom disliked her sister-in-law but felt obliged to ask, "How's Selma?"

"Fine…says 'hello' to everybody," Ben mumbled, flushing. The springs groaned as he shifted in his chair.

"Do you want anything, Ben? Can I get you a cup of coffee?"

"I had my fill of coffee on the train…Let me take a look at this handsome nephew of mine. Hey, you've shot up, Gary. You're going to be taller than me."

I smiled. His prediction delighted me. A man was supposed to be tall, not shorter than his girlfriend like Bernie. I looked forward to the day I'd tower over him.

"Where's the parakeet?" Ben asked, noticing the cage was missing.

"Didn't I tell you?" Mom said. "I left the window open, and it flew away." Tears filled her eyes. Mutely, she handed him the photo of Grandma at my *bar mitzvah*.

"Mama looks beautiful here," Ben said.

My mother threw her arms about him, hugged him for a long time. Then she took Ben to the kitchen, telling me I should watch television while they 'caught up on things.'

I wanted to have a private conversation with Uncle Ben too. My mother still had the idea that I should become a doctor, dentist, or some other lucrative profession. She also thought I had the brains to achieve one of these goals because I'd skipped the second grade. What I think happened was that a few kids had been moved up because the second grade classes were overcrowded, but my mother insisted on her own interpretation, that I was brilliant.

Whether I was or not, I wanted to ask Ben to convince her I should go to art school. I'd put together my best drawings to show him. The longer I waited, the jumpier I felt. Uncle Ben might hate my drawings. I got them out. Studying them one by one, I saw only the flaws; distorted legs on one figure; misshapen hands on another. I felt like tearing them up. I'd never asked anyone to look at and judge my drawings before, and I was terrified. What if my uncle said I had no talent?

The teakettle's piercing whistle brought me to my feet. Thinking I'd be invited to drink tea with them, I went to the kitchen.

As soon as I appeared in the doorway, my mother snapped, "Excuse me. This is private."

"But I want to talk to Uncle Ben."

"Later," Ben said with a wink. "Your mother and I have a lot to discuss."

I guessed Mom was discussing the pros and cons of Bernie with him. That might take all night. "I'm going to sleep," I said. A part of me was relieved to put off showing my drawings to Uncle Ben for a day or two.

After brushing my teeth and relieving myself at the toilet, I climbed into my mother's bed. Uncle Ben and I were going to share it, while Mom took my place on the couch. I was half-asleep when Ben shuffled into the bedroom. He undressed in the dark. When he lay down next to me, his side of the mattress sank way down. I had to hold onto to the edge to keep from rolling into him. After a while, he began to snore. I envied my mother sleeping off in the living room away from the noise.

Shortly after breakfast the following morning, the phone rang. The next few hours either my mother or Uncle Ben were on the phone. One of the calls came from Bernie to check when he was supposed to come by; another from a relative with a cold who wouldn't be able to attend the unveiling and wanted to apologize. I had the impression that the other calls were from Selma. Uncle Ben said little during his conversations with her. When he hung up after one, he secluded himself with my mother. I couldn't hear what they whispered but after they spoke Mom seemed upset. She snapped at me for nothing.

I didn't know what was wrong, only that Uncle Ben was too busy to talk to me about my art. Besides, we were about to go out to visit my grandmother's grave. My mother would say I was heartless to be thinking about myself at such a time.

While she was pouring me a cup of tea to drink with my lunch, some drops splattered onto my shirt. "You can't go looking like that. Take it off," Mom said. She got out the ironing board for the second time that day, and pressed a new shirt for me. When she was done, she rushed off to get dressed in a black shirt and skirt that she planned on wearing to the cemetery.

I answered a knock at the door. It was Bernie, shorter than usual in a shiny pair of loafers, instead of his boots. The loafers probably pinched. He moved cautiously as if he felt off balance. In her phone call with him a couple of days earlier, I'd overhead my mother tell him exactly what to wear. He had on beige slacks, and a white shirt with a plain, dark blue tie. His hair was slicked back with every strand in place. He'd shaved his cheeks and chin closely, even scraped some spots red.

Rabbi Schneider arrived five minutes after Bernie. Mom offered coffee and pastry. The rabbi asked for a glass of water, took a few sips, then put his glass in the sink. The five of us left the flat. Uncle Ben carried his sports bag and threw it in the trunk of Bernie's Buick. I figured he had something in the bag that he wanted to use at the cemetery, a prayer shawl, and perhaps his own skullcap rather than one of the black silk ones the rabbi would distribute that had sat on God knows whose head. We climbed into the car; Rabbi Schneider in the seat of honor beside Bernie; myself in the back between my uncle and my mother. Bernie flicked on the ignition and the air-conditioning. I noted he sat barely high enough in his seat to peer over the steering wheel.

There was little conversation as we rode through the city. Driving through Queens, I stared past my mother, out the side window at the orange-turquoise-white Howard Johnson, rolling hills, and large brick old age home. I'd seen them when we drove to the cemetery last year. I recognized the cemetery's spiked iron fence, the box hedges beside it. Bernie parked in a lot. We walked through the main gate onto a gravel path. A caretaker at a small stone office building gave Uncle Ben a map that he'd marked to show the location of Grandma's grave. The paths had signs like the ones on city streets. August sun beat down on our heads. Bernie's white shirt was stained with damp spots. The rabbi wore green tinted sunglasses. A Panama hat topped his skullcap. I shaded my eyes with my hand.

The rows of graves stretched on and on, made me realize that everyone ended up in this city of the dead. Next it would be my mother and Ben, then me. There was no escaping. I was going to die. I shuddered, wishing I could run away from the cemetery and Death.

A small group stood at Grandma's gravesite, waiting for us. Mr. Kessler's family was still away in the country, but he'd kindly picked up and driven a carload of people: my mom's elderly aunt and uncle from Argentina; Grandma's union friend,

Ida Mutchnik; our neighbor, Mrs. Cohen. After briefly greeting everyone, Mom walked over to examine the new gravestone.

My grandmother's name and the dates of her birth and death were cut into the shining, white granite. Nearby gravestones were dingy in comparison. Soon my grandmother's would get spotted and covered with moss like the others. Worse, vandals might desecrate her stone. In the next row were two gravestones covered with black crayon scribbling. Kids must have jumped the fence at night and marked them up. The vandals were cowards, picking victims who couldn't defend themselves.

I stared down at Grandma Etta's grave, at the grass and dirt, tried to see through and make a connection her. 'It's me, Gary. I promise I'll remember you.' Glancing at my mother, I noticed Bernie's arm was draped around her waist. "Grandma," I pleaded, "Make a magic spell that makes him disappear." I was sure she didn't like him.

The rabbi began the service. I read the mourner's prayer, "*Yisgidal, v'yisgidal...*"

The service was brief followed by a speech from Rabbi Schneider about how necessary it was to remember happy times during sorrow, and vice versa. Soon, we were walking back to the gate, my mother and her Argentinean relations speaking in Yiddish, Mr. Kessler and Bernie assisting Ida Mutchnik who tottered along with a stick. We said another prayer at the sink by the gate, washed our hands, and then proceeded to the parking lot. Mr. Kessler helped his passengers into his car. I was about to climb into the Buick's backseat when Bernie came up to me, squeezed my shoulder, and muttered, "Rough morning." Without responding, I got into the car.

Soon I was riding towards the city, anticipating showing Uncle Ben my drawings. To my amazement, Bernie drove up to Pennsylvania Station. "What are we doing here?" I asked.

Bernie left the car running, went around to the trunk for my uncle's sports bag. I'd completely forgotten it was there. Uncle Ben climbed out. The sports bag switched hands.

"Ben has to catch his train," Mom said.

"But you said he was staying a few days."

"He can't."

The prospect of showing my drawings to Uncle Ben had unnerved me, but not showing them to him was worse. I was devastated, couldn't respond when he called a general 'goodbye' to everyone in the car. Bernie, in the driver's seat again, craned his neck, and began inching out into traffic.

"Stop," my mother cried, flung open her door, leapt out. Cars and taxis honked as she gave Uncle Ben a hug. In an instant, she was back in the car.

Ben stood on the sidewalk waving as Bernie drove off. I recovered enough to roll down my window and shout, 'I'll call you, Uncle Ben.' I still hoped to talk to him about how I wanted to be an artist. Bernie drove Rabbi Schneider home. My mother took the rabbi's place in the front passenger seat, and I sprawled in the back.

Pulling down the sun visor, Mom used the little mirror behind it to study how she looked. I saw she was completely at home in the Buick. That added to my sadness, as did her invitation to Bernie to stay for supper. I suppose she wanted to reward him for all the driving he'd done. She'd dote on him the way she used to dote on me, making sure that he had the best bits of whatever she had to offer.

I dragged around the apartment while my mother prepared the meal, and the two of them talked in the kitchen. All I could think about was how Mom had monopolized Uncle Ben the night before. If she hadn't, I would have had the few moments I needed to show off my drawings.

Mom called me in for supper. I stuck my head in the kitchen door. A *yortzeit* candle she'd lit last night for my grandmother was sputtering in a little glass on top of the stove. I stood, gazing at the flickering flame. The apartment felt suffocating.

"I'm not hungry," I said.

"That doesn't mean you can't sit with us," Bernie said jovially.

I shrugged and walked away.

My mother followed me to the living room. "Look at me," she ordered.

I turned to face her.

"On a day like today, you're making trouble."

"All I said was that I'm not hungry. What's wrong with that?"

"You're rude."

"So are you! You wouldn't let me talk to Uncle Ben."

Mom heaved a heavy sigh, sank into a chair. "Selma wouldn't let him stay, not even an extra day. She even resented that he came for the unveiling."

Hearing these words, I knew I wasn't going to phone Uncle Ben. I felt sorry for him. He could barely help himself, let alone me.

"What did you want to talk to him about?"

"I wanted to show him my drawings." I hadn't meant to tell her, but I felt so beat down that the words slipped out before I realized what I was saying. I wanted her sympathy, her love.

She chewed her lip as if struggling not to blurt something back.

I sat down across from her, was silent. So was she. Through the window behind her chair, I could see the fire escape, telephone poles and wires. Kids were down on the street playing games that would go on until it got dark. They called, "Got-tcha," "You're it," "Whitey cheated."

A rustling in the kitchen reminded my mother she must return to her guest. She left me. I heard her telling Bernie, "Gary likes to draw. He counted on showing my brother his pictures. But there wasn't time."

"Let's see if I can' do something to get him cheered up," Bernie said.

For a moment, I feared he'd rush into the living room and tell me one of his stupid jokes, like, 'Where've ya been? Flushed down the toilet?' It annoyed me that he thought he could 'fix' me--like he'd fixed the Zippersteins. It wasn't like he could look at my drawings in place of Uncle Ben. What did an ignoramus like Bernie know about art?

My mother took him to the door and said goodbye. As soon as he was gone, I ran out to the street. Heat rushed at me. On the corner, a few kids had opened up a hydrant. The water hit the hot pavement and turned to steam. A girl my age dressed in red Bermuda shorts, a loose white t-shirt, and rubber soled sandals that flapped against the pavement, approached. She was a big sister or a babysitter, taking a kid for a walk in a squeaky stroller. The little boy's face looked like it was on fire. "Give the kid a drink of water," I cried. The girl went right by like she hadn't heard.

A few days later, my mother told me that Bernie was going to take me to the track. I asked whether she was going. "No," she said, "It's just you and him." I was torn, one part of me wanting to refuse, another feeling curious, So far, the only horses I'd seen were the ones the police rode in Central Park. Whenever Bernie had been waiting for my mother to get ready, I'd turned on the television to avoid talking to him. On occasion, we'd watched old Westerns. Bernie cared more about the horses than the stories. He'd told me the breeds the Lone Ranger, Tonto, Hop-a-long Cassidy and Gene Audrey rode.

As if I was doing Bernie a favor, I said, "All right, I'll let him take me."

Sunday he picked me up. He had a plastic bag with him that I assumed contained a present for my mother. To my surprise he handed the bag to me. He'd bought me a bright orange zippy shirt like the silk ones he wore. I put it on in the bathroom, then came out to show how it fit. My mother looked like she was sucking on a lemon, but she didn't say a word.

She sent the two of us off, saying, "You'll have a wonderful time." I wasn't so sure. Once I was riding through the city, my mood improved. Sunbeams sparkled on the East River. Breezes blew through the Buick's wide-open windows. I asked questions, and he told me how it was all too easy for a jockey to get bounced over a horse's head onto his shoulder or collarbone; that the fastest horses ran about thirty miles an hour. He was affable. "Beautiful day...Couldn't have better weather if you ordered it...Ever hear about the Belmont..."

"Are the races fixed?" I asked.

"Not at my track! And no animal is doped to hop up its speed. It's not worth the risk to the horse. Besides, if you get caught that's the end of you and racing."

He turned onto Highway 87, flicked on the radio. Tapping the steering wheel with his ring, he softly sang along with the music, "Maria, Maria, I just met a girl named Maria..."

At the racecourse he pulled into the employees' parking lot. Straight ahead were a weather-beaten wood grandstand and a few low buildings painted the same light-green color.

"Hey Gary, come on, I want you to meet some folks," Bernie said.

He was light on his feet. I had trouble keeping up as he rushed past bales of hay and horse trailers. He gave me a behind-the-scenes tour of the saddle, dressing, and weighing rooms, and finally, at the stable--a large cool building that smelled of horse, hay and manure--he called over jockeys and stable-hands, and introduced me as "Lil's boy."

As they talked to me, the jockeys swung their arms or stood on the balls of their feet like they were keeping their muscles limber until their races. These wiry, muscular men were no taller than Bernie. Standing among them, he no longer looked short. All the workers seemed to like and respect him.

"Where's your mother today?" they asked me. They spoke of her as "a real lady." The 'better class I'd met at Francine's cocktail party had been cold and snobbish. The racetrack people made me the center of attention.

Everyone had to get back to work. Boys who looked my age brushed down the horses in their stalls. The sleek horses turned their heads as Bernie and I walked past. One bared yellow teeth behind her black lips, and neighed. Another rolled her eyes.

"This is *Midnight*...and this is *Whiskey*...and this is *Penelope*. Bernie knew all their names, where they were bred, their bloodlines, where they'd raced.

"Look at this beauty," Bernie called and led me into the stall of a horse with a shining black coat. She danced about nervously. Her hooves looked sharp.

"Go ahead and pet her," Bernie said, but I didn't want to get any closer. "She knows you're nervous." He stroked the horse's back. "That's a pretty girl..." he calmed her.

We went from the stables out into the bright sunshine. The stands had begun to fill and we joined a crowd that was buying soft drinks, talking, rushing to seats. The races were about to start. "Place a bet for me." I begged Bernie to do it since I was under-age.

"Uh-uh, I can't," he said. "Against policy. I'm management and it won't look right."

He guided me to the top row of the stadium. We had a perfect view. Although I wasn't betting I was excited when the jockeys appeared in bright colored silk shirts, tight pants, caps, and goggles. They lined up on their horses at the starting line. Many of the horses wore cloth masks over their faces. I felt tense and silent waiting for the buzzer to sound. Finally, bang! The horses burst out of the gates. The jockeys were crouched low, half standing in stirrups cinched high up, only a few inches below the saddles. Whips snapped through the air, stinging the horses' rumps. The riders urged the horses, faster, faster. The crowd screamed. I was on my feet yelling with them. My fists clenched. My heart felt like it would burst.

Only Bernie sat quietly. But his hands twitched as if he were holding the reins. When the first race was over he said, "Come on, I want you to meet someone." Running down ahead of me, he took the stadium stairs two at a time. Bernie stopped at a row where a man, sitting on the aisle, was drawing on a sketchpad propped on his knees. Pencils stuck out of the breast pocket of his plaid shirt. His horn-rimmed glasses magnified his blue eyes. A pair of binoculars hung around his neck.

Startled when Bernie reached over and tapped his shoulder, the man looked up and said, "Why it's you, you son of a gun. Glad to see you again." In a moment, he set aside his drawing materials, slid out of his seat, and shook hands with Bernie.

"This is Gary, the kid who likes to draw."

"Draw or scribble?"

"Don't ask me. I don't know the difference."

The man turned to me saying, "I'm John," and shook my hand. I thought he'd let go, but he looked at my hand, tapped the big callous on my third finger. Whenever I drew, my pencil pressed against that spot. John touched it like he had to check whether it was real, whether I really did draw.

"Show the kid your sketchbook."

"These are studies. I do water colors in my studio."

Bernie grinned as I leafed through John's drawings of thin, long legged horses. It impressed me that he sketched the horses in motion. I imagined him looking through his binoculars, drawing, looking through the binoculars again. He must have fast reflexes to see things and respond in a flash.

His horses looked like they were running themselves to death. Their eyes bulged. Froth bubbled at their muzzles. The veins in their necks stood out. Their coats glistened with sweat. A close-up of a head showed a horse with rolled up eyes like a suffering saint. I wondered whether John had seen that look in a real horse.

"They sell for a pretty penny," Bernie mused. "So, what do you think, Gary?"

"They're good." I mumbled, afraid to say something stupid. I was thrilled to meet a real artist.

"Don't put him on the spot. What if he doesn't like them?" John laughed.

"I do like them."

How long have you been drawing, Gary?"

"My whole life."

"Have you taken any classes?"

"No. I never took any classes."

"Don't apologize. It doesn't mean you can't draw. Do you want to take a class?"

"Yes, I would."

"The Saturday classes at the Brooklyn Museum are good. I teach there. You can take my class if you want."

"Thanks."

A new race was starting. Bernie wanted to get back to our high seats where we had the best view of the track. We shook hands with John and said goodbye. The rest of the afternoon, I heard the announcer's voice--"won by a nose...running neck and neck...a photo finish...dropped his whip...falling behind..." To me the horses John had drawn were more real than the ones racing below.

I wanted so much to take the art class at the Brooklyn Museum, and was filled with questions. Who'd be in the class? How advanced would the other students be? Would I be good enough? Would the class cost a lot of money? Would my mother object? Did she know about John? I'd never been to the Brooklyn Museum, didn't know how to get there.

I glanced over at Bernie. He'd been as excited as me during our meeting with John. Mom said Bernie was a sweet guy. I wasn't ready to go that far. But I was willing to concede that he might not be as bad as I'd thought.

When the races were over, he drove back along Highway 87, the way we'd come The highway cut through the Van Cortland Park Golf Course. Golfers I saw to the right and left, made me think of Florida--and how my father hadn't taken me to see the sights during my visit. I glanced over at Bernie, singing along with the radio music, tapping his ring against the steering wheel again. He was little more than a stranger for me, but he was knocking himself out. I suppose it wasn't so much for my sake as for 'Lil.' But that was better than the nothing I'd received from Dave Geckleman.

The Buick was caught in a weekend crush of people driving back into the city from their country getaways. We inched along and the drive seemed endless.

"How did you get to be a jockey?" I asked.

"What else should I be? I'm short. I wanted it to be an advantage. It wasn't just that. My father came from Romania, a little town outside Kishinev. He'd talk about the horses in Ataki..."

I interrupted. "How did you meet the right people? How did you make contacts?" I wanted to know how a man became a Somebody in the world.

"I was sixteen, and I was a pretty good rider," Bernie said. "I went to the track and I asked the manager to give me a job. He was a big Irish guy named, McGuire. He said they didn't have anything. So I asked him to let me work for free. For two weeks I shoveled shit out of the stalls. I came earlier then anybody. I left later. And they didn't pay me a cent. McGuire, says to me one day, 'Are you going to keep this up?' I said, 'Yes.' So he says, 'I can't look at myself in the mirror. You're making me feel guilty. I gotta put you on the payroll. You're hired.' That's how I started. Then, I looked for my chances."

"Like how?"

"How? I'd look a man over, and I'd say to myself, 'What can I do for that man?' I'd run errands for the guy, bring him cigarettes, and pretty soon he knows who I am, and he needs me to do things. But all along, the important thing was I thought of myself as a jockey. I believed in myself and that gets passed on to the other man. Then, if something comes up he remembers me. One time, a jockey got sick at the last moment before a race. He was throwing up all over the place and he couldn't ride. There I was, right on the spot."

"How did you learn to ride?"

"Ha! That's a whole other thing. I was a crazy devil. The first horse I rode was half-dead. It was the fruit man's horse..."

The first chance he could, Bernie pulled off the highway and into the city to escape the stop-and-go traffic. He ended up driving through Harlem. The buildings were old and grimy, many with broken, boarded up windows. Beer cans and crumpled newspapers littered the streets. We stopped at a red light near a corner where there were some boys with stockings pulled over their hair like hairnets. They stared at us and one of them bent his arm in a "fuck you." They all laughed. Another picked up a rock. I thought he'd run over to the car and break the window. The light changed and Bernie who still had the fast reflexes of a jockey, sped off before anything could happen.

After a while, the familiar little stores of the Lower East Side appeared. Bernie circled around, found a spot near my house, and parked the Buick. We went inside. He raced up the steps. "Lil," he called as he rapped on the door. The door opened.

Mom gazed at me searchingly and said, "Did you enjoy yourself?"

"It was fun," I said.


I waited a few days before I broached the subject of my taking John's class with my mother. She sat in a chair in the living room, darning one of my socks as I related how I'd met John at the racetrack. Her silver needle darted in and out of the sock in jerks, as I talked about his art class.

"Bernie didn't say he was going to introduce you to an artist who taught classes," she said stiffly.

"I don't think he knew he'd be at the track." To my surprise, I was lying for Bernie's sake, didn't want to get him in trouble.

My answer seemed to satisfy Mom about Bernie, but not about me. "You're starting high school next week. Won't you have enough to do without *schlepping* over to Brooklyn? What about your job with Mr. Temple? I thought you were going to work for him on Saturdays."

"It would mean more to me to take the art class…"

Mom bit off the thread, held up my sock to examine her handiwork. "Didn't you sign up for an art class at Seward High? So why do you need another?"

My heart sank. We'd fought about whether I should take the art class at my high school. Her position was that I'd be wasting my time. Yet in the end, she'd let me have my way. She wasn't going to let me take two art classes. There was no way I could persuade her.

Mrs. Kessler returned from the country with her daughters. Other people came back to the neighborhood, including Jeffrey Lumpkin. I met him in the street one day, looking suntanned and taller. He asked me over to his house. I'd finished my shift at the pharmacy, so I agreed.

Like most of the boys who'd been at John Burroughs, Jeffrey and I professed to have crushes on a girl named Joan Schwartz. Spotting a phone booth. I stopped, and said, "I have to make an important phone call to Joan." Of course, I didn't phone. I just went into the booth, picked up the receiver and pretended to talk. Then, I came out, trying to keep a straight face.

"What's up?"

"You swear you won't tell anyone."

"I swear."

"I'm going to be a father!"

"I thought she was on the pill."

"She was...but it didn't work."

"Don't you know about Trojans?"

I punched Jeffrey in the arm. We horsed around the rest of the way.

'The Lump' lived in a flat over the stationery store on the Avenue. I'd passed by it all my life, but I'd never noticed the narrow, brown door on the street until Jeffrey opened it and we went up a flight of steps to the

Lumpkin flat. Jeffrey's parents worked, his father as a house painter, his mother as a first grade teacher, so we had the place to ourselves. The kitchen's white tiled walls reminded me of bathroom walls. Jeffrey bounced around, setting out milk, graham crackers and the remains of a chocolate cake.

My grandmother had taught me the Yiddish words *essen,* to eat like a human being, and *fressen,* which means to eat like an animal. Jeffrey ate like an animal. His face and clothes got smeared with chocolate frosting. Milk spilled on the floor. Cracker crumbs scattered over the Formica table. Jeffrey, his mouth full of food, confided that his grandfather was sick, that he might come to live with them and share his room.

"I never had my own room," I said.

Jeffrey looked up, crumbs over his chin and lips, "You could give me a drop of sympathy!"

I apologized.

For the next hour, we talked about starting Seward Park high school the next week. I couldn't wait. I wanted to be popular, have a good time, and even hoped I'd find a real girlfriend, not a fantasy one.

I walked home, and when I opened the door, the phone was ringing. Thinking it was Bernie, I ran to get it. I was eager to tell him my mother didn't want me to take John's class. My hope was he'd volunteer to try to persuade her.

A woman's voice greeted me, "Hi, Gary." It was Francine! She spoke in a rapid voice. "Your father's in the hospital. He collapsed yesterday. They took him in an ambulance."

"What's wrong with him?"

There were so many reasons Dad might be in the hospital. He could have started a fight while he was drunk; stepped in front of a car; fallen in the bathtub and hit his head; collapsed in an alley and been stabbed by thug who 'rolled' drunks. .

"He needed a rest. He's been having health issues for a long time."

"Health issues," I echoed. Was it a health issue to sit on a bar stool every day? My father, I assumed, was using a hospital bed to sleep off a bender.

"You should come down here and see him."

"Did my father ask for me?"

"He wants you to come."

I didn't believe her. The last visit, she'd wanted to use me for her own purposes. I said, "I'm starting school soon. My first break isn't until Thanksgiving."

"That's not soon enough. Come this week. Come tomorrow."

"I told you, I'm starting high school." It annoyed me that Francine didn't care whether I missed the first crucial days. That was the time that cliques formed, and anyone who came later was automatically an outsider.

"It's serious, Gary. You have to get here fast!"

Her alarm made my heart pound. "I'll talk to my mother." I took down the name of the hospital and the phone number and extension for my father's room.

Before she hung up, I asked, "Did you have your baby?"

"Yes, yes…you have a little brother, Abraham…You'll meet him."

The phone clicked off.

My mother came home. "Whew, it's hot out," she said, setting a large bag of groceries down on the kitchen counter. She took out a carton of milk, cottage cheese, bunch of carrots with ferny leaves. I watched her diving into the refrigerator, making space for the perishables.

"I had a call from Florida," I said.

"Florida?" In a flash, she left off her unpacking and came up to me. "From your father?"

"From Francine."

"What does *she* want?"

"Dad's in the hospital. She said it's serious, that I should go down there to see him right away."

Her face turned white. "Is it cancer?" 'The big C,' was what people in our neighborhood called cancer. They were scared to even say the word. If someone had it they pretended it was something else. A man down the street had had his leg amputated, and his wife said he'd been in an accident. When he grew thin and weak, she told people he had pleurisy. After he died my mother told me he'd had cancer all along.

I thought my father was sick because of his drinking. I'd promised him that I wouldn't tell my mother he was a drunkard. Abiding by that promise, I said, "I don't know." I went for the information I'd jotted down about the hospital. After I showed it to Mom, I told her I had a half-brother named Abraham.

Her eyebrows shot up. "Is there anything else I should know?"

"No," I muttered. I could see the news upset my mom. I wondered whether the reason Francine hadn't sent a birth announcement was because she knew it would.

Mom said, "I have to make a phone call." She took the phone and the slip of paper I'd given her into the bathroom, closed the door. I overheard her saying, among other things, "What does it mean 'his liver is failing?' Can't they do something for him?" A second call was made. My mother told Bernie to come over. I was glad he was coming. His opinion had begun to matter to me.

It was rush hour and traffic must have been inching along, but Bernie made his Buick jump and fly over the other cars. It wasn't more than a half hour after Mom finished putting the remaining groceries away that I heard his special knock, one slow and three fast taps. There was a conference in the living room, my mother and Bernie talking and me sitting in the corner with my mouth shut.

Bernie said, "Gary should go see him. What's the problem?"

"The man always ignored Gary. Now, Gary's supposed to run down there."

"He's his father."

"He didn't act like one."

"You know what they say: Two wrongs don't make a right." Bernie winked at me.

"I don't want Gary going there and getting all upset."

"He has to go or he'll regret it later. Come on, Lil. You know it yourself."

"What do you want to do, Gary?" Mom asked. "I'm not going to stand in your way if you want to go to see your father."

I was trembling. The last thing I wanted was a long bus ride to Florida with hour after hour to think about my father; whether I should love him because he'd told me stories about Finland when I was small; whether he was detestable because he'd abandoned me. I supposed that I should pity my father, but I didn't. It was his own goddamn fault he was messed up. Look at Bernie who'd been divorced three times, but was still fighting to get his life straight. He didn't spend his days on a bar stool, drinking himself to death.

I felt confused, scared, overwhelmed—and unwilling to show these weaknesses. Bernie's prediction that later I'd regret not going, influenced me. I said, "I want to go."

"All right. I'll go with you," Mom said, reached over and squeezed my hand.

"But why, Lil?"

"I know my own son. This is too much for him."

Bernie snapped, "Let him grow up! He has to do this on his own."

"Do you want me to come with you, Gary?"

I did, and I didn't; wanted to be her little boy; wanted to be a man; knew Francine and my father would want me to be on my own, that my mother's presence would cause more tension. "I'll go by myself," I said.

Bernie smiled. He expected a lot of me. I was pleased I hadn't disappointed him.

Sighing, my mother said, "We better find out about the bus schedule."

"He's not going by bus," Bernie said. "Gary will fly down. The ticket's my treat."

"Thanks," I said.

My mother looked miserable. Neither of us had ever been in an airplane. She said, "You'll take a seat near the door of the plane. That way, you can get out faster if you have to."

"What do you think is going to happen, Lil?"

She shrugged. "I don't know. It's better to be careful."

"Nothing's going to happen! It's safer in an airplane than here in New York. Look at that poor lady who was murdered in Queens a few weeks ago. Three-dozen people witnessed it, and nobody did a thing. It makes me sick," Bernie said.

He made an airline reservation for me. Afterwards, he gave me a slip of paper with my flight information. "Telephone your stepmother and tell her you're coming, tomorrow." I did. When I spoke to Francine, she said, "You're doing the right thing."

My mother threw a quick supper together, opening a can of sardines. It was one of those flat cans you roll back with a 'key,' and while she was doing it she cut her finger on the lid's edge. "It's nothing," she said and held her hand under the tap. She mashed up the sardines with cream cheese and lemon juice. We sat down to eat. Mom's cut opened again. Bernie was ready to take her to the emergency room for stitches, but the bleeding stopped. My mother gave me a small overnight bag to pack with toiletries.

My flight left the next morning, a Thursday. I was returning on Saturday. The first day of school was the following Monday, and I wasn't going to miss it. In the morning, I phoned Mr. Temple and told him I had a family emergency and wouldn't be able to come to work the next couple of days. He was kind, commiserated without pressing me to tell him what was wrong. "Call when you're free to work again," he said.

Bernie drove me to Idlewild, the airport that was renamed J.F.K. a couple of years later. At the gate, he said, "I'm going to give you some good advice. Forgive your father. The way I see it, no one's perfect." He pressed a white envelope into my hand. "Keep this safe."

"What is it?"

"A few dollars in case you need them."

"Thanks, Bernie."

We shook hands. I joined the passengers boarding the airplane. A stewardess took my ticket. My assigned seat was next to the window. I sat down in mine, putting my small bag beneath the seat in front of me. Along with my anxiety about seeing my father, I felt scared to be flying. As the airplane rose up in the air, I looked out saw that the houses and cars below looked like tiny toys. An airline hostess in a blue, tailored uniform passed down the aisle giving out juice and soft drinks. I set my coke on a little pull down table. The plane flew through a cloud. I wished I could put my hand outside and run it through the wispy air.

A few people got up to use the bathrooms. I had to see what the facilities were like, squeezed past the two passengers in my row to the aisle. Inside a small stall, I took out Bernie's envelope and found a ten- and two twenty-dollar bills. What a fortune! When I got back in my seat, I kept patting my pocket to make sure I hadn't lost the envelope. Leaning back, I daydreamed about spending all the money on art supplies, canvases, sable brushes, oil paints with wonderful names like Siena, cadmium red and burnt umber.

The elderly woman sitting beside me started a conversation, said she had spent the summer in New York at a resort, and was now returning to her home in Florida. I felt an urge to blurt out that my father was dying, and I was going to see him. I didn't. It was a cheat to make someone pity me as if I was grieving over a *real* father. The man I was going to see was less than a stranger. I'd have had no feelings towards a stranger. My father had hurt me. Francine said he'd been sick for a while. If he'd been in pain, I understood his not taking me on excursions during my visit. But why hadn't we talked more, gotten to know each other?

The plane landed at Fort Lauderdale, and I made my way through the busy airport to the outside sidewalk to wait for a shuttle. In yesterday's phone conversation, Francine had told me there was one that would take me directly from the airport to Good Samaritan Hospital. A van pulled up and the driver didn't seem surprised when I told him my destination. With so many sick old people retired to Florida, he was used to family emergencies.

Glancing out the bus window at the big palm trees and the bright sunshine, I wondered what to say to Francine when I saw her. When we spoke on the phone, I'd felt too agitated to congratulate her on her baby. I didn't know whether I should do so now while my father was sick.

The driver pulled the van up to a large square building on Flagler Street and called, "Good Sam." It took a second call for me to realize 'Good Sam' meant 'Good Samaritan'.

I climbed down with my bag and entered a hospital lobby. Like the airport, it was full of people going in and out, or sitting around, waiting. One woman knitted a long red scarf and cried. I had my father's room number, so I didn't need to consult the white-haired clerk in a pink smock at the information desk. Passing a flower store and gift shop, I came to a bank of elevators. I caught one going up. In the crowded car, two young doctors in white coats stood beside me, talking about a case.

I got off before them, began walking down a long hallway. An elderly janitor in a blue uniform was washing the floor with a string mop. I tiptoed over wet stretches of linoleum. The doors to rooms were open. This was my first visit to a hospital. I held my breath, scared that I was going to catch some horrible disease. Curious, though, I peered in the open doors, saw green-walls, night tables, sick people sunk into their beds. Some watched the televisions mounted to the ceilings. Others slept or stared in space like zombies. A fat man in a hospital gown was grunting on a portable toilet. He must have been too sick to notice or even care that people could look in and see him.

Most of the hospital rooms had two beds, but my father's was private. There he was, stretched out, unshaven, his eyes shut. Francine sat beside him riffling through a magazine. I tapped at the open door. Francine looked up, saying, "You made it." I crossed the room. There was no hug from her. She simply motioned me to take the chair on the opposite side of the bed. I sat down in that chair, and that's where I stayed while my father slept.

My father didn't have on a shirt. That startled me. It was rare that I'd seen him without one. He looked much thinner than when I'd seen him in the winter; his bones sharp; his eyes further back in their sockets; his nose larger beneath the clear plastic oxygen mask that covered the bottom half of his face. On an upright metal pole hung a bag with a dangling tube. Clear liquid from the bag slowly dripped through the tube, into a needle taped to a vein on the inside of my father's arm Another tube came from under the top sheet and emptied into a urine bottle. I sat there staring at him. He used to be a handsome man, but now he was a helpless blob.

Francine's blue eyes had dark circles beneath them. "How was your trip?" she asked but didn't wait for my reply. "I called you right away. Just after he was admitted."

"Thank you."

"He was too weak to go by car. We had to have an ambulance."

"I'm sorry."

"He's hardly eating."

The window behind her looked out on the parking lot. She kept talking in a nervous, hysterical stream. I was afraid to say the wrong thing, afraid to even move. I wished I were running through the parking lot, making my escape.

"We're not going to stay all night. We'll go back to the apartment and come back in the morning. You're finally going to meet your brother...if that means anything to you."

Several times, Francine's voice broke with sobs. I couldn't see what good my being here was, or what good was meeting this brother I'd only found out about yesterday. Touching the envelope in my pocket, I imagined Bernie standing in the corner of the room in his cowboy boots, and wanted to scream 'Why'd you make me come?'

I started hearing his voice in my head. 'Remember that Philly, the one I showed you at the racetrack, and how we calmed her down. What do you do when you see a nervous Philly? You get careful. You move slowly. You don't do anything to upset her. The woman's husband is dying. You know what I'm saying? Put her mind on something else. Ask about her kid.'

"Does Abe look like you or Dad?"

"Like both of us. By the way, it's Abraham, not Abe. Abe is common."

Bernie again, 'A gentleman always agrees with a lady.'

I managed, "I see what you mean. 'Abraham' is better."

"I think so," Francine said and smiled. "Abraham or Avram if you prefer."

"Avram's good too."

Bernie's response: 'Hey kid, you're learning how to treat the ladies!'

My father's eyelids fluttered open. He stared at me, struggled to speak, then remembered the oxygen mask and pulled it down to his neck.

"Thanks for coming," he told me and licked his dry lips. His voice was weak.

"Do you want water?"

He nodded, so I gave him the water glass. But he couldn't get the straw in his mouth unless I propped him up. We hadn't touched in a long time, hadn't even shaken hands when he picked me up at the bus terminal last December. I felt embarrassed to put my palm directly on his head or neck. Instead, I slipped my hand *under* the pillow to raise him.

He took a sip of water and rested before he asked, "How's your mother?"

"O.K." I said, glancing at Francine. She held a bit of my father's sheet in one hand, and kneaded it.

"You're doing all right, Gary?"

"Sure...fine, Dad."

He looked sad, almost as if he was going to cry.

"Don't strain yourself, Dave. Look, the aide left you a nice new toothbrush. Wouldn't you like to get your teeth cleaned?" The night table was crowded with a telephone, a water jug, a glass, a pad and pencil, and a vase of wilted, yellow roses. There was also a packet with a toothbrush, toothpaste and mouthwash--all unused.

My father turned his face aside.

"Then, let's get your hair combed."

"No."

"Would you like me to read you a newspaper?

"Don't bother. I don't need to know the news any more."

An aide brought a tray with juice and Jell-O, and Francine urged, "You should eat. The doctor is coming soon. He'll ask if you ate."

"I might not be here. I'm going on a trip."

With Dad looking away, Francine twirled her finger beside her forehead, meaning she thought he was acting loony.

A white-coated doctor came in to examine my father. He listened to his heart with a stethoscope, looked into my father's eyes and turned over Dad's thin hands. The black and blue bruises on the palms shocked me. I remembered the time he took me to Steeplechase amusement park in Coney Island. Our hands were stamped with black ink at the entrance. After we went out to the beach, we could get back in by passing our hands under a green light that made the ink glow.

The doctor and Francine went out to the hall and talked. My father looked exhausted, closed his eyes. Believing that drawing would relax me the way it usually did, I picked up the pad and pencil from the nightstand and sketched the roses. The stems looked furry in the cloudy water. I didn't know if it was their rotting or the stink of disinfectant, but something smelled badly. The pencil dropped from my hand. I retrieved it. I resumed drawing but drawing didn't bring the usual calm. The thought came to me that the black marks I'd seen on my father's hands signified he'd never leave the hospital.

Francine came in and patted Dad's shoulder. "I'm going. The hospital will call if you need me."

"Sure. You go." His eyes blinked open. They looked glassy and blank.

She kissed his cheek and beckoned to me.

"Goodnight, Dad," I said, and we left.

The shiny black Lincoln was our get-away car. Francine opened the door. I climbed in so quickly that I banged my knee and cried out.

"What's the matter?" Francine asked with the irritation of encountering another problem.

"Nothing," I reassured her. She slid into the driver's seat, snapped on the ignition, radio, and air conditioning.

I sat at her side with my overnight bag knocking between my legs, as she drove quickly through what she called 'Colored Town.'

"What's wrong with Dad's liver?"

"Cirrhosis."

"What's that?"

"It's what happens if you drink," she said, running a red light. She drove up the same highway I'd seen on my first day in Florida, the tall apartment houses on one side, and the ocean on the other.

Even by plane, traveling was exhausting. I looked forward to going to sleep in the den, lulled by the sound of waves. Francine turned into the garage. I followed her to the lobby where she checked the mailbox. "Only bills and advertisements," she muttered, stuffing everything into her large, white purse. We rode up in the mirrored elevator.

When we stepped in the door, the apartment felt different without my father. Somehow before, I'd known he was there by a smell or sound that was no longer present. The baby sitter came to greet us in the vestibule. She was the same older Haitian woman who'd cleaned house for Francine before. Today, she was dressed in a paisley print shirtwaist dress, but with her hair, braided and pinned to the top of her head, exactly like before.

Throwing her arms about me, she cried, "So sorry, Daddy sick."

Tears filled my eyes.

"How did the baby do?" Francine said abruptly.

Alicia turned to Francine. "I try to give strained squash to baby. He start spitting. I really try, but Abraham go like this." She stuck out her tongue to demonstrate. "So I try to give apple sauce. He eat that up. That he like. He eat up whole jar. He laughing and happy. Don't worry. He very, very good."

"What about the diaper rash?"

"I put the medicine on you give."

"All right, Alicia. I'll see you in the morning."

Like last time, Alicia changed from slippers to shoes, and got a raincoat and the same large purse from the hall closet.

The door closed. Francine and I walked down the hall to the living room where the small television that had been in the den before, was on at a low volume. Francine turned off the set, and said, "Come on. I want you to meet him."

In her bedroom, she turned on a small lamp. Nearly six-month-old Abraham slept in the corner of the room in a fancy crib with a ruffled canopy. I went over to get a better look. He was dressed in a blue pajama. He had my father's light hair and pale complexion. His little chest moved up and down with his breaths. His tongue clacked against the top of his mouth. Beneath his closed lids, his eyes flickered. His face lit up with smiles as if he were having a wonderful dream.

"What do you think of him?" Francine asked as she reached out and smoothed his blond curls.

"He's great." I didn't know whether I meant it, what I felt about my brother, whether I never should have come to see my father.

Francine tried to say something, stopped, then said, "You better get to sleep. We might have to go to the hospital in the middle of the night."

"Where do you want me to sleep?"

"Where else? The den."

I carried my overnight bag there. Without switching on the light, I stood by the window, watched the ocean. The hiss of the waves were a little like an oxygen mask's ssshhhh, ssshhhh, ssshhhh. My hand crept up over my nose and mouth as if I was wearing one. For a moment, I felt like I couldn't catch my breath, that my father and I were one. The trouble was I was made from him. He was in my bones and blood and Abraham's too. That scared the hell out of me.

My bed wasn't made the way it had been last time. Fresh linen was stacked on a chair. I had to open the pullout couch myself. After, I undressed I threw the sheets and blankets on the mattress in a heap, crawled inside. In an instant, I was asleep. There were no phone calls from the hospital in the middle of the night, but the baby woke up. A clock with big shiny red numbers on a table next to me read two. Abraham cried for a half hour, then fell asleep. At five, I heard him again. This time, he babbled away. I fell back to sleep. When I woke up next, it was light. I got dressed and went looking for Francine. She told me Abraham was down for his morning nap. I had breakfast. Alicia showed up as I was finishing a bowl of Rice Krispies.

Francine and I drove back to the hospital. Most of the morning, I spent glued to the chair beside my father's bed while he dozed and woke and dozed again. My back and shoulders ached from sitting there. The hands of the wall clock moved slowly, just like when my grandmother was dying.

Like in the other rooms, a television hung from an iron bar in the ceiling. I went over, clicked a button. The television barely lit up before Francine snapped, "Your father doesn't like it. You better turn it off."

I went over to the window, opened it, breathed in the humid Florida air. It was only a few seconds before Francine remarked, "Close the window. Hot as it is outside, someone in your father's condition might get a chill."

My gaze lighted on the dying roses. I asked permission to take them to the men's room and dump them. Permission was granted. I threw them in the bathroom trashcan. A stink rose from the stems. I urinated, washed my hands, grateful for anything to do that broke up the time.

Francine was restless too. A couple of times, she popped up, went over to the little mirror over the sink and combed her hair or applied a new coat of lipstick. For a while, she wandered in the hall, talking to the nurses, and then to other visitors. When she returned, she had snacks of graham crackers and apple juice from the ward kitchen. On the hour, she used the telephone on the night table to phone Alicia and check on Abraham. The only one who rang her was Tony. No one from the better class bothered to call to find out about my father.

In my boredom, I watched a fly buzzing around the window. A little later, the buzzing stopped. The fly had died on the windowsill. I gazed at the walls, noticed old scotch tape marks. I knew from what I saw in other rooms that other patients put up family snapshots. My father had no pictures.

As it was nearing lunchtime, I reached into my pocket to check that I had Bernie's envelope. The money was gone. My heart thumping, I ran back to the bathroom to look around. At last, I remembered I'd put the envelope in a drawer for safekeeping last night. I'd been afraid I'd lose it at the hospital. But now I was sorry I didn't have it on me. It would have been comforting have Bernie's envelope in my pocket, and not because I needed money.

Francine and I went downstairs to a cafeteria with orange-plastic topped tables and plastic chairs. The large room was crowded with nurses and doctors in scrubs, and visitors like us. We grabbed trays and waited on a long line for our turn. The server wore a yellow uniform, a hairnet and plastic gloves. He tapped a ladle against the stainless steel counter while he waited for Francine and I to decide. One warming tray had strips of steamed catfish. Another was filled with 'Sloppy Joe' hamburger sauce. There were containers of limp, overcooked carrots and wrinkled lima beans.

Francine looked it over and sniffed, "Do you want to eat any of this stuff?"

"I'm not hungry." The smell of the catfish made me nauseous.

"Never mind. I was going to pop back to the apartment to check on Abraham any way. While I'm there, I'll make us some sandwiches."

Francine took off for home, while I headed to my father's ward. An aide was wheeling a gurney down the corridor. Someone had died. I hurried by, but slowed down and hesitated near the door to my father's room. I was afraid I'd find the bed empty and stripped down. To my relief, my father was alive, awake and looking around.

"Where's Fran?" he asked.

"She's home. She's checking on the baby."

I sat down in my usual chair.

Because my father was dying, anything I could think of to say to him seemed stupid and cruel. Even the weather wasn't a safe topic. 'It's a beautiful day,' would only remind him he couldn't go out. I hoped he'd go back to sleep.

Dad's voice was weak. "Come closer, Gary."

My chair scraped as I pulled it closer.

"I'm glad we're by ourselves. I have to tell you something."

"What?"

"I didn't..." His hand crumpled the edge of the top sheet. "I don't know how to say it."

There was a racket out in the hall. An aide clattered lunch trays as she collected and stacked them in a cart. Someone called brightly to a patient, "Look at you. Aren't you something? Taking a walk."

My father blurted, "I didn't treat you right."

Astonished, I waited for more.

Dad looked away from me and closed his eyes. He was done. Those few words were all I was going to get. I sat mulling over his *I didn't treat you right.* If he'd made his admission a long time ago, he could have rectified his wrong. A last minute apology only got me stirred up. Had he wanted me to say how he'd treated me didn't matter? I wondered what he felt now that he'd made his confession. His face looked like a blank mask. Then I saw a tear drip out of his left eye and roll back behind his ear.

Francine bustled in wearing a fresh outfit, an off the shoulder white blouse and black slacks. It looked like the brief respite at the apartment had restored her. She took her chair and dove into a bag she'd brought, taking out a thermos of coffee, paper mugs, fruit, and American cheese sandwiches that she placed on the small portable table that swung over the top of my father's bed.

We had to push the table aside when a nurse came in to check on my father. She measured his temperature and blood pressure; emptied his urine bottle; washed him. He'd developed bedsores on his back and screamed when she touched them.

Later, a young, student nurse came in, took Francine and I aside, and whispered, "He's not doing well. It's going to be soon. You better call people."

"Like who?" I asked, thinking she meant medical people.

"Like his relatives. Like the people he knew. The people who want to say good-bye. They should come."

When I heard that, I was afraid Francine was going to call in 'the better class.' To my relief she answered coolly, "We don't need anyone else."

"I was just trying to help," the young woman sniffed and marched out of the room.

Francine said, "The fact is, your father doesn't even want a funeral. He made me promise there'd be no fuss."

I nodded. What she said was what I knew would be my father's wishes.

I thought we were going to stay late like the night before, but Francine wanted to get home. She said, "My sitter had to leave, so my brother's watching Abraham." Then she looked over at my father. He was dozing again, and she said, "He's so out of it, I don't think he even knows if we're here or not." She kissed him on the forehead, and we took off.

Taking the same route as the night before, she drove over to the apartment. A smiling Tony met us at the door. With his sunburned nose, his white pants and white sneakers, it looked like he'd moved on from golf to boating. He told Francine, "Don't worry. The baby's fine. He's sleeping."

We moved down the hall to the living room. There was a big difference from the neat way it looked when Alicia was in charge. This time, a rattle, pacifier, stacking toy, and stuffed animals were scattered over the white rug. Francine grabbed up a soiled diaper, hurried out of the room to throw it away, leaving me with her brother.

"I was just getting to it," he called after her. Tony could really turn the charm on. "Gary!" he cried, grabbed my hand, pumped it up and down. "You're taller. Too bad we're meeting under sad circumstances. How is your dad doing?"

"He's..." I shrugged. I didn't like Tony, felt uncomfortable about his looking after Abraham. The baby was helpless, couldn't tell anyone if Tony neglected him, or did anything bad to him.

"You don't have to say, Gary. I know. I've been to see him. Did you have trouble getting to the hospital?"

"I took the van."

"I wanted to pick you up? Unfortunately, I just couldn't make it. Fran appreciates your coming down here. Your dad does too. It's too bad you're staying such a short time. It would be nice for you to be around longer."

Francine returned and told Tony, "I'm exhausted."

"Of course, what am I thinking? You and Gary had a long day. Call me if you need me." He kissed Francine's cheek, and then said, "I'll pick Gary up at the hospital tomorrow and drive him to the airport. It will give us a chance to catch up."

"It's one less thing for me to worry about."

I couldn't refuse after Francine said that. Besides it was more convenient to be driven than to take the van. I'd have to put up with phony-Tony.

The following morning, Francine woke me early. Her eyelids looked swollen and half-closed like she could use some more sleep. But she was worried about my father and wanted to get to the hospital as soon as Alicia arrived. I dressed, packed my overnight suitcase, carried it out to the hall, putting it near the door. In the kitchen, I found the toast and orange juice Francine had left for my breakfast on the kitchen counter.

I hadn't yet seen Abraham awake. It was my last chance since I was going directly from the hospital to the airport. While I was chewing on my toast, Francine came in and told me, "I'm going to wake the baby up." She went to the bedroom and got him. He whimpered like he wanted to stay asleep, but Francine carried him down the hall, cooing, "Come see Ga...ry. Ga...ry's your bro...ther."

I put my plate in the sink, and when I turned around, she was standing behind me with Abraham in her arms. The baby stared at me with big blue eyes. It was as if he knew I was going away, that this was his only chance to see his big brother. Francine held him out. "Go ahead, take him. You can hold him."

"That's o.k." I said, and shook my head. I was afraid I'd hold him wrong and drop him, or that he'd start crying.

"Don't be afraid of him," she laughed. "Look, he wants to go to you."

Abraham' head wobbled a little, and he smiled. It wasn't that I didn't think he was cute. I don't know why, but I didn't want to hold or even touch the kid, and not just because I had no experience holding babies. As I backed away from him, I knew I was acting like my father would have, but couldn't help myself.

"I woke him up especially for you, Gary." Francine pushed him towards me again.

"You said we have to get going." Why didn't she see, I was going home today, would soon be faraway and probably never see Abraham again? Even if I wanted I wasn't going to be able to be a brother to him.

"There's still a little time. Alicia's not here yet. He won't bite, Gary!" Francine insisted.

The bell buzzed, the noise scaring Abraham. He burst into tears. Francine carried him to the front door. In the high-pitched voice she used with him, she tried to soothe him. "Look who's here? Who is it?...It's Alicia!"

I followed, watched Alicia put her purse and umbrella on the table and change into her gray felt slippers while she sing-songed to Abraham. "Hell-o Sweetie Boy. We up early. We not napping, today? Why you crying? You want to come to Alicia?" She held out her arms. "Yes, yes. Abraham want to come. Now he happy."

The baby's eyes were red and tear-filled. He gave out something between a sob and a sigh, and then settled against Alicia's big breasts. His thumb found his mouth. He started sucking.

'You want me stay late tonight?" Alicia asked Francine. "Any time, you need me, I stay. Uncle Tony don't take care of Abraham good as me. You want me sleep over? I do it."

"Your husband will want you home."

"Roy say 'Mr. Geckleman sick. You help out when they need.'"

Like me, Alicia didn't trust Tony to look after Abraham. I was glad to hear her offering her services, and Francine's assurances that she'd use them.

"Where's bottle?" Alicia sang. "We find bottle while mommy and brother bye-bye..."

On her way to the kitchen, she gave a disapproving glance at my overnight bag and said to me, "You going so soon? You have no time with Abraham."

Before we could get to my father's room, a nurse came out from behind the nurses' station, an older, white haired woman with thick glasses that magnified her dark eyes. She told Francine, "I'm sorry. Your husband's in a coma."

Francine shuddered, then said, "All right. All right, we'll manage."

Halfway to my father's room, she broke down, started sobbing and ran into the women's bathroom. I waited outside with my suitcase. The janitor I'd seen on Thursday was mopping the hall floor again. Slap-slap, the stringy gray mop was getting closer to my feet. I was in the way, so I went on to my father's room and saw him propped up by pillows, sleeping peacefully.

The same nurse who'd given Francine the bad news came into the room. I braced myself, expecting her to be like the student nurse, that she'd tell me that Francine and I must call people. She didn't.

"How are you doing?" she asked.

"All right."

"How old are you?"

"Fourteen."

"So young…" She shook her head.

I looked away. The room felt small, suffocating.

"Maybe you should hold your father's hand. A person shouldn't be alone while they're passing."

"He never liked that kind of physical stuff." I stared at the brown linoleum, wondering where Francine was, perhaps still in the women's lavatory, trying to get control of her tears.

"Trust me," the nurse said.

"He's unconscious, right? He won't know the difference."

"He will. I've seen many, many people die. It always calms them to feel someone's touch. He'll know he's not alone."

"Not him..."

She squeezed my shoulder and told me, "You have to handle this your own way. I better get back to work." She left, closing the door behind her.

At my father's bedside, I took my usual seat. Dad looked asleep. His hands lay limply on top of the sheet. The one nearest me lay palm up, showing the black and blue marks I'd seen the day before. I was sure that if I touched his hand—even while he was in a coma--he'd jerk it back as if flames had scorched him. To prove that busybody nurse was wrong, I took his hand in mine. To my amazement, when I tried to let go, he squeezed my hand. A part of me understood that this feeble squeeze was probably a reflex. Yet it mattered. To me, it signified that he needed and wanted me with him!

Francine appeared. She'd touched up her make-up, re-combed her hair, gone to the ward kitchen and made steaming cups of coffee for us. As soon as she walked in the room, my father let go of my hand--and I of his.

The precious moments we'd shared had passed. Now, my only duty was to be Francine's company as we sat on either side of my father's bed.

At noon, I glanced at my watch as the lunch cart rolled down the hallway. Tony was supposed to pick me up in a half hour. "Maybe I can still catch the van to the airport. Then Tony could sit with you and Dad. You'd have someone with you when...when…" My throat choked. My father's death had begun to matter to me.

"Tony will drive you. I'll be all right," said Francine with renewed resolve and strength.

"I'm sorry I won't be here.

"The important thing was, the two of you said goodbye"

I nodded. Another ten minutes passed. Francine's eyes were closed. I said to her, "When Abraham gets old enough to understand, please tell him about me."

Her lids still closed, she smiled, and said, "I will."

I went to stand by the window. Beyond the parking lot I could see the inlet from the ocean that divided Palm Beach from West Palm Beach. It was wide and looked like a sparkling lake. I imagined walking into that gigantic bathtub, the water rising around me, and wondered what dying felt like to my father.

A familiar red convertible pulled into a space in the parking lot. Tony stepped out. With his bouncy step, he hurried towards the hospital. In five minutes, he was standing in the doorway. "Are you ready?"

I picked up my overnight bag.

"I'm early. You could have a few more moments with him."

"I'm ready."

Francine's white high heels click-clicked against the linoleum as she walked Tony and me down the hallway to the elevator.

I said, "Good-bye," and Francine surprised me by kissing me on the lips. The hospital's fluorescent lights made her skin look pale. Her platinum hair floated like a halo around her head.

Riding down in the elevator, I felt a lingering feel of her lips on mine, the way I'd felt a lingering touch of my father's hand.

As we drove to the airport, Tony offered to park the car and stay until my flight left.

"Don't bother. Just drop me off," I said.

"It's no trouble. I'm glad to do it."

We argued back and forth, and finally, I gave in and said, "If you want to see me off, that's great. I appreciate it."

At the airport, he didn't turn into the parking lot. Instead, he drove me up to the terminal. Skycaps were checking luggage at the curb. Through the glass sliding doors I saw my airline's counter.

Tony gave a little laugh and said, "I'm sorry, Pablo. I forgot. Actually, I'm in a hurry. I can't come in with you." I picked up my suitcase, climbed out of his car, and slammed the door. Tony took off in a flash.

Inside the terminal, I checked in, then waited near my gate and watched airplanes taxi down the runway and lift off. Soon passengers began boarding the plane to New York. An experienced flyer now, I sank into my seat and snapped my seat belt on. The stewardess came down the aisle with a cart and served trays of roast chicken and vegetables. While I ate, I talked to the man next to me. The stewardess removed the trays when we were done. I kept open the little table that snapped down from the seat in front, took out Bernie's envelope, and began a drawing on it that would be my gift to him. First, I made a 'B,' then put a head on top, and turned it into a figure riding a horse.

The trip to Idlewild passed quickly. It was so much better than sitting on a bus for two days. In the crowd gathered around the gate, I spotted Bernie. "Gary," he called, waving. He was dressed in sandals, Bermuda shorts, and a short-sleeved plaid shirt. I hurried over. Pulling me to him, he hugged me and asked, "How's your father?"

"In a coma."

Bernie shook his head. "I'm sorry."

Since I didn't have any luggage to collect, we walked to the parking lot.

At the car, I handed him the envelope with the money. "It's all there."

"You didn't need it?"

"Nah, I didn't."

"Well, then that's all right." He withdrew the bills, stuffed them in his pocket, then noticed the picture I'd drawn on the envelope. "Say, I thought you didn't draw horses."

"Only when I'm inspired."

That's me, eh?"

"Yes."

Smiling, he climbed in the car, carefully placed the envelope on the dashboard. "It won't get wrinkled there." As we rode along the freeway, he cleared his throat and asked huskily, "Was it okay seeing your dad?"

"I'm glad I went."

"Good."

I was glad he didn't ask me to say more. I stared out the window, everything looking different after a couple of days' absence; the Lower East Side's red brick buildings and little shops; goods spread out on card tables on the sidewalk; clothes hung from hangers hooked to awnings. Housewives pulled squeaking shopping carts. The Italian vegetable man stood outside his shop, guarding his melons and lettuce. A milkman lugged a big metal tray of milk cartons into the grocery.

Bernie parked in front of my apartment house.

Stepping into the lobby, I noticed the sharp disinfectant smell and the squeezed together baby carriages and bicycles, the dingy walls. Upstairs, my mother stood in the doorway. She must have been on the lookout for us at the window. Her eyes looked red as if she'd been crying. "I have to talk to you," she said as I came inside. "Francine called. Your father died, Gary. I got the phone call an hour ago. There's no funeral."

I went into the bathroom, sat on the closed toilet lid. If I hadn't gone to Florida, I knew I wouldn't have felt as badly as I did now.

My mother knocked on the door. "Are you all right?"

"Leave him be, Lil," Bernie said. "He needs to be alone."

I stayed in most of Sunday, lying on the couch. With half-closed eyes, I could see Dad, a cigarette dangling from his lip. 'I'm here,' he said. I felt the 'ping' in my head, the feeling that said I had to get something on paper. Soon my sketchbook was in my hands, open to a fresh page. My pencil moved quickly as I drew a face I knew so well—the thin, straight nose, narrow lips, slightly sunken cheeks. I struggled over the exact shape of the skull and the set of the jaw, put in the indentations at the sides of the nose, shaded the fine skin. With a life of its own, my picture became a portrait of how my father looked as he lay dying. Those long hours by his bed, I'd breathed in his gray face, slumping body and weightless hands. I cried as I drew.

My mother offered to let me stay home from school for a week of sitting *shiva*, but Monday morning, I told her, "I'm going to school."

In the past, on the first day of school, I was nervous, sweated and shivered, and ran to the toilet every ten minutes before setting out. But today, I was calm. I ate breakfast, slowly dressed in the new clothes my mother had set out. Everything seemed unreal.

Seward Park High was on Essex and Grand, a big, four story brick building surrounded by a spiked iron fence. Hundreds of kids milled around the yard. I didn't recognize or look for anybody. The bell rang. Kids moved into the building, trying to find their homerooms. The noise in the halls was loud as they called to friends they hadn't seen since June.

Numb, I floated through the crowd, not caring where I was going. My father hadn't wanted a funeral. I fantasized that I was attending one for him right here in the high school. Francine flickered through the teenage crowd, dressed in widow's black, Tony by her side. Bernie was part of my fantasy too. Above the hallway's clamoring voices, he intoned, "Nobody's perfect. You have to show some good will to the guy."

A blow to my head woke me. "Freshman-baby," a boy cried as he smacked my head with his loose leaf. Before I could respond, he'd hurried off. Fighting back tears, I found my classroom. My homeroom teacher, Mrs. Gordon, gave me my schedule.

Instead of being in a single room all day like in grammar school, I had to change classes and go to new teachers with new kids. A class ended when a buzzer sounded. Students raced for the door and surged out in the hall. At first I didn't understand that the stairways on one end of the building were for going up, and those at the other end, for going down. On the way to my first class, I accidentally took the wrong stairway and got stampeded. With difficulty, I mastered the complicated rules for going through the halls. A white line ran down the middle. Like the 49th parallel in Korea, no one was allowed to cross it. I stuck to the wall on my right. If I needed to be on the other side, I went all the way to end of the hall, made a turn, and came back.

Every time I sat down in another classroom, I heard the same speech, "This is high school. You're not going to get away with anything." That and everything else I heard sounded meaningless. My father's death made a wall between me and everyone else. The others were trying to break it down. The blow to my head, the stampede, the strange rituals in the hallway were all imposed on someone else. Nothing reached me.

At lunchtime, I went down to a large basement cafeteria. There were slits of high windows, and rows and rows of wooden tables and benches lined up on a concrete floor. The air smelled of disinfectant. I took a taste of a watery soup, and a white bread sandwich slathered with a horrible tasting margarine, and pushed them away. Potato chips, dishes of Jell-O, syrupy canned fruit, apples and cartons of milk were also sold, but I lost the little appetite I had. Food was getting smeared on the tables. The garbage pails overflowed. When the bell rang, I made my escape to my last two classes.

At three, my school day ended. I started towards home. It was a relief to be out of school. I could focus my thoughts on my father. I could release the sobs that had been choking me all day. Blinded by tears, I bumped into Dr. Greenbaum's wife on the Avenue. She was a kind woman whom I'd known all my life.

When I was small, Mom used to take me along to doctor's appointments and disappear into the examination room in the front part of the Greenbaum apartment. I was left in the waiting room, leafing through comics. On occasion, Mrs. Greenbaum came down the hall to talk to me. Once when I was three, I'd heard her playing the piano in the part of the apartment where she and the doctor lived. I tiptoed to the living room and saw her sitting with her eyes closed as she moved her fingers over the keyboard. I crawled under the grand piano, watched her feet pressing the pedals. The music pounded through my bones. I made myself into a little ball, clutching my knees to my chest. I wanted to stay and listen, but my mother came looking for me and pulled me out.

I apologized to Mrs. Greenbaum for knocking into her, but she interrupted and said, "I'm the one at fault. My eyesight is worse and worse. I can't even watch television, except if I turn my head and look out of the side of one eye. But that makes me tired.

The only reason I took a walk today is because soon winter will be here. Once it's cold, and the streets icy, I won't be able to walk at all."

"I'm sorry about your eyes."

"Let me treat you at the candy store," she said, impulsively.

I accepted. I hadn't realized how hungry I was. When my grandmother died, Rabbi Schneider had told my mother that a mourner had an obligation to eat after the funeral, that it brought the person back to the living. I sat at the candy store's marble counter, sipping malted milk. The chocolate ice cream and milk mixture was thick. I sucked and sucked through my straw, comforted by the sweetness.

When we finished our drinks, Mrs. Greenbaum folded the paper she'd stripped off her straw into accordion pleats. Her forehead creased like she was thinking hard. "I need to find someone to read to me. Gary, how about you? You could come whenever you have time. I'd pay you."

Loyal to Mr. Temple, I told her that I already had a job. I was going to work for him on Saturday mornings. My mother wouldn't let me do more. She, I knew, would be afraid I'd get behind in my homework if I worked during the week. Also, she'd fear that it would be unsafe for me to be wandering through the streets when it started getting dark early.

"I see," Mrs. Greenbaum said, looking disappointed. "If you change your mind, let me know."

I offered to walk her home.

"Thank you. I can manage on my own," she said, and patted my hand.

I came home to an empty apartment. My mother was still at work. After doing my homework at the kitchen table, I got out the sketch I'd done the day before. I'd drawn what Dad looked like while he was dying. To me, it meant that I was willing to draw anything, no matter how painful.

It wasn't clear to me whether it was a good drawing, but it said things to me about my father that I didn't want to forget.


I settled into Seward Park High's routines with required subjects of English, Algebra, Chemistry, American History, French, Physical Education. My teachers were different than the easy-going women who'd taught me before. In fact, two of my high school teachers were men. My Math teacher had a Ph.D. and insisted we call him *Doctor* Frankel.

The French teacher, Madame Gravelle, was an old lady with long white hair that she pulled back into a bun. She'd teach us a word in French. We yelled it back, and she'd say, "*Tres bien. Encore*. Very good. Do it again." The history teacher, Mrs. Pearlman, got lost in her own thoughts. She handed out a test to see what we knew, then stood by the window looking out, not caring if we cheated. Mr. Frankel couldn't get the Algebra class under control. He'd lose his temper and shout, "Shut up."

The elective art class that I'd looked forward to all summer was the class I came to dislike the most. It was filled with black leather jacket, long greasy hair guys who hated school and wanted easy grades. The art teacher, Mrs. Weiner, spent most of her time breaking up fights. She raced about the room ducking crayons and pieces of charcoal that flew through the air. I wasn't going to learn anything from her.

Mr. Porter, my English teacher, had been an advertising executive, and gave up a high salary job to come teach at our high school. A tall guy, dressed in a checked shirt and bolo tie like a cowboy, he'd stride into the class, and roar, "Friends, Romans, countryman, lend me your ears...." Kids would shut up and rush back to their seats to flip open copies of *Julius Caesar*.

My pal Jeffrey Lumpkin was in my English class. The more I hung out with him, the more I appreciated the guy. He was funny and smart. I liked the way he got worked up about what was happening in the world, missile sites in Cuba, riots in Jackson, Mississippi because a black guy registered for college classes. 'The Lump' liked the way Bob Dylan screamed his songs. He'd go around imitating his style, and sing, "Blow'n in the Wind." He also did hilarious imitations of teachers, most of his performances taking place while we ate lunch together in the cafeteria.

Pretending to be Mr. Guttenberg, the librarian, Jeffrey twisted like a snake and sputtered, "You...you...you dim bulbs!" Or he screwed up his face, and with a falsetto voice became "the whiner," Miss Pimentel, his music teacher. "I do everything for you. I bleed for you kids. And you? You stab me in the back!"

His funniest impersonation was of the principal, Mr. Jones, who showed up at assemblies, climbed up on the stage, and started screaming because the cafeteria and bathrooms were filthy. While Mr. Jones talked, his arms shot back and forth, faster and faster. Soon, he forgot what he was saying. All he could do was stare at those non-stop pistons.

Imitating the principal, Jeffrey twisted, squirmed and schemed to get his 'Mr. Jones hands' still. One hand held down the other. With bared teeth, Jeffrey inched his mouth towards that hand. Just as he was about to take a bite, the hand exploded, shot up and dragged him out of his seat.

Jeffrey knew what was going on in the city. At his suggestion, we went to see *Ben Hur*, a film in which a Roman centurion rescues a slave from a slave ship and adopts him as his son. Another Sunday afternoon, we went to Greenwich Village and saw a foreign, black and white film, "The Seventh Seal," in Swedish with English sub-titles--nothing like the kind of American movie I usually saw. A knight went on a pilgrimage. In one scene, he played chess with a hooded monk. At the end of the game, the monk did a Boris Karloff number, pulling off his hood and showing his white skull face. The monk was Death.

I couldn't take my eyes off the knight. He was tall, thin and blond and looked like my father. Dad was half-Finnish. The Finns had a big population of Swedish descent, so his resembling a Swede wasn't surprising. Yet I was upset to see his look-alike on the screen, felt I was seeing him again. The movie ended. Jeffrey and, I left the theater. The light outside hurt my eyes. The colors of a blue car or a woman's long, red hair seemed shockingly bright. Jeffrey talked on and on about the film, before noticing I was crying.

"Hey, what's the matter?"

I shrugged, unable to speak. It was a month since my father had died, and I'd thought I was 'over it.' Apparently, I wasn't.


The autumn months after my father's death, my mother and I started talking more. When she got started she could tell a good story. She had me laughing as she imitated the kids whining when their mothers parked them in the Klein's shoe department. "I want you, Mommy...I have to go wee-wee." The moms would run off to fight battles at the bargain tables. The shoe salesmen weren't able to sell shoes because they had to baby-sit. The children walked about in the high heels, broke up pairs by kicking shoes under the seats, tossed loafers around like balls.

One afternoon, she was ironing. With each shirt, she began with the collar, then went onto the cuffs, and then finally the sleeves, the shirt's back and front. While she flicked the silvery, hissing iron over the damp cloth, I sat spellbound on her bed, listening to her reminisce about Argentina. She talked about her Buenos Aires school, childhood best friend, a handsome boy she'd liked. I watched her press her red dress, then gently place a hanger inside.

She lifted the hanger hook, making the dress ripple down like a smooth, waterfall, and hung it over the closet door. I'd seen it hanging like that before, and it had meant nothing, was no more important than a saltshaker or a lampshade. But this time, I had to draw it. The dress hung there, full of my mother's hopes. When she went off to prepare supper, I sketched it. I felt like I understood her.

In December, she started working Christmas overtime at Klein's. Bernie didn't see much of her. I didn't see much of either of them. I was happy when he came over one evening to pick up a camel hair coat my mother had brought home from Klein's. She was still trying to improve the way he dressed.

When I let him in he said, "What's that on your hands. Did you cut yourself?"

I had a few spots of red paint on my hands that I hadn't been able to wash off. A boy in my art class had considered it hilarious to dribble paint on my desk. Mrs. Weiner had been too harassed to even notice.

I explained what had happened to Bernie, and he said, "Don't worry, it will wear off."

"I still have to go to that art class."

"You don't like it your art class at school?"

"I hate it," I said.

"Sounds like you need a better class."

Two days later, Bernie came over and gave me a Brooklyn Museum circular, listing the spring art classes. The cost was twenty-five dollars a class. I'd saved up enough money from my delivery boy job, but Bernie told me, "Don't worry. You have a scholarship." That meant if my mother would let me take the class, he was going to pay. He ran his finger down the list of courses to the one beside his friend, John Flynn's name. "You should study with John. If you draw horses, you can make a bundle."

"I can't draw horses."

"Why not? You're an artist. You're drawing all the time."

"It's hard to explain. You have to have a feeling about something before you draw it."

"Pick what you want. Maybe, later, you'll change your mind and take John's course."

Several courses were listed for 'young adults,' and I chose the beginning sketch class. The kids who came to the museum would want to draw, unlike the ones in my high school art class.

A few days later, my mother was free one evening, and Bernie took us out to dinner to the Italian restaurant in Greenwich Village that he liked. After we'd eaten and were waiting for desserts of pie and ice cream, Bernie broke the news to my mother about my starting a class at the Brooklyn Museum in January.

"Enrichment, Lily. Let the kid have some enrichment."

"Enrichment," my mother sniffed. "Why does he have to go all the way to Brooklyn? You mean to say there's nothing in the city?"

"My friend, John, says he should study at the Brooklyn Museum."

"Your friend says? Who is this friend who knows better than me what's good for Gary?"

"He's an art expert. What's the big deal about going to Brooklyn? It's not the end of the world. Gary can jump on the train and get off at Prospect Park."

"When is this class?"

"Saturday mornings."

Turning to me, my mother asked, "What's going to happen to your job, Gary? If you can't show up on Saturday mornings, Mr. Temple's going to hire someone else."

"I'm quitting there. I have a different job." I'd just decided to take Mrs. Greenbaum's offer.

"Where?"

"Mrs. Greenbaum is going blind. She asked me to come read to her."

"Since when did you talk with her?" my mother said in a flustered voice.

"I met her on the street when..."

She cut me off. "Do what you want, Gary. Take the art class. Quit at Temple's. Go read to Mrs. Greenbaum."

A bewildered-looking Bernie asked, "Who's Mrs. Greenbaum?"

"A neighbor," Mom said in a sharp tone that indicated the discussion was over.

The next day, I ran over to Avenue A where Dr. and Mrs. Greenbaum lived in an apartment in a new, beige brick building. All the surrounding buildings were smaller, and made of red brick that had darkened to a dull maroon. I ran up the steps of the building. Among the name cards on the brass plate besides the buzzers was one that said "Morris Greenbaum, M.D." I rang and rang as if my life depended on Mrs. Greenbaum's being at home.

Her voice came over the speaker, "Who is it? What's wrong?" She sounded alarmed like my ringing had scared her.

"It's me, Gary."

"Gary who?"

"Gary Geckleman."

The buzzer sounded. I rode the elevator up the sixth floor. Mrs. Greenbaum was waiting at her open door. Her thick glasses made her blue eyes enormous. "Come in, dear. Come. What a nice surprise to have a visitor. I'm here all by myself."

She didn't even ask why I'd come. I followed her small, slender figure down a long hall past the waiting room where I used to sit and leaf through comics, past the examination room, and round a corner to the living room where I'd once crept under her piano. The huge living room looked the same—a piano, many paintings, overflowing bookcases, green walls and carpeting.

I said, "If you still want me, I'd like to be your reader."

Mrs. Greenbuam was standing by one of the bookcases. She ran a finger over a shelf of books, skimming the spines like a xylophone player. "Look at all these books," she mused. "When I was a little girl, I went to the library every week and brought home three or four books. When I went to Hunter College, I majored in English. I suppose I've worn my eyes out, reading. I have a room full of books, and I can't read any of them. I'm so glad you're going to be my reader."

We agreed I'd come twice a week, starting after the New Year, and after I gave notice that I was quitting to Mr. Temple. My mother didn't like me working on school days. But I didn't think she would make any trouble. My impression was she accepted but didn't wish to talk further about my working for Mrs. Greenbaum.


I looked forward to beginning my class at the museum. The night before the first class, I barely slept. Waking up at daybreak, I ate a bowl of cold cereal. To my surprise, my mother rose early too. It was barely light out, but there she was pressing my shirt and pants so I'd look good.

The only times I'd been to Brooklyn was when I'd gone to Brighton Beach with her. Bernie was driving me to the first class because she was afraid I'd get lost in a strange neighborhood. He showed up at half past nine dressed in the camel hair coat that she'd bought him on sale at Klein's. It had big, padded shoulders, but tapered down, getting narrower as it dropped to a hem just below his knees. The cut made his legs look shorter.

The Buick was parked a block away. I bounced down the street, full of excitement. "I'm having trouble keeping up with you," Bernie laughed as I jumped into the front seat. He drove down Canal Street to the Manhattan Bridge. Traffic was heavy, but, as always, he knew exactly when to make his move and cut into a crowded lane.

"Thanks for taking me," I told Bernie. I felt so grateful he'd made Mom agree to the art lessons, and for his paying for them. I'd thought Uncle Ben would be the one to help me. It hadn't turned out like that.

"I like driving…when I bought my first car, it was a big deal. My mother and father couldn't believe it. They were so impressed. I'd pick them up and take them for a ride. My folks didn't care where we went. They just got a kick out of riding in the car. For me, it's still the same thing. So don't thank me. I'm glad to drive you."

Big columns lined both sides of the highway on the approach to the bridge. They reminded me of the Roman columns I'd seen in *Ben Hur*. On the lower level of the bridge, the guardrails blocked some of the river view. A train flashed by, crossed the bridge, and disappeared underground. After class, I'd take the return train when it was time for me to go home. Bernie drove onto Flatbush Avenue. We passed through a poor neighborhood, went by the Brooklyn Academy of Music and Grand Army Plaza. The Grand Army Plaza arch was like the one at Washington Square in Greenwich Village. This one, though, was decorated with bronze bas-reliefs of horses and chariots like the ones in *Ben Hur*. I glanced at Bernie's blunt profile. For a flickering moment, I imagined him as a Roman soldier in a silvery helmet and breastplate, racing a horse-drawn chariot.

After the arch, he turned onto Eastern Parkway, a wide avenue lined by six- to eight-story high apartment houses. A walkway ran down the center of the avenue. Crown Heights Orthodox Jewish families were out taking their *shabbes* strolls. The men wore black hats and side locks, the boys skullcaps, the women brimmed hats and long skirts.

Bernie pointed out the sights: Prospect Park; the Botanical Gardens; the public library. He also showed me the subway stop I'd have to go to later. Soon, he pulled up in front of the museum, a big, white building. I hopped out, said 'goodbye,' and he drove off.

Since I was early for my class, I decided to look around. I went inside, climbed up a flight of broad steps to the main floor. Wandering through a row of big, dark rooms, I saw Egyptian mummies, John D. Rockefeller's furniture, statues of naked women. I had butterflies in my stomach. What if the teacher told me I was a lousy artist; the other kids didn't like me; I'd come on the wrong day; Bernie had forgotten to send in the check for twenty-five dollars…

At eleven, I went to my classroom in the basement where I found eight other students. I didn't realize that the one with a ponytail and braces was the teacher until she introduced herself. Judy Glick gave each of us a charcoal stick and a board with paper tacked on. We bundled up in our coats and scarves, and trooped off to sketch in Prospect Park.

The sun shone weak and watery over the lawn, paths, trees, and the few walkers, bicyclists, and horseback riders who braved the weather. We art students each picked a different spot and started drawing. Judy slipped from one person to another, giving advice. She told me to squint my eyes, that in the blur, only the important lines would stand out. Another thing I learned was that if I was drawing something big like a tree, I should get up close to it, and when I drew, make the image fill my paper. At the end of the two hours we were back in the basement of the museum handing in our boards and charcoal, and washing our hands.

Judy said, "See you guys next week."

I raced away to the subway with my rolled up drawings under my arm. When I got home, Bernie was there. He asked me,

"How's it going?" I showed him my drawing. He glanced at it and said, "I wish I knew how to appreciate that stuff." I felt hurt.

The next Saturday I was back at the Museum, and the Saturday after that too. The weather was bitter in February. The cold made my eyes tear, burned my cheeks, numbed my toes. We couldn't sketch outside. Classes were held in the museum. The students drew the sculptures and copied paintings. The museum rooms were wonderful, but they could be stuffy and dirty. Cobwebs hung from the ceilings. Parents and their noisy children crowded around us as we worked. We had to retreat to the basement classroom early to receive Judy's comments.

She saw so much that I'd never noticed before. At a class when we were attempting to draw each other, she told us, "You should go to the ballet. You'd get a good look at ideal bodies. You'll see that women have shorter torsos and longer legs than men."

I respected her, was nervous when she looked over my sketches. Around the middle of April, she stopped making suggestions to me like she did to the other kids. I assumed she hated what I'd drawn. I was crushed. One afternoon I worked up my courage, and asked, "Why don't you say anything about my drawings any more?"

"Oh Gary, I'm scared I'll ruin what you're doing. You're the artist here."

"But I want you to tell me what you think!" I said.

"All right."

Not to say I wasn't thrilled to be singled out from the others as the artist! Tingling with excitement, I looked forward to when I could be by myself and turn the compliment over and over in my thoughts. Who could I tell? My mother? Bernie? Neither would do. Perhaps, Mrs. Greenbaum. Twice a week, I went and read aloud a new chapter of *David Copperfield*. A couple of times when I'd arrived, I'd found her looking through art books with a magnifying glass.

After handing in my drawing board to Judy, I rushed outside. The sky was gray and filled with clouds. It began to rain. I hurried towards the subway past bare sycamore trees, dirty clumps of snow. At the end of the block, I waited for the light to change. Rain gushed down. I raced towards the subway.

Before I could duck inside, Bernie's Buick pulled up beside me. He reached over and threw open the passenger side door. I climbed inside, slamming the door shut. My clothes were soaked, my picture ruined. Bernie drove down Flatbush Avenue. The car windows fogged while the Buick's wipers whisked back and forth at double speed. I rubbed a little clear circle on the windshield with the heel of my hand. People on the street were dashing into stores or standing beneath awnings. We passed the Brooklyn Academy of Music where kids with violin and cello cases huddled in front.

"How'd it go? Am I getting my twenty-five dollars worth?" Bernie asked.

"My teacher thinks so."

"I heard. She talked to my friend John." Bernie's face lit in a bright smile. "I'm proud of you."

"Thanks. How come you picked me up?"

"The track's closed because of the rain. Besides, there's some place I've been wanting to take you. John gave me the idea."

"Where?"

"You'll see."

We went to the Metropolitan Museum of Art. Bernie spoke in a whisper as he tiptoed over the polished floors. His idea of art appreciation was standing in the middle of a room, and glancing around quickly, then going on to the next room. The only pictures he got up close to were a few battle-scene paintings with horses, and one of a half-man, half-horse called "The Centaur." After twenty minutes, he said, "I'm no art connoisseur," and went off to the gift shop saying he'd hang around there until I was done.

I forgave him for not appreciating my sketches. If he couldn't even stand paintings by the great artists, why should he want to see what I'd drawn?

I never expected him to take me to an art museum again, but in fact, he and I went to most of the ones in Manhattan, including the 'orange squeezer' Guggenheim, on Fifth Avenue with a pop art exhibit of paintings by Andy Warhol, Robert Raushenberg and Jasper Johns. When I'd seen the paintings at the Metropolitan, I'd known I could never paint silver and lace and skin that looked so real you could almost touch it. But Andy Warhol had a comic book style that I believed I could master, if I wished. I felt encouraged.

We also took in the Museum of Modern Art. Bernie liked the glass walls and light, was impressed with the well-dressed men and women wandering through the rooms. He and I studied a picture called *Cache-cache* or "Hide and Seek." There was a big leafy tree with all kinds of things hidden in it. Bernie found a blue baby with a huge head at the root.

"Well, look at that. These artist guys are pretty smart, aren't they?" Bernie said, and went over and collapsed on a bench.

Museums bored him to death. He'd been in agony, but he'd taken me any way, and when he drove me home, he said cheerfully, "I'm getting an education." Bernie'd left school in the seventh grade, and what he was showing me was how to educate myself. It was completely different from the education I received in my high school. There were no teachers, blackboards, or textbooks. I just had to drink up what I saw, Paul Klee's funny little toy boats, the way Jackson Pollack threw paint around like a mad man.

After one of our museum visits, I decided I wanted to try oils. I had enough *bar mitzvah* gift money in the bank, as well as savings from my jobs, to allow me to buy canvas, turpentine, and tubes of oil paints. First, I got flake white and cerulean blue. On another occasion, I bought Indian red, lampblack and viridian. Experimenting, I dampened a canvas with turpentine and brushed colors over the canvas. I didn't know what I was doing and had a lot of failures. When I gave up on a picture, I white washed the whole canvas so I could use it again. There was one painting I did that I liked. It was of different shades of red. Some brush strokes in the picture were light and airy, others thick so the redness looked like a deep hole that went right through the back of the canvas. That one success inspired me to keep plugging away on my own.

My art classes, museum visits, and oil paint experiments kept me stirred up. I started dreaming of oceans of colors, reds, blues and greens. They were so beautiful that I didn't want to wake up. I saw things differently, was hypnotized by the designs suggested by raindrops on a window, individual hairs on my arm, football players on a television screen.

Much of the time, Bernie was at my side, a second father, to whom I felt ever closer

6. Mrs. Greenbaum

Except for my teachers, I didn't know many women college graduates. Mrs. Greenbaum was one of them. I looked up to her, and was bewildered when she said, "Morris says that I'm a *luftmensch*, that I'm not practical…that I'm moody…" Once she told me that she was 'an ugly old woman.' Sometimes, I got a last minute call canceling a meeting. Or she came to her door, said she had a headache, and pressed two dollars into my hand.

The first time she turned me away, I told her, "Don't pay me. You can't help it if you don't feel well."

"Take it. Your mother once did me a big favor."

"What favor was that?" I asked.

Mrs. Greenbaum looked away and murmured, "I said more than I should."

On the days I did read to her from *David Copperfield*, Mrs. Greenbaum sat across from me, her eyes closed, a blissful expression on her face. In many ways, she spoiled me, feeding me pound cake and cocoa, plumping extra pillows on my chair, asking whether my throat was hoarse, or I was tired.

I told her that I was taking an art class. "How wonderful," she exclaimed. "I'd love to see some of drawings." I was shy about showing them. Every time I came she asked, "Did you bring your drawings?" Finally, I brought along two nature sketches I'd done in Prospect Park. Using her thick magnifying glass, she studied each one closely.

"Why these are fine!" she said. "Are you going to be an artist?"

"Maybe," I said, looking down. "A commercial artist."

"You should become a real artist, the kind who's serious and has pictures hanging in museums."

I wasn't sure if she knew what she was talking about, but I loved her for believing in me. I wanted to, but couldn't bring myself to repeat my teacher Judy's complimentary remark about my talent. Mrs. Greenbaum didn't seem to need additional testimony.

From that afternoon on, instead of my reading Dickens to her, we spent most of our time leafing through the shiny, thick pages of big art books. I saw Auguste Renoir's beautiful children dressed in blue; Matisse's dancers; Picasso's cubist women; Marc Chagall's brides and grooms, *menorahs* and little red and green Jewish villages floating through the sky. Chagall, Mrs. Greenbaum explained, was inspired by Yiddish expressions like *luftmenschen*, which literally meant people who lived on air.

One of our meetings we spent walking around her living room like it was a museum, and looked at the pictures on her walls--her nephew Ronald's sketch of an outdoor Paris café; a watercolor of red and white roses; another of squiggly yellow and black lines called, "Tiger;" a large oil painting of a young woman playing the piano.

Speaking of this last one, Mrs. Greenbaum said, "I bought it when my Aunt Fanny died and left me her diamond ring. I knew my aunt wanted me to have something that gave me pleasure. I sold the ring. What do I need diamonds for? I'd much rather look at this beautiful painting."

Of all Mrs. Greenbaum's pictures, the one that fascinated me the most was a Ben Shan crayon sketch of a bald man with bulging eyes, a choked-looking neck and swollen hands. Black

Hebrew letters swirled over his head. The man was in anguish. This picture was so different from the depictions of crucifixions, Greek myths, portraits of aristocrats, or the cubist and pop art pictures that I'd seen at the New York museums. Ben Shan, like Marc Chagall, proclaimed he was Jewish.

I asked Mrs. Greenbaum, "Was Ben Shan ever in a concentration camp?"

"I don't think so. He lived on a commune in New Jersey, made up of Jewish garment workers, people like your grandmother and mother. In the cold months they sewed, and in the spring and summer they took care of the farm. But he might very well have had the Holocaust in mind when he drew this particular picture."

Every time, I came over, I took a few minutes to revisit the Ben Shan print. Drawing at the Brooklyn Museum, I still sketched things outside of myself, tried to copy what I saw, or what other artists had drawn. But inspired by Marc Chagall and Ben Shan, I'd begun to have an inkling that much more was possible, that I could tell my own story.

Each semester, I took another Brooklyn Museum art class paid for by Bernie. Also, I continued to be Mrs. Greenbaum's reader. She became my friend, someone I could talk to about anything—my memories of my grandmother; that my mother had a boyfriend, and I felt like 'a fifth wheel;' that I knew I couldn't become a first class artist unless I received training at art school; that I desperately wanted to attend one instead of going to college;

that my mother didn't want me to be a starving artist; that she expected me to attend one of the city colleges.

The winter of my third year of high school, Mrs. Greenbaum began sending away for art school catalogues. There was a small pile of them on the lid of her piano, including ones from the Parson's School, and the Rhode Island School of Design.

"You know I can't go to art school," I said one snowy afternoon as we sat in her living room.

In response, Mrs. Greenbaum gave airy waves of her hand and said, "It doesn't hurt to dream. Apply in the autumn. You might get a scholarship."

"What about my mother."

"Perhaps, she'll come around."

"I need more than tuition money. There's room and board, books, art supply and travel expenses."

"You could work part-time."

"I'd work. I'd do anything to go to art school. But I won't be able to earn that much waiting on tables or working in the library."

"You'll pay what you can. As for the rest, we'll see. You never know what will come up."

In this moment, it seemed to me that Dr. Greenbaum was right. His wife was a *luftmensch.* Usually, I didn't see much of him. When he wasn't seeing patients, he rattled around in some other corner of the big apartment and left Mrs. Greenbaum and me in peace. Today, though, he slipped into the room, went over to the piano, and began leafing through the catalogues.

"Can I help you with something, Morris?" Mrs. Greenbaum asked, her voice thin and high, different from when she'd been talking with me.

"Don't mind me," the doctor rumbled. "I just wondered what these things were doing in our house." Then, he turned on his heel and walked out.

Later, just as I finished putting on my overcoat, scarf hat and galoshes, he caught me as I was about to leave, and asked, "You're almost finished with high school. What are you thinking of doing when you're done?" He talked down to me like I was still a little kid.

"I'm thinking of enlisting in the air force," I said. Some of the older boys at my school intended to join the military after they graduated and serve in Vietnam. A few others talked about going up to Canada to avoid the draft.

Dr. Greenbaum nodded as if he were impressed by my boast.

What I'd told him wasn't true. I wanted to be in school and get a student deferment. Firstly, the dangers of being a soldier scared me. Secondly, Mrs. Greenbaum had said, "Art's like piano playing. You have to practice every day." She was right. If I missed a day or two, my hands were clumsier when I drew.

I lied to Dr. Greenbaum because I despised him. A lie seemed the only way open to me to express my contempt. I feared if I were openly rude to her husband, Mrs. Greenbaum wouldn't want me to work for her any more.

For years, my feelings for Dr. Greenbaum had been the opposite of those I presently felt. I'd admired the doctor because he'd looked after my sick grandmother without charging my mother. Then, last summer, I'd overheard a conversation between my mother and Mrs. Kessler that changed my outlook.

Mom and Mrs. Kessler had drunk coffee in the kitchen, while I sat in the living room, watching one of my favorite TV programs, "The Fugitive," a show about a man falsely accused of murder. Every week, he escaped to another town and searched for the real criminal. When the program was over, I turned off the television and was about to begin reading an assigned English book, "Of Mice and Men." But I put it aside and started listening to the conversation in the kitchen when I realized Mrs. Kessler was talking about the Greenbaums.

"She's ten years older than him. Everybody knows the only reason he married her was for her money. She paid for his medical school tuition. After he graduated, he wasn't interested in her. He didn't make a scandal by divorcing her. That would have hurt his practice. But he played around whenever he could."

"Let's not talk about Dr. Greenbaum," my mother broke in, curtly.

I'd been shocked. Dr. Greenbaum wasn't a saint. He cheated on his wife. It had taken me a couple of days to work out that my mother had been one of the women Dr. Greenbaum had selected as prey. I recalled the phone call she'd received shortly after Grandma died that had upset her so much. It had never occurred to me before that the caller had been Dr. Greenbaum. He'd asked her to be his mistress when she was lonely, grieving, at her weakest. I was proud that she'd turned him down. Even though she had, every time I mentioned Mrs. Greenbaum, a flush flitted across her face. I suppose she was afraid she might have encouraged the doctor by accepting his offer of free medical care for Grandma.

A neighbor woman was holding the elevator for me, my excuse to run away from Dr. Greenbaum. On the street, I looked up and saw a moon in the sky even though it was still afternoon. The weather was colder than earlier, although the snow had stopped. Shivering, I walked home and thought about Mrs.

Greenbaum. She'd said my mother had done her a favor. I shared the same opinion.

Bernie and my mother were still dating. His courtship, he joked, was lasting longer than any of his marriages. My mother said she wasn't ready. She wanted to wait for me to move out before she'd marry him. Her assumption was that I'd live at home while I went to a city college like CCNY. She wouldn't be able to marry Bernie until I graduated, found a job, and could afford my own place.

Meanwhile, Celia Kessler--the girl who used to jump on my mother's bed like a kangaroo, who tormented Tiny, my grandmother's parakeet--was sporting a diamond engagement ring. She was going to get married to an Orthodox guy. There'd be seven rabbis at her wedding to recite the seven blessings. Mr. and Mrs. Kessler weren't even religious. Their idea of a nice *shabbes* was going out for a ride in their new car. After years of slaving away at his shoe factory, Herb Kessler had saved up and bought the latest Ford model, a Mustang. His idea of a good time was to drive his family around in the shiny car, and top the afternoon off with a meal at a Chinese restaurant.

Celia was changing all that. There were no more Saturday rides, and no more eating Chop Suey. She'd made her mother buy new dishes, and brought them to a *mikvah*, a ritual bath to kosher them. Right before she married, she was going to bathe in the *mikvah* to purify herself. Every time I saw Celia, she was busy crocheting one of those skullcaps in incredibly tiny stitches that orthodox girls make for their boyfriends.

Having lost so many relatives during the war, my mother wasn't often invited to a celebration. When she was, she made the most of it. She became a bridal consultant and peacemaker at the Kesslers'. Should the wedding dress be brocade, chiffon, organdy or taffeta? Should it have a 'sweep,' 'chapel,' or 'cathedral' train? There were arguments and tears. No problem was solved before another took its place. What color should the bridesmaids wear? Should Celia's veil be 'flyaway,' 'fingertip,' or 'ballet-length?' Should the cousins in Rockaway be invited? What kind of flowers? Mrs. Kessler insisted there had to be a sculpted ice swan at the wedding *smorgasbord*.

The biggest problem was finding a place to hold a kosher wedding party. Mrs. Kessler wanted it to be fancy. Mr. Kessler said it shouldn't cost 'an arm and a leg.' To save money, they were going to have to rent a hall in Queens or the Bronx rather than closeby in Manhattan. Mr. Kessler worked late at his shoe factory, so Bernie was recruited as chauffeur. He drove Mom and Mrs. Kessler from one end of the city to the other. Finally, they found 'Gold's,' a hall on 172nd Street off the Grand Concourse in the Bronx. It had a chapel and a next-door hall where the dancing and meal could take place.

The wedding invitation read 'black tie optional,' but it wasn't optional as far as Mom was concerned. Bernie and I had to go to the tuxedo rental shop to have our measurements taken. My mother needed a new dress, one that wouldn't offend any of the groom's Orthodox family. She'd noticed one at Klein's that was high-necked, long sleeved and a dark wine color. During her lunch hour, she inspected the lining; checked to see if the seams were finished; made sure the material was cut on the bias; looked for tiny holes or snags. The dress was perfect, except it cost too much.

A miracle happened. The following week, the dress she wanted went on sale. The moment it was marked down, Mom bought it, along with a new hat, and shoes. That night, she took the dress out of the bag, unfolded it gently, and held it up against her to show me how well the silk draped.

On the wedding day, Bernie showed up in a tuxedo and shiny black patent leather shoes. He carried a corsage in a shiny white box with a cellophane lid. My mother hadn't expected flowers. When she saw the box, she said, "You brought me roses." But she guessed wrong. Bernie had brought her a white orchid. My mother lifted it out carefully, saying, "It's still cold from the florist's."

Bernie helped her pin the orchid on her dress with a pearl-topped pin that came with the corsage.

"What do you think?" my mother asked me. She looked so happy.

"It's nice, Mom," I said.

"You look good too!"

Downstairs, Bernie tucked her into the Buick's front seat, while I plunked into the back. We started driving towards the Bronx, and then up the Grand Concourse towards Gold's on 172nd Street. From the outside, it didn't look like much. There was a Waldbaum's drug store at street level, and we had to climb up a narrow flight of steps. But when we stepped inside, there was a carpeted, lit-up lobby with vases of orange and white gladiolas. I noticed a good-looking young man in a mirror on one wall, wondered who he was, then realized--to my amazement—that it was myself.

Off the lobby were the two rooms I'd heard about, the big hall with a wooden dance floor, the chapel. The guests arrived. Everyone from my neighborhood seemed to gather in the hall, including the Greenbaums. Mrs. Greenbaum was dressed in a tailored blue suit and tinted glasses. I waved. She couldn't see me from across the crowded room. I went to the bar for a soft drink. A long table displayed plates of chopped liver, cocktail frankfurters, and smoked white fish, as well as an ice swan with a bowl of fruit salad between its wings.

Everyone snacked on the food, and then we were ushered next door into the chapel. Folding chairs had been set up on either side with an aisle between. Women sat to the right, men on the left, separated in the orthodox style. Bernie sat beside me. In front was a flower-decked *chupah*, wedding canopy. A rabbi stood beneath. The ceremony began. A procession passed down the center aisle of bridesmaids, groom's attendants, ring boy and flower girl. The groom, David, walked between his parents. His black hair emphasized his pale, white face. His parents had their arms around him as if they were holding him up. I thought he looked younger than me, but here he was getting married.

Finally, the bride appeared with Mr. and Mrs. Kessler supporting her on either side. Everyone was staring at Celia. I was surprised how beautiful she looked in her white satin gown. Her veil floated around her. Her skirt rustled. Her train flowed behind. I could barely recognize the Celia I'd known most of my life, the Elvis Presley fan that used to sing, "Don't step on my blue suede shoes," swivel her hips like Elvis and play a make-believe guitar. I was certain that she'd wink or make a face at me as she passed. She did glance over my way for an instant. While everyone's attention was on her, and nobody noticed me, I couldn't resist, and stuck my tongue out. Celia saw but kept a neutral smile.

Prayers were said and the rings exchanged. Celia and her mother circled the *chupah*. The seven rabbis began blessing the couple, each in turn. From next door, came the sounds of the waiters setting up tables for the sit-down meal. The smell of pot roast and roasted potatoes made me hungry. I glanced over the rest of the congregation and spotted my mother sitting between some orthodox women in elaborate *shaytels*, wigs. She looked hypnotized, her mouth slightly open, and her hands clasped.

The groom smashed a glass underfoot. Everyone called out, "*Mazel Tov*." It was time for the meal. The big hall had been transformed, circular tables set up around the room, each covered with a pink cloth, and set with gleaming plates, glasses, silver and a centerpiece of flowers that guests could take home later. Against one wall was a sweets table with cookies, marzipan candy, sugarcoated pink and white almonds, and best of all, a three tiered wedding cake. The bride and groom's families stood in a receiving line before the long main table at the front. Everyone lined up to congratulate them before we sat down for the meal.

The main table was on a dais and looked down on the dance floor. The bride, groom and their immediate families took their seats high up like royalty, while off to one side, an accordionist, clarinetist and violinist set up their music stands, took out their instruments and began to play. On cue, the waiters came around serving soup, and taking orders for entrees of pot roast, chicken or fish. While we ate, the music paused and relatives and friends went to the front and gave speeches honoring the bride and groom.

Between courses, people surged up to the dance floor. My mother was tapping her foot, and Bernie looked a little tipsy from champagne. The bride and groom were hoisted up on chairs and carried around. The groom's Yeshiva boy friends competed in doing the Russian scissors dance. A circle formed as they crouched down and kicked out their feet. Everyone clapped and cheered. One tune blended into another. People sang in Yiddish and Hebrew.

I bumped into Mrs. Greenbaum at the edge of the crowd. The noise was so loud, that she didn't hear my first 'hello.' Looking confused, she peered at me.

"It's Gary," I said.

"Gary!" Her face lit up. "Are you having a nice time?"

"Sure."

"Tell me dear, is your mother here?"

"Yeah, she came." Actually, Mom wasn't far off, but poor Mrs. Greenbaum couldn't see.

"Please, do me a favor. Bring her over. Do bring her over, dear."

I crossed the room to my mother and told her. Mom said, "What's it about?"

"I don't know."

My mother turned to Bernie and said, "It's the lady Gary reads to. I'll be back in a second." While she took off for Mrs. Greenbaum, I headed for the sweets table with Bernie. The Yeshiva boys were still going strong. They'd formed a large circle and were doing the *horah*.

At the end of the dance, I noticed that my mother and Mrs. Greenbaum had disappeared. I assumed they were in the lobby where there was less noise and they could hear each other.

People started to leave. Celia and David took off. The band packed up their instruments. The Kesslers moved about saying good-bye. Herb Kessler smoked a cigarette in quick puffs and told people, "Thank you for coming."

"Have you seen my mom?" I asked him.

"Right there," he said.

My mother was coming toward Bernie and myself. "Let's go," she said.

I wanted to ask what Mrs. Greenbaum had said to her, but it was impossible. Mom had to stop to say a few last words to this person and that. I thought we'd never leave. Finally, we made it outside. We walked down the street to the Buick. On the way home, Mom and Bernie talked about the wedding, while I sat in back, silent. Bernie dropped us off, and my mother and I went upstairs to the apartment.

"What did Mrs. Greenbaum tell you?"

"Give me a chance to change out of this dress."

We both changed. Mom came into the living room in her bathrobe and slippers. She looked pale without her make-up.

"What did she want?"

"She wants to send you to art school."

My mouth felt dry. "What did you tell her?"

"She talked me into it."

"You mean it?"

"I told you 'yes.' How many times do I have to repeat it?"

"I'm just surprised." I sank onto a chair.

"She told me you were talented…and I'd had a few drinks…and I was at Celia's wedding…"

A few months ago, Bernie who'd been able to fix so many things, including the Zippersteins, had tried to convince my mother to let him send me to art school, but she'd refused. Mrs. Greenbaum, though, had achieved what I thought was impossible. She was hardly a *luftmensch*. She'd selected exactly the right moment to make her offer, when Mom was tipsy, and at a wedding.

"She insists on paying all your expenses, even if you go out of town."

"If I go out of town, you and Bernie will be able to get married."

My mother flushed. "Celia was always only a little kid…but here she is married…I'm being selfish, I know, but I want to move on with my life."

I hugged her and said, "You're not selfish. You're wonderful."

As I dozed off that night, the Jewish-gypsy wedding music throbbed in my ears.

The next morning, I stood across the street from the Greenbaum's beige stone apartment house, having come to thank my benefactor, and hear from her own lips that what my mother had told me the night before was the truth. Gazing up, I looked for some sign of life behind the windows in her apartment. It was late morning, but no shade was raised to let in the light; no curtain fluttered. I didn't dare go across the street and ring the bell. The Greenbaums were probably worn out by the wedding and fast asleep.

I was thinking about leaving and returning later, when I noticed the man who lived next door to the Greenbaum's, returning from walking his dog. Recognizing me, he waved and held the door open. I crossed over and slipped inside the apartment house with him. We got in the elevator with the dog, a dash hound with long drooping ears and sad, brown eyes. I hesitated at the Greenbaum's door before knocking. Mrs. Greenbaum opened the door, dressed in a plaid bathrobe over a nightgown. Her hair was sticking out in place like it hadn't been combed.

"Did I wake you?" I whispered.

"Oh no, I was up, but Morris is sleeping. I was expecting you!" She ushered me inside with a loving smile.

We tiptoed down the hall. Once we were in the living room, I told her, "I came to thank you."

"But you shouldn't thank me. I'm doing exactly what I want." That reminded me of Bernie when he'd said similar things whenever I thanked him.

Dr. Greenbaum appeared in a blue terry cloth bathrobe and flip-flop slippers. His eyes had dark bags beneath them. He turned and stared at me. "What are you doing here so early, Gary?" he rumbled.

"I invited him over, Morris."

"At this time? It seems like he's always hanging around."

Mrs. Greenbaum said, "Please Gary, go into the kitchen and wait. Morris and I have something to discuss."

I slunk off to the kitchen, a large, dim room with an old-fashioned stove, and big, deep porcelain sink. The window looked out on an alley with garbage pails.

I strained to hear what the Greenbaums were discussing, but couldn't make out a word until the doctor's voice rose, and he said, angrily, "How dare you do this without consulting me?"

My heart pounded. It sounded like Mrs. Greenbaum might not be able to send me to art school after all. I crept towards the living room. Hidden at the edge of the door, I could hear my fate being decided.

"It's my own money, Morris. My father put it aside for me."

"All right, it's your money. But why should you spend it on this kid? What is he to us?"

"What were your women to us?"

"You're doing this to punish me?"

"I'm doing this because he has talent…and because his mother did me a favor."

"It's your *facaktah*, shitty money. Do what you want. I wash my hands of it."

I ran back to the kitchen, not wanting Mrs. Greenbaum to know I'd eavesdropped. Soon, she came to me. Her face looked gray. "I'm afraid I'm having on of my headaches," she said.

"I better go."

She nodded. "You'll come tomorrow. We'll talk about art schools."

I left the apartment without encountering Dr. Greenbaum again, ran out the door, down the stairs. When I got home, my mother was just getting out of bed. We drank coffee together in the kitchen.

"Where've you been?" she asked, stretching her arms overhead and yawning.

"I went to thank Mrs. Greenbaum." I didn't relate how brave Mrs. Greenbaum had been.

7. The Art Exhibit

Something unusual and wonderful happened to me. I had
my first art exhibit the summer after I graduated from high school.
My teacher from the Brooklyn Museum had a friend who owned a
small Greenwich Village gallery, and talked her into sponsoring
me. I was so excited that I delivered invitations beforehand to
everyone I knew. I even mailed one to Francine who wrote back a
letter of congratulations and sent me a photograph of herself and
three-year-old, Abraham. He was a handsome boy who resembled
our father.

The photograph was in my pocket as a good luck charm
when I greeted people at the gallery, Bernie, Uncle Ben, and Mrs.
Greenbaum of course, neighbors like the Kesslers, salesladies
from Klein's, Jeffrey, Milt, and my other friends from school. In
September, I was going to go to art school in Providence, Rhode
Island, which felt as distant as Africa. This was my opportunity to
say goodbye to people I cared about.

I'd been nervous, but became exhilarated and happy.
Many in the crowd had never been inside a museum, but they
looked like they were enjoying themselves. "We're proud of
you," they kept telling me. All of my pictures told a story, not just
my own, but those of the people who'd come. At the bottom of
the pictures, I'd written phrases I'd heard people say in a swirl of
letters like I'd seen in Mrs. Greenbaum's Ben Shan print.

Sylvia, a girl at school, had told me her Aunt Ethel
claimed she was the kidnapped Lindbergh baby. So, I'd drawn a

baby wrapped in a pink blanket and wearing a Jewish star. Below, I'd written, "We told Aunt Ethel the baby was a boy. We said she wasn't the same religion as the Lindbergh's. Aunt Ethel didn't care. Lindbergh was a Fascist, so it made my father mad. He was always looking in the newspapers for Jewish kidnapped babies to see if he could get Aunt Ethel to switch to being one of them."

"A divided bedroom," a picture with an old man on one side of a curtain, a teenage boy on the other, was inspired by what Jeffrey Lumpkin had told me. I wrote on the curtain, "My grandpa's sick, so he's living with us now. My mom put some hooks in the ceiling of my bedroom and hung a sheet between the twin beds. The amazing thing is she thinks she made two separate bedrooms. I said to her, 'Mom, a sheet doesn't keep out the noises grandpa makes. He's moaning and snoring and snuffling, all the time. Can't you put him in the living room?' So she gives me the evil eye, and says, 'You'll adjust.'"

"My life is in my clothes" was a portrait of Lena, a humped, toothless old woman who swept the halls of the buildings on our block. I wrote. "She wore a pink blouse that my mother had given her. I'd seen it on my mother a hundred times. So it was strange seeing it on someone else—as if the woman Mom had been when she wore that blouse, no longer existed."

"Beneath everything, he's an angel" was a picture of a wide-grilled Buick on a car lift, and beneath the car was a grease monkey with large wings. That drawing was of Bernie.

My grandmother used to tell me how the borders between Poland and Russia often changed overnight so that her parents never knew exactly where they were. I drew my father slumped over a bar counter. The picture was called, "Am I in Russia? Or Poland?"

The picture I liked best was of my grandmother with her parakeet, Tiny, perched on her head. I called it, "The invisible third," and inscribed along the bottom, "My rabbi taught my Hebrew Class that where there are two together, there's always a third. He'd meant the third was God."

The End

Made in the USA
San Bernardino, CA
17 August 2014